Life After Love

by

KG MacGregor

Bella
BOOKS

2014

Copyright © 2014 by KG MacGregor

Bella Books, Inc.
P.O. Box 10543
Tallahassee, FL 32302

Printed in the United States of America on acid-free paper.

First Bella Books Edition 2014

Editor: Katherine V. Forrest
Cover Designer: Judith Fellows

ISBN: 978-1-59493-428-5

PUBLISHER'S NOTE

Other Books By KG MacGregor

Anyone But You
Etched in Shadows
The House on Sandstone
Just This Once
Malicious Pursuit
Mulligan
Out of Love
Photographs of Claudia
Playing with Fuego
Rhapsody
Sea Legs
Secrets So Deep
Sumter Point
Undercover Tales
West of Nowhere
Worth Every Step

Shaken Series
Without Warning
Aftershock
Small Packages
Mother Load

Dedication

It was 2004 in London, Ontario, when I first met Linda Hill, publisher of Bella Books. She spoke at a gathering of readers and writers, and fielded questions about why she published lesbian books. She called it the best job in the world, and described her philosophy of signing not just books, but authors she could introduce with confidence. She had a covenant with readers, a promise to deliver quality books featuring characters they would root for and want as friends. I knew then I wanted to write for Bella.

A few months later at a conference in New Orleans, I wedged myself next to her at a table filled with other Bella authors, and I made my case. At that time, I had self-published four books, but they were languishing from lack of distribution. I put them in Linda's hands and boasted of several others in various stages of development, pleading with her to bring me aboard. The next few months were anxious as I awaited word, but my efforts paid off in 2005 when Bella published *Just This Once*. That yellow emblem on the spine next to my name filled me with pride.

Over the next nine years, we partnered for nineteen more books. With access to Bella's sterling editors and meticulous proofreaders, I grew as a writer, collecting awards and accolades I'm honored to share. I never imagined such a successful career, nor that my books would be sold in bookstores all over the world.

I humbly dedicate this book, my twentieth, to the staff of Bella Books—the real-life women who polish my work, design the covers, set the type, answer the phones, pack the boxes and bring my books to readers. Let's do twenty more.

About the Author

A former teacher and market research consultant, KG MacGregor holds a PhD in journalism from UNC-Chapel Hill. Infatuation with *Xena: Warrior Princess* fan fiction prompted her to try her own hand at storytelling in 2002. In 2005, she signed with Bella Books, which published the Golden Crown finalist *Just This Once*. Her sixth Bella novel, *Out of Love*, won the Lambda Literary Award for Women's Romance and the Golden Crown Award in Lesbian Romance. She picked up Goldies also for *Without Warning*, *Worth Every Step* and *Photographs of Claudia* (Contemporary Romance), along with *Secrets So Deep* and *Playing with Fuego* (Romantic Suspense).

Other honors include the Lifetime Achievement Award from the Royal Academy of Bards, the Alice B. Readers Appreciation Medal, and several Readers Choice Awards.

An avid supporter of queer literature, KG currently serves on the Board of Trustees for the Lambda Literary Foundation. She divides her time between Palm Springs and her native North Carolina mountains.

Visit her on the web at www.kgmacgregor.com.

CHAPTER ONE

"UPS Ground gets this to Denver by Wednesday, Edgar." Bea Lawson slapped the last ribbon of packing tape to the oversized package and counted out the elderly man's change for a fifty-dollar bill. "Thanks a lot for stopping in."

She appreciated customers like Edgar who spent their dollars locally instead of online. It was great for her business, Pak & Ship, the postal services franchise she'd opened six years ago in Ballard, one of Seattle's most eclectic neighborhoods. Now coming off her busiest holiday season yet, she felt great about her investment of cash and sweat equity.

Bea enjoyed her work. There was just enough physical labor to guarantee a good workout every day, and the record-keeping provided a constant intellectual challenge. She also enjoyed the interaction with customers—most of them, anyway—plus she could bring her rescue dog Dexter, a pit bull-Labrador mix, to the shop. Best of all, she owned her franchise outright, having paid off the last of her small business loan four months ago.

With the holiday season behind them, her assistant manager and oldest friend, Kit Hurlocke, was coming in at eleven instead of eight thirty like Bea, but she too worked six days a week. They needed another employee, someone who would stick. Her two most recent hires had lasted only a few weeks before sliding into sloppy habits that forced Bea to let them go.

Kit was due any minute and would take over the counter, giving Bea a chance to catch up on paperwork and take Dexter for a walk. She was preparing her bank deposit when a familiar face arrived.

Allyn Teague shook her straight blond hair from her knit cap and pulled off her gloves so she could wriggle the key into her mailbox. Allyn worked from home but used Pak & Ship as her business address, as did many home-based workers who wanted someone around to sign for packages. She stopped in three or four times a week to pick up her mail.

"Looks cold out there," Bea said.

"Already feels like snow. They say we're in for seven inches between now and Sunday."

Dexter came trotting out of the back office at the sound of Allyn's voice, his tail thumping loudly against a stack of cardboard boxes. Sixty pounds of solid muscle, he was mostly chocolate brown with patches of white on his chest, legs and face. His amber eyes remained riveted to Allyn because she usually brought him a treat.

"He's been asleep under my desk all morning, but he hopped up the second he heard you. I'd say you're his favorite customer."

"He's my favorite dog." Allyn was tall and a few pounds on the heavy side, but it was the color of her eyes that made her stand out—turquoise so bright Bea had mistaken them for contact lenses until Allyn assured her they were her very own.

She'd gotten a peek at Allyn's driver's license when she rented the box several years ago and knew she was three years younger, turning thirty-two in July. She also knew she was married to Melody Rankin, and sometimes got mail addressed to Allyn Rankin-Teague. They lived nearby in Redwood Heights, a newly built cluster of faux Victorian homes on lots the size of postage stamps.

Allyn allowed Dexter to lick the treat from her outstretched hand. "Most days his is the happiest face I see."

"I'm going to take him for a walk as soon as Kit gets here. Want to come along?" Though they were only acquaintances, Allyn was the kind of person Bea liked having around. She was always cheerful and quick to flash a friendly smile, even when she had to wait in line longer than usual for service.

"Wish I could, but Fridays are my busiest day. I still have a half-dozen calls to make before close of business, and I always try to have dinner ready by the time Melody gets home."

Melody sometimes came into the shop with Allyn on Saturdays, but rarely on her own. She was pear-shaped—large hips with a thin torso—with wavy brown hair cut above her collar, and even taller than Allyn, though her round shoulders suggested she'd spent years trying to disguise her height. Always businesslike, sometimes impatient.

Bea had reached out several times, inviting them to basketball games, parties or Pride events. Allyn always promised to run it by Melody but they never followed up. Some people were just homebodies, Bea thought.

"I'll see you Monday, Dexxie. Be a good boy."

"Hey, a bunch of us are going to the Huskies game tomorrow night. They're playing Stanford." She was getting a blank look. "Women's basketball. It starts at seven if you're interested."

"Oh, thanks. I'll see if Melody's up for it."

In other words, no.

Kit sidled up behind Bea as Allyn walked out. "I sure hope I'm around when that woman realizes you're flirting with her."

"Geez! You scared the crap out of me. And I wasn't flirting with her."

"Whatever you say." Kit was, in the words of her bulging bicep tattoo, a Big Ol' Dyke, sixty-one years old with a silver crew cut and a face weathered by years of tromping through the elements to deliver the US Mail. She wore a set of rainbow triangles around her neck like dog tags, and had more friends than a kid with a bag of Skittles.

Bea straightened the collar on Kit's polo shirt, dark green just like hers with a Pak & Ship logo on the chest. "Come on, I was just being friendly. Besides, she's married, and you know I'm not the kind to mess with that."

"All I know is your face lights up like a kid at Christmas whenever she walks in."

"Maybe you're just comparing it to the look on my face when you walk in. I tend to smile at most other people."

Kit sneered. "Watch it. I was once a postal worker, you know."

Bea clipped Dexter's leash in place. "She's threatening us, boy. We'd better get out of here now."

* * *

With shaking hands, Allyn set the carving knife on the block and took a step back. "If this is your idea of a joke or something, it's not funny."

"It isn't a joke." Melody looked at her grimly across the granite-topped island in their designer kitchen. Most days she went straight to their bedroom to change into sweatpants and a T-shirt, but not today. She'd retreated to the bedroom but emerged still wearing the thick gold scarf over her pantsuit as if ready to walk back out the door at any moment. "I'm so sorry, Allyn. I don't know what else to say."

"Sorry?" Allyn had felt an undercurrent of tension for several weeks but chalked it up to stress at work. Never once had she imagined Melody would walk through the door and announce she was leaving. That couldn't happen. They were married. Everyone they knew held them out as the perfect couple.

Melody overreacted to everything. That's all this was. Anyone would feel like running away after laboring the way she had over a critical grant application. She'd been chained to her desk upstairs every night for the last seven months, on top of having to travel back and forth to Tucson. "You just need a break, sweetheart. It's not fair how they've piled all this work on you, but once you get it finished, you'll have your life back. *We'll* have our life back."

"I don't want it back, Allyn. That's what I'm trying to tell you. Everything has fallen out from under me this year. It's nothing you've done, I swear. I've changed."

Allyn couldn't comprehend her stony-faced expression, much less her bizarre declaration. "What do you mean you've changed? We love each other. That's all that matters."

"I still love you. I swear. But the way I feel about everything is different. I've been trying for weeks to figure out what to do about it, and the only solution is for me to leave."

Panic and confusion knotted the muscles in her abdomen. This was the woman she loved with all her heart. The only woman she'd ever loved. The woman she expected to grow old with. "You want to leave your job? Fine, I don't blame you. You want to leave Seattle? That's fine too. We can sell the house and move to Peoria if you want. But you don't get to leave me. Whatever this is, we'll work it out together. That's what being married means. I'm always going to be there for you, and I go where you go."

"You know I love you. That'll be true until the day I die."

Allyn drew in a deep, shaky breath and still couldn't get enough air.

"I'm so sorry. None of this is your fault, Allyn. I just…" Her voice trailed off as she turned away.

"All this time I've been asking if something was bothering you. You kept saying no, it was just work. I knew it was more than that. Why are you throwing all this at me now? You should have been talking to me."

"I wanted to but I didn't know how. I knew you'd want answers and I don't have them. All I can tell you is nothing feels right anymore." Melody drifted into the living room where she perched on the arm of the couch and folded her arms, halfway between settling in for a talk and dashing out of the room.

It was surreal to watch her lick her fingers and rub at a scuff on her ankle boot. Did she seriously think her fucking boot was important at a time like this? Of course not. This was her typical behavior when she wanted to avoid conflict. Ignore. Deflect. Downplay.

"I turned in my notice at the provost's office two weeks ago. Today was my last day."

"*And you're only telling me this now?*" Hearing herself shriek, Allyn closed her eyes and mentally counted to five. Melody always shut down when confronted. If she wanted answers, it was crucial to remain calm. "Never mind, that doesn't matter. My business is going pretty well. We've got some savings. We can always move into something smaller and rent out the house for a couple of years. You want to go back to school or something? Fine, whatever you need. Life's too short for you to be miserable at work every day."

Melody hissed as she inhaled through gritted teeth, a gesture Allyn recognized as a sign she was feeling boxed in and would disengage completely if the conversation persisted. "You haven't heard a word I've said."

"I heard every word. I'm just having a hard time believing you're ready to throw your whole life away. Where is this even coming from? You've been out of it ever since you started on this grant. That's been what?" She counted on her fingers back to July. "Six months? Seven? And it hasn't been easy. In case you didn't notice, I took care of everything around here…and I stayed out of your way so you could finish. Then out of the blue you tell me you're not happy anymore and now you want to *take your life in another direction.*" Despite her intention to stay calm, her last words came out heavy with sarcasm.

Melody began pacing the rug in their family room in small, deliberate steps as though trying not to step on the lines in the pattern. Only when her back was turned did she finally answer. "We turned in the grant application last October."

"Then what…" A wave of incredulity ripped through her as she realized Melody had been pretending to work for the last three months. "What the hell is going on with you?"

"What's going on is I met somebody!" she barked, spinning around to face her. "A woman who lives in Tucson. We fell in love, and I'm leaving because I got a job in the provost's office at the University of Arizona. So there. Now you know all there is to know. Are you happy? I didn't want to tell you because I knew how much it would hurt."

"Oh, my God." With that, all the pieces suddenly fell into place, forming the ugliest picture Allyn could have imagined. "What an idiot I've been! All those nights I felt sorry for you having to work so late at your desk. You were up there pouring your heart out to some other woman. 'Poor, poor Melody! They're even making her travel on the weekends now.' You disgust me!"

Melody's bright red face was proof the accusations were hitting their mark. "This wasn't something I planned, Allyn."

"The hell you didn't! How does somebody have an affair without planning it? How do they quit their job and get another one without planning it? It looks to me like you planned it all the way down to the last detail."

"That's not what I meant. I'm just saying it happened all of a sudden. I wasn't looking for it. Honest. But then I couldn't get back to where we were no matter what I did."

"*It happened?* Now you're making it sound like you're the innocent victim here. Just last summer we were talking about having a baby."

"I guess that scared me more than I realized. That's about when it all started."

Allyn clenched her fists, fighting a rage that made her want to hurl the nearest ceramic vase into the fireplace—or at Melody's head. "Don't you dare try to rationalize any of this. I'm your *wife*, goddamn it. If you have doubts about something, you're supposed to work through them with me, not another woman. I can't believe you just strung me along till you got all your little pieces in place, and all this time you knew you were leaving. If I hadn't dragged it out of you, you'd have walked out of here without telling me a thing and left me wondering for the rest of my life what I'd done wrong."

Melody shook her head vehemently, but she wouldn't meet Allyn's eye. "It wasn't like that. I didn't want to say anything until I was sure. I've been trying all this time to get those feelings back, but I couldn't."

"And how did you try? Did you talk to me about it? Did you turn off your fucking computer and come downstairs to spend time with me? What about when you were off on your romantic weekends? Did it ever cross your mind to take me somewhere instead? No, you didn't think about anyone but yourself. And now you expect me to be understanding because this just *happened* to you?"

"I can't talk to you when you're like this." Melody stormed past her to the master bedroom, the heels of her boots pounding the wooden floor like hammers.

Several seconds passed before Allyn followed to find her retrieving a bulging suitcase from underneath the bed. "Fucking hell! You fucking came in here and packed while I was cooking your dinner." She almost never swore but adrenaline had taken over.

"I was honestly hoping we might be able to talk like mature adults and I wouldn't need to go tonight, but I should have known you couldn't do that. You're too emotional. I'm afraid if I stay here much longer, we'll both end up saying hurtful things we can't take back. It's best if I go stay with Jillian and Tiffany till you calm down."

"Calm down? Seriously? You just dumped a world of shit on me and now you think I should calm down?"

Again Melody's face burned bright. This whole confrontation had obviously been staged to end without any sort of negotiation, including her escape to Jillian and Tiffany's. She'd made her decision already, and apparently expected Allyn to accept it.

Allyn's mind raced frantically. This couldn't be happening. "We're legally married, for God's sake. You made a commitment to be with me forever and I'm going to fight for you. You do *not* get to just leave."

"Would you really want me to stay if you knew I wasn't happy?" Despite her flustered look, Melody showed no signs of giving in. Her forehead was wrenched in a steely frown. "We were different people when we got married, Allyn. People change a lot in eleven years."

That was bullshit. It was only two years ago they'd gotten married in the eyes of the law. Why would Melody have gone through with that if she'd harbored doubts about their future?

"I don't want to hurt you, Allyn. But I can't just manufacture feelings that aren't there anymore."

The nightmare was getting worse with every callous word out of her mouth. Allyn couldn't let this happen, couldn't give up, couldn't lose the one person she loved more than life. She had to get control of herself and talk Melody out of leaving. "I can't let you throw away our life. What do you want from me? You want me to calm down? You want me to sit quietly and keep my mouth shut so we can talk it out? Fine, I can do that. Just tell me whatever it is I need to do to fix this."

Melody sighed and slumped on the edge of the bed, intent again on staring only at her boots. Her dark brown pinstriped pantsuit was the nicest she owned, and she'd probably worn it today because her co-workers had thrown a going-away party for her.

"I hate it when you quit listening. You get fixated on what you want and you tune out everything else that doesn't fit. There's nothing for you to fix. I didn't decide all this today. It's been coming for a long time. Talking about it isn't going to help."

"You mean it isn't going to help *you*. You're walking out of here with all the answers and leaving me to wonder what the fuck happened."

"What more could you possibly want to know?"

"Everything, starting with who she is."

Again Melody shook her head. "You don't need to know her name. I know how you are. You'll go online and download every little piece of data you can find. That's what you do with everybody. Her life isn't any of your business."

"That happens to be my job, and you know damn good and well I don't do it with everyone." Her business, which she ran out of their home, was recruiting top-level employees for the tech security industry. That gave her access to dozens of databases from which she could produce a work history for almost anyone in the country with only a few keystrokes. The only time she'd ever used her work skills for personal reasons was to check out a woman their friend was dating—and she realized with fury she'd done that at Melody's request. Now Melody had the nerve to throw it back in her face.

"All I'm going to tell you is she's a grant writer like me. She posted something in a forum and I thought she sounded really smart, so I messaged her with a couple of questions. That was last July."

Had this really been going on under her nose that long? She searched her memories for the last time they'd made love. At least a couple of months ago, before Thanksgiving.

"After that we started emailing back and forth. It was all professional. Then we had a chance to meet in September when we were both in DC."

Allyn's anger at Melody's feigned innocence gave way to a palpable hurt. The weekend trips to Tucson had started soon after that, and though she dreaded the answer, she forced herself to ask, "Is that when you slept with her?"

The silence was louder than if Melody had screamed her reply.

"How could you do that? Didn't you tell her you already had a wife? Does she even know I exist?"

"She does."

Of course, and they probably laughed at her for stupidly cooking all of Melody's meals and doing her laundry while they screwed around behind her back. Melody deserved to be tossed out of the house with everything she owned, but Allyn couldn't bear the thought of losing her. "You took vows with me. You made promises to be with me forever—only me."

Melody was both stubborn and proud. Also slow to admit when she was wrong. For all Allyn knew, she was leaving because she knew she'd screwed up and couldn't bring herself to ask for forgiveness.

That was it. Allyn had to forgive her right now…convince her they could put it behind them, no matter how difficult it would be. All of this might even blow over in a few days—as soon as the consequences kicked in and Melody realized how serious it was.

"I forgive you, Melody. For everything. You don't need to leave. Not tonight. Not ever. If you don't want to talk about it anymore right now, we don't have to say another word. Just like it never happened. I'll stay out of your way for as long as you need. I'll even sleep in the guest room upstairs so you won't feel any pressure."

Time would heal this.

Melody stood and gave her a patronizing pat on the shoulder. "I don't mind talking as long as you're not flying off the handle. We're both smart…rational. Let's go sit down and have dinner. After this long we ought to be able to have a conversation without fighting. I care about your feelings, Allyn. The last thing I want is to see you hurt more than you have to be."

More than she had to be. Why did Melody think it was necessary to hurt her at all?

Allyn mindlessly went through the motions of putting dinner on the table, but didn't set a place for herself. As calmly as she could manage, she said, "I'm too upset to eat right now, but I'll sit with you because I want to hear how this happened."

"So I'm supposed to eat by myself while you sit there and stare at me? What's the point of that?" Melody instantly switched from conciliatory to combative. "I'm trying to do what you want and answer your questions, but you don't really want to talk. All you care about is making me feel guilty. Dinner's just a big charade."

"No, acting like nothing's wrong would be a charade. Lying to me about how hard you were working on that grant and why you were going to Tucson was a charade. Sleeping in our bed and letting me feel like your wife was a charade." With every sin she ticked off, her pride and sense of righteousness swelled, and she rebelled against the notion of remaining calm for Melody's sake. "But the biggest charade of all is you pretending to care how I feel. It's clear you don't give a fat fuck about anyone but yourself."

"I knew you couldn't be mature about this." Melody slammed her linen napkin on the table. "I should have packed everything while you weren't here and left you a note. The only reason I didn't is because you never leave the goddamn house."

"Right, since I work ten hours a day and still find time to be your personal maid. When was the last time you lifted a finger around here to help with anything?"

Melody lunged for her suitcase but Allyn grabbed it first and shoved it toward the door.

"Thanks a lot, Allyn. At least now I don't have to question whether or not I'm doing the right thing."

"Yeah, well...don't give it another thought. Now get the hell out of here."

Allyn slammed the kitchen door so hard behind her that it rattled dishes in the cabinets. Burning with fury, she watched through the window as Melody whipped out of the garage in her Honda Accord, barely missing a parked car before she peeled down the street.

It was only when the taillights disappeared that the enormity of Melody's betrayal hit her, and she began to cry from anger, humiliation and heartbreak. She had no idea what to do next.

CHAPTER TWO

"De-fense! De-fense! De-fense!"

Bea rose to her feet and joined the chant, despite her doubts the Washington Huskies could stop Stanford, the top-ranked women's basketball team in the country. Year after year, Tara Vanderveer reloaded the Cardinal with All-Americans who made the rest of the Pac-12 look like high schoolers.

To the crowd's delight, the Huskies stole a pass and ran the court for a breakaway layup, but it was too little too late. The clock ran out on a double-digit loss.

"I can't wait to see how much it snowed while we were in here," Kit said as she helped Bea into her down jacket. "Bring on the crazy drivers."

"Snow's good for business," she answered. Her shop would get extra foot traffic the next few days from people who didn't want to chance driving to the post office on slippery roads.

"I suppose you'll expect me to risk life and limb to come to work tomorrow."

"You know how busy Mondays are. Besides, they should have most of the streets plowed by then."

"I guess that means yes." Kit looked over her shoulder and lowered her voice. "I saw you and that programmer from Redmond talking. Did you get her number?"

"I got her email address." The fact that Debbie D'Angelo had spent a good part of the evening goofing around with a gaming app made it unlikely Bea would follow up, though she had nothing per se against gamers. What she had was a problem with gamers who couldn't stop playing while other people were talking to them, or seemed not to realize there was a basketball game going on.

"And? Are you going to ask her out?"

"I doubt it. She's a little on the young side."

"Aw, she's not that much younger than you. Besides, you're still cute." She ruffled Bea's hair. "You've got that Black Irish thing going. Who's going to resist those big green eyes?"

Bea swatted her hand away. "I doubt Debbie even noticed. She was too busy zapping space aliens or something. That's what I mean by too young."

"It doesn't matter who it is, you always find something wrong. Too young, too old. Too silly, too serious. Some people might get the idea you aren't interested in dating anybody."

"Maybe I'm not." Bea knotted her scarf as they stepped outside into three inches of fresh snow on top of the five they'd already gotten. Kit knew her as well as anyone, and it was clear she was trying to push buttons. "You have to admit you envy me every time Marta's dad comes to visit. In fact, I distinctly remember you offering to sleep in Dexter's bed if I'd let you hide out at my house."

"Yeah, but that's only two weeks a year. The other fifty are heaven on earth."

"I'll remind you of that next time you complain about your wife not letting you play softball anymore."

Kit snorted. "She's saving me from myself. And I'm doing the same for her by not letting her sit on the condo board. She'd kill somebody. Relationships are all about compromising and taking care of each other."

Bea knew all about how relationships worked. She'd been lucky enough to have one that was damn near perfect, but now she had neither the time nor emotional energy to build another. Dating was fine, and she'd finally given herself permission to enjoy a little casual sex if the chemistry was right, as long as there were no expectations about everlasting love. One-nighters were all she needed, if that. Once it became clear the relationship wasn't going anywhere—which always seemed to happen right away—she saw no reason to drag out the inevitable, saving everyone a lot of grief. As far as she was concerned, her life was on track. She had a profitable business, a home of her own and the best dog in the world.

They reached the parking lot to find most of the vehicles indistinguishable from the others, each a giant blob of snow. Kit's red four-wheel-drive pickup stood out in a row of small sedans.

"What about Marta's friend, the French teacher?" Kit asked. "She liked you a lot."

"She was nice, but geez. Twenty-six years older than me and ready to retire. You guys must think I'm desperate."

"You just got finished saying Debbie was too young. Age is a state of mind."

"So why don't you fix them up with each other? No one ever believes me when I say this, but I'm in a good place right now. I like my life just the way it is."

Kit went silent as she inched her way past a stream of pedestrians to the exit, but picked up where she left off the instant she pulled onto a plowed boulevard. "We Skyped with Wendy last week. She told us to keep at it, that you'd wear down eventually."

Bea sighed heavily. "I should have known. Don't you guys have better things to talk about?" Kit and Marta were among the few friends who knew the truth about Wendy, but that didn't mean she wanted them in her business.

"When was the last time you got laid?"

"Now there's a pervy question if I ever heard one."

"Can't remember, huh?"

"Actually I can, but I'd forget it if I could. It was after Belinda's wedding last fall when I went back to the hotel with that woman from Spokane. Kirstie something or other."

"The one with the long red fingernails? I bet that was interesting."

Bea shook her head at the memory. "I meant that about you being a pervert, you know. Those fingernails weren't even the worst part. It just felt weird being with somebody I hardly knew, like we were both actors putting on a performance. None of it was real."

"Sex doesn't always have to be real. Sometimes it's just fun."

"I know, but not that time."

As they turned onto her street, Kit said, "Lucky for you, I'm out of ideas for now but that doesn't mean I'll stop trying. You're too good a catch to stay single. I suppose we can try to be more discerning about which lonely lesbians to throw at you."

"That's so big of you."

"Smartass."

When they stopped at the curb in front of her house, the curtains parted in the living room, framing Dexter's silhouette in the picture window.

"Just look at that and tell me why I'd want to come home to anything else."

"You got me there. See you tomorrow."

By the time Bea walked through the front door, Dexter was on his usual tear through the house, racing in a circle from the living room to the kitchen to the hall and back.

"Did you miss me?"

He paused long enough to lick her hands and face before his excitement got the best of him and he dashed off to run his circuit in reverse. The mayhem ended with him whimpering at the back door, begging to be let out to the fenced-in backyard.

"Go play in the snow."

She laughed from the back porch as he ran off more steam, stirring up a plume of snow in his wake. She'd never had a dog before—only a pair of stray cats named Chloe and Fletcher—and considered herself lucky to have found one so perfect on the first try. It felt good to know she'd always be loved. He'd be glad to see her no matter how long she'd been gone. He wouldn't pout or give her the cold shoulder, and though he adored practically everyone he met, he'd never go home with anyone but her. Best of all, she didn't have to deal with his prickly family.

Her two-bedroom bungalow was barely a thousand square feet, plenty for the two of them. She'd practically stolen it from the bank at the height of the mortgage crisis when her business started turning a profit. It was less than a mile from her shop, allowing her to walk to work, most days with Dexter.

"Come on, Dexxie. Time to go to bed."

He darted by her in the direction of the bedroom.

"No! I didn't mean now. I have to dry your"—he leapt onto the center of her down comforter—"feet."

* * *

Allyn double-checked the settings on her phone in case she'd somehow turned off the notifications. Melody hadn't returned any of the half-dozen voice mail messages she'd left in the past two days, nor answered any of the texts.

Jillian and Tiffany were ignoring her too. She'd always considered them shared friends, though Tiffany worked with Melody at the university. They'd probably known about the affair for months. No telling what lies Melody had told them to win their allegiance.

On a quick drive by their house earlier that day, she'd spotted Melody's Accord in the driveway but it was blocked in by their cars and covered with snow. It was possible she'd flown down to Tucson already to be with that woman and get ready for her new job.

She'd learned on the Internet that roundtrip flights to Tucson cost four to five hundred dollars, meaning Melody had spent at least two thousand on her trips back and forth since October, ostensibly for work. Perhaps that woman—she couldn't bring herself to think of her as a girlfriend or lover—had fronted the money for tickets. Allyn managed their household finances and, in looking back over their records, had found no paper trail of their affair. Not that she'd expected to, as Melody had a personal credit card and her own checking account. She'd been faithful about depositing her half of the household expenses into the joint account, but Allyn wasn't sure how much longer that would continue.

The red, green and blue flickers of digital displays on appliances and electronics offered the only light in the house after dark, but that didn't matter. She didn't need light to sit and brood. She could barely concentrate on anything but her misery. Somehow she'd have to gather her wits tomorrow, since her Monday calendar was filled with calls.

When had the woman she loved with all her heart turned so cold? The cheating was bad enough, but refusing to take even a morsel of responsibility? And then blaming her for getting upset about it as though sleeping with someone else was perfectly acceptable behavior? Had Melody really expected her to swallow being cast aside without fighting back?

Perhaps she had. Early in their relationship Allyn had given up her job at Microsoft to work at home because Melody didn't like her traveling so much to college career days where she recruited the best and brightest for her company. Even as recently as two years ago when they bought this house, Allyn had given in though she preferred the older one in Belltown because it seemed more genuine than a newly built Victorian. She could honestly say she'd always cared more about making Melody happy than pleasing herself. That's what devoted partners were supposed to do for each other. Why hadn't Melody done the same?

That wasn't fair. Melody too had made sacrifices, like indulging Allyn's loathing of decorating for Christmas, an artifact of her dysfunctional upbringing. They spent most holidays with the Rankins—

An unbearable pain pierced her chest as she imagined losing the people she'd come to know as family. Sheryl Rankin was more of a mother to her than her own, and Melody's sisters were as dear as any friend could ever be.

Allyn couldn't bear to think they'd abandon her once they learned what Melody had done. If anyone could talk some sense into her, it was Sheryl.

She'd barely slept since Friday, and was so nauseous she couldn't keep anything down. The result was a pounding headache that calmed only when she imagined Melody coming back through the kitchen door to say she'd made a colossal mistake. They'd have a difficult road ahead, but Allyn would ease it with absolute forgiveness. It was the only way to get back the life and love they'd shared.

The chime on the hall clock signaled midnight. She had a call scheduled at six a.m. with someone on the East Coast, a new business client she needed to impress so he would come to her first when he had openings in his company for tech security. She couldn't pull that off without several hours of restful sleep.

Getting that much needed sleep was its own problem. The bed they'd shared was too familiar, the empty space an inescapable reminder that Melody was not only gone, but likely spending the night in the arms of someone else.

Allyn stumbled down the dark hallway past Melody's office to the guest bedroom. It was fitting. She felt like a guest, living her new life in this room until her old one came back.

CHAPTER THREE

Bea tapped each box and envelope with her pen and counted aloud as Chuck, the UPS deliveryman, watched. "All there, five pieces."

Chuck handed her a stylus so she could sign the electronic delivery slip. "Of course it's all there. Would I short you?"

"Maybe at first." This was their running schtick ever since the day she'd hurriedly signed off on his delivery only to have him return an hour later with an errant package they both had missed.

The oversized packages wouldn't fit in the mailboxes, so Bea stepped into her office to fill out the yellow slips she used to notify box holders to come to the counter.

Dexter crawled out from under her desk and stretched his stocky legs.

"You lazy boy. You didn't even get up for Chuck. I guess that means you're not interested in going for a W-A-L-K."

He huffed his disagreement.

"Or a T-R-E-A-T."

Either he'd learned by the tone of her voice when she was teasing him, or he knew exactly what she was spelling, because his ears went up and his tail began to wag.

A soft buzzer above the door signaled the arrival of a customer and she returned quickly to the counter. Allyn Teague was near the front of the shop checking her mailbox.

"Look, Dexxie! Your buddy's here."

He trotted out and stood with his front feet on the counter, his tongue already lapping with anticipation.

"Oh, sorry. I forgot to bring anything," Allyn said hoarsely from across the room.

Bea couldn't remember the last time that happened, but she didn't want Allyn to feel she was obligated to bring a dog treat each time she came in for her mail. "I've got some here in the drawer if you'd like to do the honors."

Allyn covered her mouth and coughed. "I've got the flu or something. I don't think I ought to come any closer." Even at a distance of fifteen feet, her puffy face and red-rimmed eyes were obvious.

"Sorry to hear that. You probably shouldn't have walked down here as cold as it is. Don't worry about your box getting full. I'll save it for you. Or call me. I can drop it off."

"Thanks."

Before Bea could tell her to feel better, she'd lowered her sunglasses and left.

* * *

Will call tonight at 6.

The short text was Melody's first communication since walking out five days ago, and Allyn couldn't stop staring at it.

For the past two days she'd reined in her impulse to contact Melody via phone, text or email. The breaking point had come Monday night when she'd followed half a bottle of wine with a stream of sobbing voice mails that eventually turned bitter, leaving her even more humiliated because she'd done it to herself. After sleeping it off and paying the price with a hangover, she began a self-imposed cooling off period.

Now her restraint had paid off with Melody finally reaching out.

Allyn's emotions had run the gamut all week. Sometimes she'd cry for hours on end, usually while scrolling through their digital memories or wandering from room to room recalling where and when they'd bought things together. Then something would trigger her anger—the closets and drawers Melody had cleaned out surreptitiously, the password protection on her desktop computer, the missing photos from their shared albums—and it was all Allyn could do not to destroy the rest.

Mostly she was anxious, rushing through her phone conversations with clients so she wouldn't tie up the line, and checking her messages constantly. Cereal was the only thing she could keep down, and even then barely half a bowl. The bathroom scales showed her down four pounds in five days.

Melody's deceit was so much more obvious in hindsight. The clues had been there all along—an overall lack of warmth in their everyday interactions and an avoidance of intimacy, both explained away as a product of fatigue from her long hours at work. There also was her request that Allyn not call when she was traveling because it might interrupt a meeting, and the times Allyn heard her talking in her office upstairs, which Melody brushed off as "thinking aloud."

When the scheduled hour came and went, it was all Allyn could do to resist placing the call herself. Melody had been clear she would be the one to call. Clearly she felt no moral duty to honor her—

The phone rang twice before Allyn allowed herself to answer. "Melody?"

"Hi, Allyn." Gentle, even sweet.

"Honey, I'm so sorry about all those messages I left the other night. I lost my head…and let my emotions get the best of me."

"It's okay. What did you do? Open a bottle of wine and wave it under your nose?"

Allyn laughed heartily, far more than the lame joke was worth. She'd never been one to hold her liquor, and it was a running joke that the mere whiff of alcohol always went straight to her head. "I poured out all the alcohol in the house yesterday, so you can rest assured that won't happen again."

There were a million things she wanted to say, but this felt like coaxing a feral cat to eat from her hand. Too much too soon would spook her.

"Are you doing okay, Allyn?"

"Not really," she said, her voice cracking. A few seconds passed while she gathered herself. She didn't want to cry, not after her spectacle the other night. "It's hard to sleep, and I can't seem to keep anything down. Work's a disaster because I can't concentrate on what I'm doing. I know none of that is what you want to hear, but it's the truth."

It was Melody's turn to go silent, leaving Allyn on pins and needles as she waited to hear why she'd called. Five days was long enough to realize what a drastic move this had been.

"There are a few things I wanted to talk to you about."

"Where are you?"

"Please, Allyn. That's not important."

"It is to me."

Melody sighed. "Fine, if you must know, I'm in Tucson. I started my new job on Monday but I didn't call to talk about that."

That's why she'd orchestrated storming out on Friday night. She probably already had a plane ticket to Tucson on Saturday.

A new job fifteen hundred miles away didn't have to mean the end of their marriage. Allyn could work from anywhere.

"Are you still there, Allyn?"

Too much silence as she processed each tidbit of information. "Yes."

"Do you remember Kim Rothwell? We met her at that fundraiser for the Gay Men's Chorus. She's an attorney. I asked her to draw up some papers for me because I figured you'd want to use Jeremy. By law, we have to file for separation and then wait ninety days before the state will grant a divorce. I knew you wouldn't want to deal with the details, so I asked Kim—"

"Oh, my God…don't do this, Melody. Please just stop and think about it. We were together nine years before we could get married. We didn't rush into it, and you shouldn't rush out. You're talking about wiping out our whole life together in just three months. We've had hard times before. When your dad died, everyone was so worried about you, but I got you through it. Remember? I'm the one who held you every night when you cried yourself to sleep."

"I'll always be grateful for that, but—"

"And think about what you're doing to me. You're the only person I've ever loved, the only person I've ever been with. I've never even looked at another woman."

"Please let's not do this again, Allyn."

"I gave up a good job to work at home because you didn't want me traveling so much."

"Come on. Don't even think about throwing your job in my face. You're making more now than you ever made at Microsoft. You said yourself they eventually phased out that whole department. You might not even have a job at all if I hadn't pushed you to set up your own business."

"The point is, I've always done everything you asked me to do. I deserve better than to be left in a bowl of shit while you run away to your shiny new life."

"Don't start this again, or I'm going to hang up. Is that what you want? Remember when you were still smoking? You kept trying to cut back a little at a time, but you couldn't quit that way. It had to be all or nothing."

"You're comparing leaving me to quitting smoking? Cigarettes don't have feelings, you asshole!" Hanging up on her would have felt good but only for an instant. Getting Melody to set aside her pride and talk again after that would be next to impossible. "And I just lost my cool again. I'm sorry. This has all been such a shock that I can't even think straight."

"I'm not blaming you for anything. Believe me, I know I deserve all the shit you can throw at me, but there's nothing else I can do. I'd give anything for you not to hurt."

"If you really mean that, come home. We'll work this out… whatever it takes."

"I can't." Her voice quivered a bit but there was no mistaking her resolve. "Kim said the main thing we had to agree on was what to do about the house, and that's the other reason I needed to talk to you tonight. If you want to buy my half and stay there, I'm willing to sell at a fair market value, but we'd have to get an appraisal."

Allyn bristled again at the businesslike way her feelings were being trampled. "You know goddamn well I can't afford this house by myself. You're the one who picked it out. We bought it thinking we'd have children together. Remember that? You walked back and forth between those two bedrooms upstairs talking about which one our son or daughter should sleep in."

"You're making this so much harder than it has to be. Just listen for a change. I have the names of a couple of agents and you can pick whichever one you want. Or you can send me some names and I'll pick one. Redwood Heights is pretty hot right now so we should get a decent price, probably more than we paid for it. It would be nice to have some extra cash."

"For lawyers."

"Whatever. I know you don't want this to happen, but there's nothing either of us can do at this point. You should get the separation papers from Kim in a couple of days, and I hope you'll cooperate soon on selling the house. It would save us a lot of money and aggravation if I didn't have to go through the attorney to force the sale."

"Then I guess I'd better hang up so I can get started on my honey-do list, just like I've done for the last eleven years. I thought I knew you so well. I never had any idea you could be such a cold-hearted bitch."

"Call me whatever you want if it makes you feel better. Like I said, I know I deserve it. But it isn't going to change a thing."

Allyn wasn't sure how much longer she could hold her temper in check. She could picture Melody's smug face, the one she wore when she was convinced she was right and everyone else was wrong. "Do you even care what you're doing to me? Does it matter to you that I'm sick to my stomach all the time? That my head hurts so bad I can hardly move?"

"I'm sorry. I don't know what else to say. There's no easy way to do this. But we have to get through it to come out on the other side."

"Except you don't have to get through anything. You have your nice new life in Tucson and somebody who's going to make you forget all about what you're doing to me. This isn't fair." She shuddered to imagine the nameless, faceless girlfriend sitting nearby, patting Melody on the arm or shoulder as she endured the invective. "What does your mother have to say about this? I can't imagine she's very proud of you right now."

"Leave her out of this," Melody said sternly. "I mean it, Allyn. You can't go messing up things with my family."

"They're my family too."

"What could you possibly get out of making them think less of me?"

Despite her implied threat, Allyn knew she couldn't involve the Rankins. If they took Melody's side—as any loyal family would do—it would devastate her.

After half a minute of strained silence, Melody said, "There's one last thing. I need to come back to the house to get the rest of my stuff. Jillian's brother is going to haul it down for me in his cargo van, but we need to come on Saturday to pack it up. I'd really appreciate it if you could go somewhere for the day…give us the house. We have a lot to do and I don't want to spend the day fighting, especially with other people around."

The idea of Melody's "people" traipsing through her house was infuriating. "That woman is not coming into this house. Do you hear me?"

"She won't, I promise. It'll just be me, Jillian and her brother. Ten o'clock to about two. Obviously, I want to take the dining room furniture because that was my grandmother's… and my desk. I can send you an email with the whole list, but I promise not to take anything that isn't mine."

"I saw that you already helped yourself to some of the photos."

"Just the ones of my family."

"Nothing of me, I noticed. You're just going to erase those years. Our wedding, our honeymoon in Puerto Vallarta. It must be nice to feel so happy with your new life that you don't even need your memories. Maybe I can look into some kind of surgery...a lobotomy or something. They can fix it so it never happened."

"Stop, Allyn. You're doing it again."

"Doing what? Pointing out what a low-life sack of shit you are? Yeah, I'm doing that again."

"For Christ's sake...will you please be gone on Saturday so we don't have to go through this again?"

"I'll think about it." She ended the call, reveling in this small flash of power, the first time since Friday she'd felt anything but helpless.

CHAPTER FOUR

Bea nearly stumbled when Dexter stopped to inspect a juniper bush. She'd been focused on the two-story house, light blue with slate-gray shutters and an honest-to-goodness white picket fence enclosing the front yard. Affixed to that fence was a For Sale sign.

She didn't usually make home deliveries, but Allyn hadn't picked up her mail in almost two weeks. By all accounts, this year's flu was hard to shake, and she was worried Allyn's had progressed to something more serious.

There was only one car in the driveway, a black Volvo coupe she recognized as Allyn's. The drapes were drawn in every room, a likely sign no one was home.

A sturdy porch banister made the perfect hitching post for Dexter, a cautionary move to keep him from jumping in case someone answered the door. His tail twitched with anticipation as she rang the doorbell a second time.

"Looks like we wasted a trip, Dex."

She'd given up and started down the steps when she heard the latch turn.

Allyn appeared, squinting and shielding her eyes. She looked ghastly. No color in her cheeks, no shine in her hair. She was dressed in yoga pants, a sweater two sizes too large and bedroom slippers.

"Special delivery. Your mail was stacking up, and Dexter and I got worried that you couldn't shake the flu. Looks like we were right."

"Thanks, I appreciate that. I've been meaning to come by but I didn't feel up to it." She brightened a bit when she noticed Dexter, who was dancing with excitement. "I bet you're waiting for a biscuit."

"Sorry, I've tried to teach him not to beg, but he always associates you with treats."

"I'll go get him one. I have a whole jar I bought just for him."

When she returned, Bea nodded toward the real estate sign. "You're moving?"

"Afraid so," she said, her voice carrying a hint of sadness even as she smiled at Dexter. "You like that? Let me see if there's another one in this pocket."

"Now you're spoiling him." Over Allyn's shoulder, Bea could see all the way through to the kitchen, and she noticed the dining area was devoid of furniture and the rug rolled up. "So where are you going? Not far away, I hope."

"I don't know. I haven't started looking yet."

There was no mistaking her choice of pronouns. If something had happened between Allyn and Melody, that would explain not only the missing furniture and For Sale sign, but also her hollow look and disappearance over these past two weeks.

Or maybe her use of "I" only meant that Allyn was tasked with finding a new home because her work hours were more flexible than Melody's. It would be a shame if they were struggling financially and their furniture had been repossessed. Some people lived beyond their means. Sudden job cutbacks or unexpected expenses could be devastating, and the mortgage on a home this nice had to be quite high.

Whatever the reason, it was none of her business.

"That flu must have been killer. Feeling better?"

Allyn grunted and shook her head dismissively. "I wasn't really sick, just…everything sort of went all to hell. My wife found someone she likes better than me."

"Oh, my gosh, Allyn. I'm so sorry."

"Thanks. It's fair to say I'm not handling it very well."

"No one handles something like that well." Though she'd never had to deal with a cheating lover, Bea certainly had known her share of heartache, and it was useless to tell Allyn the hurt would pass. Even though it was true, she wouldn't believe it until she was ready. "Is there anything I can do to help? I don't know what it would be…Dexter would love to have you along for a walk if you feel like getting out of the house."

"I appreciate the offer, but I doubt I'd be very good company."

"You don't have to be. We don't even have to talk at all. Just grab your sneakers and let's go get some air."

Allyn looked at her dubiously, but nonetheless disappeared into the house and returned wearing dark sunglasses, a brown bomber jacket and blue and gold trainers. "I can't go far. I'm supposed to go meet my attorney this afternoon."

Broken relationships were bad enough without having to deal with attorneys. That was the downside of having the state recognize your marriage.

"You can lead the way if you want," Bea said. "I can't be gone that long either. I told Kit I'd be back in an hour or so. She's in the shop by herself. I really need to hire some more help."

They let Dexter set the pace, which meant stopping every few feet to let him sniff the ground.

After a few minutes of troubled silence, Allyn finally spoke. "When I first met Dexter, I couldn't believe how friendly he was. You always hear about what a vicious breed pit bulls are."

"Yeah, they get a bad rap. If you ask me, it's the owners who are vicious. Dexter's basically a mush ball."

"So how come you named him after a serial killer?"

Bea laughed. "That's what they called him at the animal shelter. I tried to change it a couple of times, but nothing else would stick. There were seven others in his litter. I picked him because he was the most independent, kind of like me. I didn't want him to be lonely when I went out."

"Why didn't you just get two of them? They could have kept each other company."

"Are you kidding me? One Dexter is about all I can handle. He's all over my furniture whenever I turn my head, and he eats more than I do."

Allyn slipped another treat from her pocket and rewarded him when he sat. "I would have liked having a dog around the house, but Melody didn't want the hassle."

"Yeah, they can be a pain sometimes but they're more than worth it if you ask me. He's great company, and I never have to worry about him getting mad at me or being in a bad mood." Nor did she have to worry about him cheating on her. "Even if I ignore him all day, all I have to do is show him a little attention and he turns into a bouncing pile of joy. Like happiness in a fur coat. Maybe you should get one now."

"No, I couldn't do that. Melody will come back when she gets this insanity out of her system. It's like an eleven-year itch or something. There's no way this other woman is going to give her the kind of life she had with me." Though her words were optimistic, her voice shook with doubt. "I think we both got complacent. We took what we had for granted instead of making each other feel special. Relationships take a lot of work, even the good ones. Or especially the good ones. You have to pay attention all the time so you can be sure you're both growing in the same direction."

Allyn obviously considered this only a temporary setback, and Bea hoped for her sake she was right. "It would be a shame for you guys to lose such a nice house. Maybe you should offer it out on a short-term lease while things shake out."

"That's what I thought too, but Melody's really pushing to sell it. Maybe it just hit her all of a sudden that we had this huge mortgage hanging over our heads. So much pressure to deal with every day. It's a lot more house than we need. This way we can start over with a clean slate. Who knows? If she needs a change, we might even decide to leave Seattle."

Her musings didn't seem realistic to Bea in light of the fact she was on her way to see an attorney this afternoon. More like the denial phase of grief.

"Look, I know you're feeling awful right now. I don't blame you one bit. But we've all been there at one time or another and if you ever feel like talking to somebody, I've got a pretty good ear. Or even if you just want a change of scenery and a friendly face or two, give us a yell. Dexter and I take a walk every day."

"We've all been there?" Her voice took on a bitter edge. "Have you ever had someone you love lie to you for six months? Start a secret life with somebody else? Kick you out of your own house?"

"Not that, but I went through a really painful situation a couple of years ago. It's tough when somebody else has all the control. I couldn't even—"

"So you haven't actually been there," Allyn said bluntly. "Melody was the person I planned to be with until the day I died. I don't mean to be rude, but if this hasn't happened to you, then you don't have a clue what it feels like. Nobody does unless they've lived it."

"You're right, Allyn. But I know it hurts." She also knew it was little consolation to hear that others had survived heartbreaking ordeals. Everyone dealt with grief in their own way.

"Hurt doesn't even begin to describe it." Allyn emptied her pocket and tossed two more treats toward Dexter. "I need to be getting back. Enjoy your walk."

Bea watched her walk away, wishing there were something useful she could say. Whether Allyn believed her or not, she knew exactly what it felt like to lose the one person she thought she'd have forever.

* * *

Jeremy Bronson was primly dressed in a pale blue shirt with a yellow tie, and his short blond hair glistened with styling gel. As he reviewed the papers from Melody's attorney, Allyn quietly calculated the cost of his professional expertise at roughly five dollars per minute and hoped he was a fast reader.

"I'll be honest with you, Allyn. I never thought we'd be doing this."

"That makes two of us."

Jeremy had handled their paperwork eight years ago when she and Melody filed for legal recognition as domestic partners, and again after they stood in line at city hall for seven hours with hundreds of other gay and lesbian couples who married on the first day Washington's same-sex marriage law took effect.

"As divorce filings go, this is more or less a standard first offer, or as I like to call it, wishful thinking. Just because we're a no-fault divorce state doesn't mean both parties should be equally accountable. You're going to incur quite a few expenses, and under these circumstances it's perfectly reasonable for you to ask Melody to cover those."

There were moments when Allyn wanted to take Melody for every penny she might earn as long as she lived. Then her rational side kicked in, the one that held out hope Melody would realize her mistake and beg to be forgiven.

"How much expense are we talking?"

"If your real estate agent is right about your appraisal, you should make a modest profit on the sale of your home, but realtor fees and closing costs could wipe that out and maybe then some. There are also moving expenses to consider, plus the things you'll have to replace if Melody claims them in the settlement. And of course, my fees."

If she were to drag her feet—perhaps by refusing to negotiate with potential buyers on the price of the house—it would buy time for Melody's epiphany. On the other hand, selling right away might be the only way to show Melody how much she'd lost, like the alcoholic who had to hit rock bottom before realizing she had to change.

He rubbed his chin as he continued to study the document. "Melody is asking for a strict division of marital assets by value.

Typically that means she doesn't actually want half of your shared possessions such as house furnishings, but half their monetary value. My suggestion is we cross that out and stipulate that she's entitled to half the house settlement, her vehicle, her personal items, such as clothing and electronics, family heirlooms and any assets she brought to the relationship eleven years ago."

"She took those things with her when she moved out. Does she seriously expect me to write her a check now for her half of the rest?"

"That's what she's asking, but we'll strike it. My experience is that people rarely push for that in a final settlement."

"So what am I supposed to do with all that furniture? I can't afford a house big enough to put it in."

"No, and I would advise against purchasing another house right now anyway. Following a divorce, most people experience a decline in their standard of living but you can mitigate that by controlling your expenses until you feel financially confident again. Rent something small, an apartment or a condominium. Then pick out the contents of the house you really want to keep and sell the rest on Craigslist."

It was true she didn't need a lot of space—one bedroom and an area she could use for an office. Even if Melody came back, there was no reason they needed a large home, especially since it was the idea of having children that had sparked Melody's anxieties in the first place.

Jeremy looked over their most recent joint tax filing, shaking his head. "No way. We're definitely crossing that off."

"Crossing what off?"

"I was looking down this list of joint marital assets, and it includes the pensions you've both earned during the marriage. Melody was barely vested in the state employees' pension, while you've put quite a bit away in a Roth IRA. That means you'd owe her money, but under the circumstances of your separation, that's completely unacceptable." He continued to redline items on the divorce agreement. "In fact, it's our position that you shouldn't have to endure any financial losses at all, certainly nothing out of pocket. We'll ask that Melody cover all closing costs on the sale of your home if it's sold at a profit. We'll also insist that she pay your attorney fees. That isn't unusual in a situation where one of the partners has broken the marriage contract. Her lawyer may strike all of these changes, but we'll put the bigger ones back in. Who knows? If she's really eager to get on with her life, she might even accept our revisions right away."

"I don't want to make this easy for her." She didn't want Melody to get on with her life, certainly not more than she already had—a new job, a new home and a new lover to keep her warm at night. There were no pieces for her to pick up in Tucson. "But I don't want to make her so mad that she won't ever consider coming back. I still believe this is just a phase. It's exciting to have an affair with someone. The glamour will wear off when everyday reality sets in."

Though he listened patiently, she could tell from his sympathetic look that he wasn't convinced. "Allyn, I know these situations can be very difficult to accept, but it's my experience when people get as far as filing one of these, the marriage usually doesn't recover. It all seems quite sudden to you, but keep in mind that Melody has had several months to adjust. While you still have strong feelings of love and trust, that probably isn't true for her. Nothing is certain, of course, but I think it's wise for you to prepare as if it's going to end."

It was only when he pushed a box of tissues across his desk that she realized she'd begun to cry.

"You were smart to bring this agreement to me. Some people just sign it because they're still trying to please their former spouse. They don't realize what they might be forfeiting. They expect to be treated fairly because they still feel married. Melody believes she can get away with taking advantage because you're vulnerable and she's probably accustomed to getting her way in the marriage. Am I right?"

Allyn nodded, unable to speak.

"She profoundly abused your trust and you shouldn't trust her anymore. My job is to make sure she doesn't continue to abuse you in this settlement. I've had many clients who were willing to make concessions just so they could put this painful chapter behind them. But then when the hurting stops, they realize they've sacrificed too much. It's entirely possible one of you will feel that way. I want it to be Melody. Not you."

* * *

Allyn's hand shook so hard she could barely scroll her computer screen. Through her tears, she read again Melody's email response to Jeremy's revised settlement, hoping against hope for a clue as to what she could do to erase its devastating message.

I just got your copy of the divorce agreement, and all I can say is WOW! If you think by sticking it to me you can make me change my mind, I've got news for you. I'm even more determined than ever to divorce you even if I have to take out a loan to do it.

It's very sad to think we could have at least been friends after so many years together but you had to go and ruin that by being petty and vindictive. Now that you've reduced our whole marriage to dollars and cents, consider it the price of our friendship. I hope it was worth it.

Attached was a scanned copy of Jeremy's document, signed and dated without changes. In three short months, their marriage would be over.

CHAPTER FIVE

Before she settled on the Ballard location for her franchise, Bea had explored the district of North Seattle. In particular, she liked Broadview, since it was densely populated and several miles from a US Post Office. The problem back then was there was already a Pak & Ship in the neighborhood. Now, seven years later, that franchise was for sale and she was considering making an offer. Another small business loan, two or three more employees—likely doable unless there were problems she didn't yet know about.

Pak & Ship was one of the fastest growing franchises in the country, so it was difficult to understand why anyone would want to unload one, especially in a prime location. A bustling supermarket anchored the shopping center while a pharmacy, bank and hardware store brought additional traffic. Plenty of parking, easy access. This store should be raking in money but the asking price didn't reflect that.

The glass door was propped open with cardboard folded into a makeshift doorstop, which probably meant the owners were too cheap to run the air conditioner on one of the hottest days of the summer. Where else were they cutting corners?

She got her answer the moment she stepped inside. Dirty shelves, stained carpet and merchandise displayed in the wrong bins. There were boxes stacked askew in random places throughout the store, and the counter was littered with mailing labels and envelopes that might never make it to their intended destinations. Why on earth would customers trust this Pak & Ship with their personal mail?

As she browsed the packing supplies, she checked out the counter clerk, a dark-haired woman who appeared to be in her early twenties. Her attention was glued to a game show that played on a TV mounted in the corner. It was telling that Bea had wandered the store alone for five minutes and the woman hadn't offered to assist her.

This Pak & Ship was failing because the owner had turned over his business to apathetic employees with no oversight. She had little doubt she could turn it around if she hired and trained the right help, and split her time between the stores.

The clerk barely took her eyes from the TV screen as she collected the money for Bea's modest purchase. She probably worked for minimum wage and cared little if customers came back or not.

As she turned to leave, a woman entered the store and walked straight to the mailboxes on the far wall. Tall and bone thin with silky blond hair, there was something familiar about her. It was only when she looked up that Bea caught a glimpse of her turquoise eyes and realized who she was.

"Allyn? Allyn Teague?"

Allyn also took an extra moment before recognition set in, but then gave a tentative smile. Not a huge grin by any means... kind of wistful in fact. She'd lost weight—a great deal of weight—to the point that her breastbone was prominent across the scoop of her tank top. "Bea Lawson. Aren't you a little out of your neighborhood?"

"Just doing a little competitive intelligence," she replied, keeping her voice low. Not that it mattered, since the clerk was absorbed in her game show again. "This franchise is for sale and I'm checking it out. I figure Kit could help me turn it around. You remember her, the woman who works for me."

"With the Big Ol' Dyke tattoo." Allyn brushed her upper arm.

"That's the one." Bea hadn't seen Allyn since the short walk they'd taken together last January, and recalled now that she'd sent in a notice by email to have her mail forwarded to this branch. "I take it you live in this neighborhood now."

"Yeah, I have an apartment a couple of blocks from here. Quite a step down from Redwood Heights, huh?"

"I wouldn't say that at all. I always liked this area. In fact, I would have put my store here if there hadn't already been one." Bea was glad for the sudden rain shower, a staple of August, that kept them huddled on the sidewalk in front of the store. Though Allyn had never been what she'd call a friend, she often wished their last conversation hadn't ended on such a caustic note. "I don't want to be nosy or anything, but how are you doing?"

Allyn smiled grimly. "I'm…fine, I guess. I owe you an apology. You wouldn't believe how many times I've thought about that day we went out for a walk and I snapped your head off. Everything was so raw back then. One minute I felt like my heart would stop beating, and the next I'd be mad that it didn't. I took that out on you, and I'm sorry."

"It's okay. I could see you were in a really bad place." She wouldn't make the mistake again of presuming to know how Allyn felt.

"It was a tough time. Selling the house and all our stuff. Dealing with the lawyers, and then having to tell everybody what happened when I didn't even understand it myself."

"You look like you've lost a lot of weight." Way too much, in fact.

"I had some trouble eating after Melody left. Then my stomach got all screwed up. Some days it feels like I'm getting back to normal, whatever that is. I just try to put one foot in front of the other and keep walking."

Seven months was a long time to grieve, especially since it seemed to be taking such a physical toll. "How's work going?"

"Busier than ever. It turned out to be a good place to put my energy."

Bea could relate to that. If not for the demands of her store, she might never have pulled herself out of her funk.

The rain lessened but not enough that Allyn could walk home without getting soaked.

"Can I give you a lift?"

Allyn scrunched her nose as she peeked out from under the awning. "It's just a little water. I won't melt."

"No, but your mail will get wet." Bea raced to her car and leaned over to open the passenger door. "Dexter's going to go crazy when he picks up your scent and realizes you've been in my car."

"How is my little buddy?"

"Still amazing. Sweet as ever. Hey, we're going to Summerfest tomorrow in Kirkwood. Why don't you come with us? There's music, street performers and my personal favorite, the best bratwurst in Seattle."

"Thanks, but…" Allyn shook her head. "I just don't think I'd be much fun."

"You don't have to be fun. You just have to have fun. Have you been out much since Melody left?"

"With other people? Not really. It feels creepy to hang out with our old friends knowing some of them still keep up with Melody. I got invited to a party over Memorial Weekend—I didn't go—but I found out later she and her new girlfriend were there. They'd flown up for the holiday so Melody could introduce her to everyone." Her voice got louder and more resentful with every word. "It would have been a disaster if I'd gone because I probably would have cried and yelled and made a general fool of myself. I don't have any idea what she's told any of our friends, but mostly I'm worried someone will report back to her about me. I don't want her to know I'm still a mess after all this time."

Bea was hesitant to reply, worried one tiny spark would ignite the air around them. The alternative was increasingly awkward silence. "I totally get it. And since you're not seeing any of your old friends, that's all the more reason you should come with Dexter and me tomorrow. I have to warn you though that some of my pals might be there, but we don't have to hang out with them unless you want to."

Allyn sighed but nodded slightly, more like surrender than enthusiasm. "I don't know, Bea. If I go...how do I say this? It's not like a date or anything, is it? Because I'm not up for that sort of thing. And I'm not really up for socializing with a whole bunch of people either. You know, I probably shouldn't go."

"Just chill a minute. It's not a date, and like I said, we don't have to hook up with anybody. Just say hi if they walk by. The fact is, I get tired of always being the only one there not attached at the hip to somebody else—not that I mind being by myself. It's just that sometimes I feel like a third wheel, so I kind of make it a rule not to hang around the same people too long. And when I start to feel like everyone's pairing off, I leave."

"I guess I could handle that."

"Cool. Keep in mind though if anybody sees us they might think we're together, but that's actually good because it means they won't be trying to fix either of us up with anyone else. You wouldn't believe the women they want me to meet. They're either twenty or sixty. Unemployed or retired. Tattooed or Botoxed."

Allyn finally laughed, the first chortle that sounded both genuine and spontaneous.

"Seriously, do I look that desperate to you?" Bea joked. "I mean, I know I'm not a prize or anything, but I could get a date if I really wanted one. It just so happens I prefer my dog to most people. He's not the best kisser, but..."

"Oh, no. Don't even go there. You're creeping me out."

"I've always said dogs were great company. Make of that what you will." She started the car and eased out of the parking space. "Now tell me where I'm going so I'll know where to pick you up."

On the short drive to Allyn's apartment complex, Bea could hear Kit's mocking voice playing in her head. Was she flirting with Allyn? She hadn't meant to. Catching a woman on the rebound was always a bad idea, especially a woman who was so obviously devastated.

Not only devastated. Damaged. The drastic weight loss was more than just "a little trouble eating," and her willingness to cut herself off from everyone she knew because of Melody was borderline paranoia.

Yet there was something Bea found compelling, whether it was just the chance to reach out to another human being and let her know the world was still a decent place, or some deep-seated desire to be a rescuer. She remembered the old Allyn as sweet and easygoing. Bea wanted *that* woman back.

CHAPTER SIX

"It's not a date," Allyn repeated as she dusted her cheeks with blush. The last time she'd bothered with makeup was over a month ago when she'd gone shopping for clothes that would fit her much thinner frame.

Blessed with a smooth complexion and eyes so blue that even strangers commented on them, she'd never been one to go overboard when it came to cosmetics. Her brows were naturally sculpted and her blond lashes so long they didn't need mascara to stand out. Still, a little foundation and eye shadow highlighted what she thought were her best features. After what she'd been through, anything that made her feel better about herself was worth doing.

It surprised her to realize this morning that she was looking forward to spending the day with Bea. "And Dexter," she reminded herself aloud. The lesbian community in Seattle was large enough to hold two completely independent social circles, meaning there was a good chance she wouldn't run into any of her old friends. Even if she did, the worst that could happen was someone telling Melody they'd seen her out with Bea Lawson. Considering Melody had once remarked that she thought Bea was cute, it wouldn't be the end of the world if word got back to her. In fact, it might even trigger a little jealousy.

She tugged on a new pair of knee-length stonewashed jeans and tried on several tops, settling on a rust-colored off-the-shoulder knit. One advantage to being thinner was being able to wear a tank top underneath instead of a bra, and she loved the freedom.

In all, she'd dropped thirty-three pounds off her five-nine frame, from a size fourteen to an eight. It was true she'd had stomach issues after Melody left, but by the time she got her anxiety and depression under control well enough to start eating again, she'd become fascinated with her power to move the scales. It was satisfying finally to be in control of something, and it was visual proof of the harm Melody had inflicted on her. But then her periods stopped, and her doctor told her she was flirting with anorexia, which he characterized as a mental health disorder. She couldn't allow Melody to break her that way, since it would only add to the list of reasons she'd left. *I always knew Allyn had mental issues.*

She'd finally learned the other woman's name from a real estate document she'd signed as a witness to Melody's signature, and was able to put together bits and pieces about who she was—Naomi Frankland, a grant writer in the College of Letters, Arts and Science at the University of Arizona. She was twenty-nine and from Flagstaff where her father was a minister. Probably named her for the Biblical character. Allyn would have loved being a fly on the wall for Melody's trip home to meet the family. *Dad, this is my new lesbian lover, who happens to be married to someone else.*

At least Melody had the good sense to keep their photos off Facebook, but Allyn managed to find one of Naomi in the university's newsletter. Short hair, plain face with pale features. From her broad shoulders and the obvious muscles in her arms and neck, she looked like an athlete. Odd, since Melody hated anything having to do with sports.

The same general physical description could apply to Bea, except Naomi was plain vanilla whereas Bea was far more distinctive. Bea's triangular face, dark shaggy hair and wide green eyes reminded her of anime, the Japanese cartoon figures.

Melody was right about Bea, but cute wasn't quite the right word. Striking was more like it.

The last step to getting ready was collecting her jewelry— onyx earrings that matched her tank top, a silver wristwatch woven into a black leather bracelet, and her wedding ring, a wide gold band with diamond insets she'd taken to wearing on her right hand. If the day ever came that Melody returned, she wanted to be able to say she'd never stopped wearing it. That would prove her love was unbreakable.

Bea saved her the anxiety of waiting by knocking on the door ten minutes early. She wore a loose, white cotton shirt tucked into casual gray shorts, cuffed so they hit her mid-thigh, and sports sandals. An attractive outfit for its simplicity. It was the first time Allyn could recall seeing her in anything but khaki pants and a dark green shirt with Pak & Ship stitched on the pocket.

"Hey! I didn't mean to get here so soon but there's hardly any traffic. Guess everyone's in church but us heathens."

"It's okay. I'm ready."

Dexter barked and stood on his hind legs as Bea held firm to his leash.

Allyn was pleased he seemed to remember her, and she cradled his head to deliver a kiss to his snout. "Are you expecting a treat? Is that why you're prancing around? I don't have any. Maybe a slice of ham."

"Forget the treat. He'd much rather get sweet-talked and scratched behind the ears."

"It's nice he remembers me."

"He wouldn't forget his best buddy. I think he missed you when you moved over here. We went walking one day in Redwood Heights and he got really excited when we went by your old house."

"I haven't been back there at all." She'd never even met the new owners, opting to handle the closing by mail after their agent said Melody wouldn't be attending. Per their final agreement, they'd split a tidy profit of twenty-eight thousand, though Melody had paid closing costs and attorney fees out of hers. Allyn had banked her windfall in hopes of sharing it if they ever got back together. "I don't miss it. It was always…I don't know, too cookie cutter for me. That's fine for an apartment or condo, but houses ought to have more character."

"If by character you mean creaky floors and noisy pipes, then mine qualifies. It also has dog toys in every room."

Before they got in, Bea hitched Dexter's harness to a seat belt in the backseat.

"I get the feeling I'm taking his spot," Allyn said.

"Actually, I am. If it weren't for that harness, he'd be in my lap trying to drive."

It was good to have Dexter around because he lent a casual aura to the day. Allyn had no idea why she'd even said yes to coming along in the first place. Events like these—festivals, fairs, craft shows—had never been high on her list. Too many people milling around, ridiculous traffic and parking, and no place to sit if you got tired. At least those were Melody's complaints, which made them Allyn's too.

"We never went to many things like this," she volunteered. "Melody worked all week at the university and hardly ever wanted to do anything on the weekends except relax."

"Whereas you worked at home all the time. I bet you had a bad case of cabin fever."

"I got used to it." Just one of the many accommodations she'd made so Melody would be happy. "I must not have cared about it too much because I've hardly been out of the house since she left."

"Today's all about having fun. If you need proof, just look over your shoulder. Dexter gives out smiles for free."

The instant she turned around, Dexter's tongue swiped her face.

"What'd I tell you? It's impossible to feel bad around a dog."

* * *

With two bratwursts in hand, Bea stopped to survey the crowd so she could navigate her way back to where Allyn waited with Dexter. Their blanket was spread on the hillside. Allyn, shielding her eyes against the sun to see the action on the lake, was laughing. It was nice to see her enjoying herself.

"Here you go, mustard and sauerkraut. What did I miss?"

"All of the boats are falling apart as soon as they hit the water."

"Ah, the Cardboard Regatta. Whoever paddles the farthest without sinking wins."

"Who dreams up these silly things?" Allyn took a bite of her brat, leaving a dab of mustard on her chin.

Bea nonchalantly reached out with her napkin and wiped it away. "I suppose it could be a metaphor for the futility of life."

"The Fatalism Festival?"

"That's in the fall, in Fauntleroy," Bea quipped, relishing another smile from Allyn. "Next up is the Canine Carnival."

"In Canada!" they shouted simultaneously.

Allyn took another bite and broke off a generous chunk for Dexter. "It feels good to laugh."

"It looks good on you too." Kit would definitely consider that flirting, and Bea would be hard-pressed to disagree. "Everyone looks good when they smile. Don't you think?"

"I guess." Her face had fallen, and she gave the rest of her brat to Dexter. "I haven't had much to smile about for a long time. Some days I tell myself that's it. I've cried enough, yelled enough, walked the floors enough, and I convince myself it's time to put it all behind me. Then I come across a photo or a trinket, something that reminds me of what I've lost, and all I can think about is getting it back again."

"It must have been really devastating. I felt so sorry for you that day. I wanted to give you a hug but something told me you wouldn't go for that."

The crowd around them cheered, but by the time they looked up, the spectacle had passed.

"Melody's the only person I've ever…you know, been with. She had a couple of girlfriends before we met, and now I wonder if she had any others while we were together. You think you know somebody, and then you find out it's all just a mirage. How am I supposed to have faith in anything after that?"

Bea was surprised to hear Allyn speak in such a starkly personal manner. If she'd been holding all her old friends at arm's length to avoid word getting back to Melody, this might be the first time she'd talked about her feelings with anyone.

"The worst part isn't even that she left. It's how cold she's been about everything. I just don't see how a person who promised she'd love me till she died could suddenly treat me like I didn't even exist. It's like I was hit by a truck and lying in the road, and she stepped right over me. All I wanted was one small acknowledgment that she cared whether I lived or died, and I got nothing. No calls, no emails. Not even a text on my birthday."

"When was your birthday?"

"Eight days ago."

"Let's celebrate now. I'll buy you a beer."

Allyn shook her head. "Drinking's about the worst thing I can do. I'd just get depressed, and the next thing you know I'd be calling her and making a fool of myself again."

Again. Guess she'd done that before. "Allyn, have you talked to anybody about how you're feeling? I'm not trying to stick my nose in your business, but it's hard not to notice that you've lost a lot of weight. Too much if you ask me, and you just gave most of your lunch to Dexter. I'm worried you're not taking care of yourself."

"I'm fine. I just want my life back."

Bea hated to be the bearer of bad news, but she was pretty sure that old life wasn't coming back. "Are you sure that's what you want? Even if in your heart you really want to forgive her, you'll always know what she did. Could you honestly take her back without constantly wanting to check her phone and email to make sure she wasn't cheating on you? What about the first time she tells you she has to travel for work? Anyone who would do something like that once could do it again. The woman treated you like shit. She doesn't deserve you."

Allyn wiped a tear away before turning all of her attention toward Dexter.

"Look, I know you didn't ask my opinion," Bea went on, "and it's easy for people like me to sit on the outside and act like the voice of authority. It's just that I got the feeling from the way you've been talking that you already realize you can't trust her again and maybe you needed somebody to tell you it was okay to feel that way."

"I would trust her again if she asked me to...if I thought she was really sincere."

Bea didn't believe that for a minute, but she had to respect that Allyn did. They didn't call it "clinging to hope" for nothing.

"I appreciate you listening," Allyn said. "It's true I haven't really talked to anybody about how I was feeling. Certainly not any of our old friends."

"What about your family?"

"Oh, hell no. My parents live in Centralia. I called about a month after we filed the papers and my mom said not to make such a big deal out of it, it wasn't a real marriage anyway."

"Oh, God. I think we might be related," Bea said with a chuckle. "The only way my folks can accept me as a lesbian is if I don't act on it. It's a church thing."

"With my mother, it's an ignorance thing. Willful ignorance."

The crowd began to disperse, a signal the water show was over. Allyn held Dexter's leash while Bea rolled up the blanket.

"They're doing Shakespeare at two o'clock. *A Midsummer Night's Dream*. Should we make our way over to the stage?"

Allyn had already started walking in the direction of the car. "Would it be okay if we called it a day? I'm getting kind of tired."

It was true they'd walked a lot, and Allyn had held onto Dexter much of the day. Still, it was hard not to think her readiness to leave was related to their depressing discussion of Melody.

"I'm sorry if I bummed you out, Allyn. Sometimes my mouth runs a little faster than my brain. I probably came off as insensitive. If you feel like talking some more, we can find a place to relax. I can even drop Dexter off at home if you want to go somewhere and grab a coffee…whatever you want."

"I appreciate the offer, but I really am tired. I'm not used to spending a whole day on my feet."

"You're sure it wasn't anything I said."

"Not at all. To be honest it felt good to have somebody listen. It may not seem like it but I've all but given up on Melody coming back. The problem is knowing it and accepting it are two different things. And you're right—even if she did come back, I'd never be able to trust her completely."

During the ride back to the apartment, Allyn sat twisted in her seat so she could feed Dexter pieces of kibble. It was a good strategy for avoiding conversation, Bea thought, but she didn't want this to be their only day out.

"I don't suppose you play softball."

Allyn tilted her head pensively. "That's the game with the stick, right? No, wait. It's called a bat."

Bea laughed. "I take it that's a no. Too bad. We have a ragtag team in the Wednesday night recreation league. Kit's the coach. Our season's almost over, but I was hoping you'd come along and hold a glove out in right field. Otherwise we might have to forfeit this week because four of our players are on vacation."

"Right field? I played first base in high school." She held up her left hand. "That's where they put the southpaws."

"Are you kidding me? Can you hit?"

"Maybe…if I can remember which end of the stick to hold."

"Please tell me that means you'll come. Six fifteen at the Ballard Playground. Your old stomping grounds. I'd pick you up but I'm at the store till six. I barely have time to get there."

"I don't have a mitt."

"We can fix that. I'll ask around for a lefty." In her head, she was already planning a trip to the sporting goods store, whatever it took to get Allyn on the team. "This is going to be so cool."

"I can't believe I'm letting you talk me into this. I haven't played in fifteen years."

"No pressure. We play for fun, and we usually go out for burgers afterward."

"I don't know about that part," Allyn said. "I'll probably need to come home and soak in the tub."

Bea pulled into the parking lot at the apartment complex. "Thanks for coming with me today. I had a good time. So did Dexter. He really likes you."

"I like him too."

Kit's voice was in her ear again, mocking her about going in for a goodbye kiss. Allyn wasn't a romantic interest. She was a woman coming off a tough breakup who needed a friend.

"Hey, Allyn?" She reached out and clasped the slender wrist as Allyn was exiting the car. "I hope this means we're going to be friends. I'd like that a lot."

"Sure." Her face began to turn red. "You know I'm not…"

"Same here." She held out her fist for a bump. "Friends."

CHAPTER SEVEN

It was nice to see the celebratory camaraderie of the softball dugout hadn't changed in all these years. When it came to sports, grown women still behaved like excited teenagers, and from the moment she arrived, Allyn was made to feel one of the gang.

"I still can't believe I said yes to this," she muttered playfully as she slipped the dark green T-shirt over her white one. She'd spent every spare moment of the last three days working out in the fitness room of her apartment complex so as not to make an utter fool of herself, and now the muscles in her thighs screamed every time she moved.

"You did," Bea said, "and you're totally rocking that shirt, if I must say so myself. Did you happen to notice that lovely Pak & Ship logo?"

"I'm a walking billboard."

"That's right. No pressure though. You don't have to feel embarrassed if you drop a ball or strike out while wearing a shirt with the name of my business on it."

"Your confidence is gratifying," Allyn said dryly.

"Our record is two and six. We lose a lot, but nobody really cares as long as we have fun." Bea lowered her voice. "Except Kit yells at us every single game to take our heads out of our asses. Don't take it personally. She's just frustrated because Marta won't let her play anymore. Bad shoulder from carrying that mail pouch."

Though everyone welcomed her, Kit acted the most enthused about having her on the team. She'd been all smiles, and repeatedly slapped Bea on the back for bringing her along.

"Oh, and by the way. See that woman in the bleachers wearing the shirt like ours? Red hair and glasses? That's Kit's wife, Marta. She's half-saint, half spitfire. You'll meet her after the game at JoJo's."

Their opponent was Hawthorne Medical Supply. The name was familiar but Allyn couldn't place it. It was possible they'd contacted her for potential IT hires, someone to secure their customer network. She'd look it up when she got home.

When Pak & Ship took the field, Allyn warmed up by tossing grounders to the infield and getting a feel for how everyone threw. It was impressive how much zip Bea put on the ball from third base, and while their stated objective was to have fun, it was clear this team was more competitive than their record let on.

The first two outs came quickly in the form of a pop fly to shallow center and a line drive back to the pitcher. The third batter was caught looking at strike three.

"Nothing to this game," she said to Bea when they reached the dugout.

Since she was last in the batting order, she went all the way to the end of the bench to cheer on her teammates. Kit had a rule against swinging at the first pitch to put more pressure on the pitcher, but they squandered a base on balls with a double-play grounder and ended their half of the inning with a long out to left.

It was like that for three more innings until Hawthorne threatened to break it open with a two-out double. Needing just one more out, Pak & Ship intentionally walked the next batter to get a force on every bag.

"Allyn Teague!"

She was shocked to hear her name, and even more disturbed to realize the base runner was Jillian, Melody's friend. With her hair pulled back through her cap, Allyn hadn't recognized her earlier at the plate.

"Wow, look how much weight you've lost. I hardly recognized you."

"I've been on a fitness kick," Allyn answered gruffly, not taking her eye off the batter. Was Jillian stupid enough to think helping Melody hide her infidelity would have no effect on their friendship?

"How have you been?"

Allyn was saved from answering by a sharply hit grounder to her right, which she fielded and tossed to second to get Jillian out. By the time she got back to the dugout, she felt as if she might throw up.

"Great play!" Bea said, slapping Allyn's thigh with her glove. "You got us out of a jam. Now we need to get some hits."

"This was stupid. I shouldn't have come."

"What's the matter?"

"That woman playing third base, the one we just walked." Allyn nodded across the field. "I didn't realize it until I saw her up close. That's Jillian Rosenfeld. She's Melody's friend, the one who helped her cheat on me."

Bea followed her gaze with a sneer. "Gotcha. So how do you want to handle this? I can try to smack one down the line… right about shin level. That's where I get the most bruises."

"What I'd really like to do is leave. I know I can't because we'd forfeit, but since you asked, that's how I'd handle it if I could. I bet she'll go straight home and call Melody to tell her she saw me."

"What's wrong with that? You're out here having fun with a great bunch of women."

There were many things wrong with it. She'd hoped never to see any of Melody's conniving friends again. She didn't want details of her life to find their way to Tucson, and she damn sure didn't want Melody thinking she was off the hook for causing so much pain now that Allyn was obviously enjoying herself again and making new friends. Anyone who could be that cruel didn't deserve a clear conscience.

"You can leave if you really want to. They'll let us play with nine." Bea started tossing up a ball so that it fell gently into her glove. "Of course, then she'd probably tell Melody she ran you off."

"No fucking way. I'm not giving her that kind of power over me."

"Damn right you're not."

Kit clapped her hands twice. "Let's go, Bea! You're on deck."

As promised, Bea hammered one down the line. Jillian jumped out of its path rather than risk injury and endured a fair bit of teasing from her teammates as a result.

Allyn was delighted to see that Bea had her back and was willing to go out there and exact revenge on her behalf. For as long as she could remember, it was Melody who stood up for her, who gave her a lift when things weren't going her way. It was only now she realized no one had been on her side for a very long time.

When the inning died with Bea stranded on second, Allyn grabbed both gloves and carried them out to the field. "Thanks. I owe you one."

"I missed. Maybe I'll get another shot if we go extra innings."

They reached the last inning in a scoreless tie and Allyn came to the plate with one out and nobody on base. Her line drive sailed up the middle for a base hit, and when the center fielder bobbled the ball, she raced for second.

"Tag up on a fly ball," Kit yelled from her coaching box at third base.

If she did that, she'd end up on third where she'd have to endure more small talk from Jillian. She'd rather see Caroline strike out.

Instead she hit the second pitch high in the air to center field. With her heel on the bag, Allyn watched Kit for the signal to run. It came the instant she heard the ball hit the fielder's glove, and she raced to third as fast as her feet would go.

Kit was on her knee pointing at the ground. "Get down!"

No way was Allyn going to slide. Pouring it on, she touched the corner of the bag on a wide turn and dug hard for home.

"No!"

It was too late to stop. Bea, who'd been in the on-deck circle, scurried to move the bat out of the way, her eyes wide and mouth agape. Then she broke into a smile and began jumping up and down.

The catcher had hustled down the line to back up the throw to third, leaving home plate uncovered. Allyn crossed with ease.

Their teammates poured out of the dugout for a celebration on the field, and Allyn let herself get swept up in the excitement. They didn't have to know she'd only run for home so she wouldn't be trapped on third with Jillian.

"Hey, you!" Kit stormed over to the huddle and glared at her menacingly...before bursting into a grin. "Remind me to go over the hand signals with you before our next game."

Bea chucked Kit on the shoulder. "I'm pretty sure I saw her give you a hand signal when she ran by."

* * *

"I wish I'd had a camera. The look on that third baseman's face was priceless." The observation came from Marta, who seemed as happy as Kit about having Allyn join their team. Bea suspected they were reading more into her friendship with Allyn than they should.

The after-parties were as much fun as the game itself, especially on those rare occasions when they won. JoJo's, a Ballard sports bar, was their favorite postgame hangout, and tonight they had the outdoor seating on the patio all to themselves.

They would relive today's epic finish for years to come, but as far as Bea was concerned, the highlight was seeing Allyn humiliate Melody's friend. She doubted seriously Jillian would be sharing that part on her call to Tucson, but Allyn was probably right that she'd update Melody on everything else.

Kit pounded her beer mug on the table and shook her finger, a typical over-the-top display that was all for show. "Who runs for home when the base coach is yelling like a banshee for you to get down? What the hell were you thinking?"

"You mean right at that moment?" Allyn sipped her lemonade and looked about with feigned innocence. "I was thinking you were crazy if you thought I was going to slide. I haven't played this game since high school and I didn't want my first time back to end in the emergency room."

"Besides," Bea interjected, "the throw beat her there. If she'd slid, she probably would have been out. It was genius."

Kit threw up her hands. "I know. I'm only mad because I didn't think of it."

"It wouldn't have worked. If you'd been waving me around, their pitcher would have run over to cover home."

Bea raised her mug in a toast. "To Allyn, who outfoxed everybody, including our coach."

She was glad and even a little surprised when Allyn agreed to join them at the sports bar. After her near meltdown on the field over seeing Melody's friend, Bea was sure she'd hightail it out of there, probably never to be seen again. Instead she'd faced down a demon and won.

Allyn pushed her chair back and stood. "On that note, I need to get home. I have a call tomorrow morning at six a.m."

"Why so early?" Marta asked.

"I start most days like that. The guy I need to talk to is in Raleigh, so it's already nine o'clock in his office. He doesn't care what time it is out here."

"I'll walk you out," Bea said, resting her hand on Allyn's shoulder. "I'm really glad you came. In case you haven't figured it out, so is everybody else. We've only got two more games this season, but we'd sure like to have you back."

"Wouldn't want to waste my brand-new mitt." Allyn paused before getting into her car. "I appreciate you going to bat for me—pun intended. I had no idea you were serious about smacking her on the shins."

"What can I say? I just went with the inside pitch." With a wink, she added, "That's my story and I'm sticking to it."

The party had broken up by the time she returned to the patio, leaving only Kit and Marta at a long table of empty plates, mugs and pitchers. Bea knew the two of them well enough to expect the third degree.

"Can't wait to hear this story."

"Don't even start. It's not what you think. We're just friends."

"What's going on with her? She's lost a lot of weight. Is she sick or something? That would suck." Kit never had been one to mince words.

"She's not sick. She's had a hard time. What she's been through, that screws up your head."

Marta looked back and forth between them. "What do you mean, what she's been through? I thought she was just one of your customers."

"Used to be but she moved after she got divorced," Kit explained.

"It was ugly. Never saw it coming. Her wife got involved with somebody else last winter. Blindsided her with divorce papers. She's hardly been out of the house since. Tonight might have been the first time she's had fun in forever." There was no reason to share the drama about how Allyn knew Hawthorne's third baseman.

Kit poked her playfully. "So what's this about being just friends? It's obvious you two have some chemistry. She was practically glued to your side all night."

"Pffft! That's because she didn't know anyone else but you, and you're not exactly what I'd call a human welcome mat. I had a hard time convincing her to come out...she doesn't trust anybody. Hell, she might be fucked up forever for all I know. I think that woman really did a number on her, so do me a favor. Don't go giggling and making jokes about us, or she'll get freaked out and that'll be all she wrote."

Marta placed a hand over Kit's mouth. "She won't say another word."

"Thank you."

The second her mouth was free, Kit said, "One more thing. Please tell me this isn't just you being a good Samaritan. Once she loosens up a little, you move on to phase two, right?"

"I can't fathom why my personal life is so important to you. Maybe if I were complaining all the time, that would make sense." Bea didn't like the edge in her voice, but that's what it took sometimes to get Kit to see that she was pushing the limits of her patience. "You know perfectly well how I feel about getting involved with somebody. And you know why. Don't make it your mission to put me somewhere I don't want to be."

"Whoa!" Kit threw up her hands defensively. "You don't have to get mad about it."

"I'm not mad." She was, but it was her own fault. "I realize I send you mixed messages. Sometimes I try to humor you instead of just asking you to drop it. You guys are my best friends and I should be more honest with you about how I feel. I promise I'll tell you if something changes, but for now, it's not happening."

They smoothed their rift with a couple of jokes and parted on solid footing, but Bea found herself struggling already with her promise. What she couldn't tell them was that Allyn was the first woman in four years to make her feel it might be possible to move on.

CHAPTER EIGHT

Bea fine-tuned the radio dial in her car to sharpen the signal as she moved farther from Seattle. The Mariners were back east playing a doubleheader against the Red Sox. If she were at home instead of driving, she might have asked Allyn over for lunch so they could watch the game on TV together.

On the other hand, another invitation to hang out could have been too much too soon. It was only a week ago they'd gone to the festival. After playing softball on Wednesday, they'd gone out on Friday for a movie to catch a summer superhero blockbuster at the end of its run in the theaters. Allyn thought it a remarkable coincidence they were the last two people in America to see it.

It was undeniable Allyn was loosening up a bit, laughing more easily and talking about things other than Melody. One thing she hadn't done was ask Bea about herself, which was perfectly understandable given everything she'd been through. Bea knew all too well how a devastating breakup could suck up one's emotional energy, leaving little for others. If their friendship continued to grow, she would share with Allyn how she'd learned that particular truism.

She'd been having serious talks with Dexter about Allyn. Unlike Kit and Marta, he was a good listener and didn't push her in one direction or the other as she tried to unpack her feelings. She'd been adamant to everyone—herself included—that she was pursuing only friendship with Allyn, all the while knowing it wasn't normal to be so excited about spending time with a friend or so concerned with looking nice and acting cool.

Allyn Teague might very well be someone she could fall for, but not until she put the ordeal with Melody behind her. It wasn't possible simply to turn off that switch—Bea knew that too—but the final stage of grief was acceptance. Allyn would get there eventually, whether she wanted to or not. There was no other way to go on living.

"We're almost there, Dexxie." Bea straightened his purple bandana which she'd chosen because it matched her shirt. He always got antsy at the end of a long ride as if cued by the stops and turns once they pulled off the freeway.

They made this trip the first Sunday of every month, a two-and-half-hour drive across the Canadian border to Vancouver. After four years of first Sundays, the car seemed to drive itself, finally pulling into the circular driveway in front of a two-story brick home with tall white columns framing the front door.

The Huangs were second-generation Chinese-Canadians with strong family ties to the old country. Dr. and Dr. Huang, a psychiatrist and a pediatrician. Their children were grown and gone except for Wendy, their eldest.

Bea gave Dexter a few minutes in the yard before ringing the bell, which was answered by a short stocky woman in her early twenties. "Hi, Krystal. You doing okay?"

The woman crouched behind the door to stay clear of Dexter. A dog phobia since childhood, she'd explained. "I'm fine. Wendy's in the sunroom. I'll bring lunch out in a few minutes."

"How is she?"

"She's running a little fever but made me promise not to tell anyone. She was afraid The Doctors would call you and tell you not to come."

"You want me to do anything?"

"Just don't let her talk too much, and call me if you think she needs to cough."

Bea knew the way to the sunroom, and so did Dexter, who always stayed on his leash inside the elegant house. He was too excitable to be allowed to run wild amidst the fine furniture and artwork, especially since his toenails might scratch the polished hardwood floors.

The sunroom was aptly named on a beautiful day such as this one, with floor-to-ceiling windows that overlooked a colorful tiered garden. In the corner facing out was a state-of-the-art wheelchair, its occupant paralyzed from the neck down.

Wendy Huang, her former wife.

* * *

When it came to housekeeping, Allyn was glad for her small apartment. Fifteen minutes with a vacuum cleaner. Five with a dust cloth. Another five with a sponge mop in the kitchen and bathroom. Clean sheets and towels. Laundry folded and put away.

She couldn't remember the last time her entire home and office were in order. Probably sometime in her old house when a cleaning service came in twice a month. It was the only way they could manage in such a large place, given their long workdays.

Once in a while she wondered if she might have discovered Melody's secret had she gone into her office to clean. She certainly would have been curious as to why Melody thought it necessary to lock her desk and file cabinet, or to protect her computer with a password. She'd taken no notice of those things until the night Melody left.

For the first time since she'd lived in the apartment, she raised all the windows to let a fresh breeze blow through. It was a gorgeous day, sunny and warm, and there were distant voices emanating from the courtyard pool.

Her home wasn't the only thing that was open. For months she'd closed herself off from the rest of the world, interacting with people only on the phone at work or as necessary when she shopped or ran errands. The turning point had come the day she ran into Bea at the Pak & Ship.

With no allies from her former life, Allyn appreciated what Bea could offer as a friend. She'd barely known Melody, so Allyn didn't have to worry that she might have been complicit in keeping secrets, or that her head was already full of Melody's one-sided tales of what went wrong.

It felt good to have someone in her corner, a friend all her own.

Only one major chore remained—deciding what to do with the photos, cards and mementos of an eleven-year relationship. For the past two days, she'd collected those items in a haphazard pile covering her coffee table. With each piece she added, her feeling about their disposition alternated between anticipation and dread.

The impetus for her task was an article she'd stumbled upon online after taking a pop psychology quiz on emotional well-being. "Life After Love" promised insight into getting back on track after divorce, and though she'd doubted initially that any of the techniques would be relevant to her unique situation, there was one idea that struck her as potentially worthwhile. It was, after all, indisputable that she spent too much time tormenting herself with the tangible memories of her years with Melody, wondering where and when it all went wrong. One of the suggestions was to remove those painful reminders of heartache from her everyday life—collecting each and every one, sealing them in a box and storing them where they couldn't be accessed easily. When her heart was healed, the author said, she could once again open the box and appreciate the memories without breaking down over what she'd lost.

Allyn doubted she'd ever recover from the hurt, but she had to learn to get through the days and weeks without making herself more miserable. Three times now she'd put aside her despair to step out with Bea, only to return home afterward and mire herself in the minutiae of her old life. The destructive cycle guaranteed she'd never escape her sorrow.

She knew all the cards and photo albums by heart, enough to choose which ones to place in the box without looking at them one last time. Even photos of her family and old friends were filed away if they included Melody in the mix.

The more difficult step was dealing with several thousand digital photos she'd organized in dozens of folders with titles such as *Maui–2009*, *Allyn–30th Birthday*, and *Rankin Reunion*. It was tempting to scroll through them again but that would take hours and undoubtedly leave her in a flood of tears. Instead she methodically transferred all that she associated with Melody to a flash drive, and then deleted them from her computer.

The flash drive went into the box, which she then sealed with an entire roll of double-strength strapping tape. She shoved the box onto the top shelf of her closet with a *thunk*, resolved to leave it there until she felt strong enough to look through its contents without crying. Or until Melody came back.

* * *

Her smile growing wider with every step, Bea crossed the room and kissed Wendy lightly on the lips. "Hi, sweetie."

"I've been waiting for you." The ventilator filled her lungs with air, allowing her to speak as she exhaled. "I like you in purple."

"I know. That's why I wore it. Dexter too. Did you see his bandana?"

"Dexxie…I bet Krystal's hiding in the kitchen."

Every word came with colossal effort, but Bea had learned it was no use to discourage her from talking. According to Krystal, this regular visit was the highlight of Wendy's month.

Hers too, for that matter.

"I brought you a couple of audiobooks. Emma Donoghue. You're going to love her."

"She's a lesbian."

"Yes, indeed. The Doctors will love that too."

That was her playful nickname for Wendy's parents. To this day, they had never formally recognized their daughter's sexual orientation, let alone her legal marriage, but they grudgingly accepted Bea's visits as a necessary evil because they made Wendy happy. The Doctors often managed to find somewhere to go on the first Sunday of the month—a movie, a scenic drive or a visit with their son and grandchildren. It worked best for everyone if their paths never crossed.

Bea poured a few drops of water from a pitcher on a washcloth and dabbed it on Wendy's neck and face. "Krystal says you have a fever today. How are you feeling?"

"How would I know?"

"Your sense of humor is morbid. Please tell me you terrorize The Doctors this way too. I'd hate to think I was the only one you jerked around."

"You're special," she rasped. "Did you bring a ball?"

"Sure did."

Wendy loved to watch her play with Dexter in the backyard, something Bea suspected was her quiet way of preserving energy. That was especially likely on a day she was under the weather. Talking wore her out when she was struggling to breathe, though she always tried to hold up her end of the conversation.

The tall windows allowed Wendy to see the entire backyard. Bea tossed the ball from one end of the lawn to the other, taking extra care to stay out of the flower beds, lest she provoke the wrath of Doctor Mom. Dexter showed off his newest trick, nearly turning a somersault to snatch the ball out of midair.

Through the window, she saw Krystal bringing in a tray.

"That's enough, Dexxie. Let's go back and see Wendy." She took a moment to wipe his paws before leading him back inside.

"I wish I had his energy," Wendy said.

"Don't we all? He wears me out." She nudged Krystal aside and took the soup spoon. "Let me do that. Smells like seafood."

"It's shrimp bisque."

"Bet it's not as good as what we used to get at Pike Place," she whispered after Krystal left. "One of these days I'm going to spring you for a week or two so we can go back to some of our old haunts."

"I want a burger from JoJo's."

They liked to plot their great escape but both knew those were pipe dreams. Bea had neither the resources nor expertise to care for Wendy outside her home. The best they'd been able to manage was a week-long visit here at the house when The Doctors went on vacation to London, and nearly every waking moment was shared with an attendant. The nights had been special though, since she'd managed to stretch out alongside Wendy in her hospital bed.

"Speaking of JoJo's, we won our softball game on Wednesday, one to nothing. We're still pitiful but it was nice to celebrate for a change."

Wendy took a bite of soup and held it in her mouth for several seconds. One of the dangers of her condition was eating too fast and aspirating. After swallowing, she closed her eyes, which was her signal she didn't want another bite just yet. "I wish I could see you play."

"You want me to ask Marta to shoot a video? I bet she'd do that. She said after our last game she wished she had a picture of everybody's faces when Allyn ran right by Kit at third. Kit was yelling for her to slide but she—"

"Who's Ellen?"

"Not Ellen. Allyn. A-L-L-Y-N. Cool name, huh? I asked her about it once and she said her father's name was Alvin and her mother was Lynda. Anyway, she used to have a mailbox at the shop but then she and her wife split up and she moved up to Broadview." She went on to explain how she'd run into her while checking out the other franchise.

"You still thinking about buying another one?"

"I don't know. I sent a query to the owner but didn't hear anything back. The timing kind of sucks right now because Michael just quit. Trained him all summer and now he says his course load at the UW is too much. I need to quit hiring students and find somebody who wants a permanent job. Maybe Allyn can give me some pointers. She's an employment recruiter."

For reasons she couldn't explain, she'd steered the conversation back to Allyn. Everyone had dogged her about finding someone to date, but Allyn was hardly what she'd call a friend. The only thing she'd admit to at this point was mild intrigue, but it was more than she'd felt for anyone since the accident.

Wendy often asked if she was seeing anyone, and while Bea had reluctantly told her about the women she'd dated—and even the one she'd slept with—it was only for Wendy's peace of mind. Ever since her prognosis of a tenuous life in a wheelchair, she'd been adamant that Bea needed to move on, and with her parents' unqualified support, she filed for divorce to prove her resolve.

Bea couldn't contest it, no matter how much it hurt. The Doctors had their stately home and the financial means to meet all of Wendy's needs, which included round-the-clock care and all-too-frequent hospital stays for pneumonia. She'd offered to move to Vancouver to be close, but Wendy said no. It was guilt, she admitted. Guilt for ruining Bea's life by getting hurt. It wasn't right that both of them should have to pay for her recklessness and stupidity.

Bea had already paid. The life she'd planned was gone forever.

CHAPTER NINE

The new owners had replaced the solid front door with etched glass, the kind that gave a modicum of privacy while letting in light. It was a good idea, Allyn thought, remembering how dark the foyer was. The drive by her old house was a final act of catharsis, an extension of her weekend chore to pack up her former life.

It was time to move on.

Following Bea's directions, she turned into the alley behind the Pak & Ship and parked in a space marked Employees Only. The store closed at six—eight minutes ago—but Bea promised to leave the back door unlocked.

Allyn had been in the back of the store before and knew there was a small office behind the closed door where Dexter usually spent his day. "Is anyone home?"

"Be right out. I'm changing clothes," Bea called. Moments later she appeared wearing tapered gray slacks with a black pullover. Upon closer inspection, it was a loosely tatted sweater over a sleeveless shell of the same color. Very nice, and more feminine than she'd expected of Bea, yet the softer look suited her.

"You look great but I have to admit it's weird seeing you in something besides green."

"Tell me about it. When I first opened the store, I was all gung-ho about looking professional and making sure people recognized my logo. That's the kind of stuff they teach you in franchise seminars. Some days I think about trading in the uniform for normal clothes, but then Kit would want to do that too, and next thing you know she's wearing a T-shirt that says 'Fuck Queers. I'm Queer.' No thanks."

Allyn laughed. Now that she knew Kit better, she could appreciate Bea's reluctance. "Any word on that other franchise? I notice they've cleaned it up and gotten rid of the girl who sat in there and watched TV all the time."

"I think the owner must have realized he could make money on it if he just hired a better manager. He pulled it off the market."

Allyn started the car while Bea locked the back door of the shop, and she found herself surprisingly nervous as she backed out. It was the same feeling she'd had the night before when she called to invite Bea to dinner. It was weird to feel that way over someone who'd made it clear she wanted only friendship. "Have you been to this place before?"

"No, but I went online and saw the prices. That's why I decided to dress up a little. Not the dress though. I'm saving that for a special occasion."

"*The* dress?"

"Correct," Bea said. "One is enough, but it's a killer. Maybe I'll let you see it sometime. You look great too, by the way."

"Thank you." She'd bought something special for tonight, a dark print dress that hugged her figure and a chocolate brown slim-fit blazer. "I wanted to go somewhere different, somewhere Melody and I hadn't been. I found this article online about how to get over a divorce. It says not to just sit around and wait for your feelings to change. You have to change your actions and start doing new things. I thought I'd done that already since

I moved and sold the house, but that's not enough. What I've really been doing all this time was pulling myself into a shell, making my world smaller and smaller. That's totally the wrong way to handle it."

"I don't think there's a right way or a wrong way to get over something like what you went through, Allyn. People have to process things their own way."

"I know, but I've been stuck. This article said you have to take charge. Make things happen." She went on to describe her weekend task of boxing up all the mementos and storing them at the top of her closet. She was proud of herself for reaching these conclusions, and admittedly looking for Bea's approval.

When they reached the restaurant, an upscale bar and grill in Ballard that featured Italian cuisine, she turned her car over to a valet.

"Dutch treat, right?" Bea asked as they scanned the menu.

"Sure." She would have gladly paid since this was her invitation. It was better, however, to set a precedent for how friends should handle the check.

After they ordered, the waiter lit a small candle at their table and Allyn noticed for the first time that Bea was wearing a tinge of lip gloss. While that struck her as somewhat out of character, she couldn't help but be pleased that Bea too had made an extra effort to look nice for their night out.

"You know," Bea said, tipping her head and squinting pensively, "I was thinking about what you said in the car about taking charge instead of sitting around and waiting for things to happen on their own. It sounds good on paper but you still have to wait for the time to be right. If someone had told you five months ago to box up all your memories and get on with your life, you couldn't have done it because you weren't ready. It took all this time for you to be willing to listen to that kind of advice."

Allyn's defenses kicked in at the idea that Bea wasn't giving her proper credit. "You think it's just a coincidence I happened to stumble across that article at the exact moment I became ready to let go of the past?"

"No, but maybe you found it because you were subconsciously looking for it. You know, ready to notice it. What do you think happened to make you feel like that?"

She had to admit, at least to herself, that she'd gone searching for online tips on getting over a painful divorce, something she hadn't considered at all until recently. "Well, for starters, I've had a very busy week…thanks to you. I know I wasn't exactly a barrel of laughs when we went to the festival, but afterward I was glad I went. It was way better than staying at home with the curtains drawn and wishing I had my old life back. And playing ball the other night and going to JoJo's…oh, and the movie. All that was fun. And look at me now. I actually called you up and asked you to dinner. It's like every little step makes the next one easier."

"Everything gets better with practice. That goes for liking yourself too." Bea smiled and raised her wineglass for a toast. "You need to be your own best friend first."

"Exactly. I started thinking if Melody actually did come back, what she'd find was a zombie who was in a bad mood all the time. I need to fix that. I want to be somebody she'll want to be with."

Bea's smile faded and she clasped her hands as she leaned across the table. "It doesn't always have to be about Melody, you know. In fact, if pleasing her is your main objective, then maybe you're not quite ready to move on."

"I never said I was doing it just for her." She sighed and folded her arms, fully aware she was pouting but unable to stop. "You make it sound like everything I've done is fake."

"I'm sorry. That's not what I meant. What you did with all the pictures and stuff, that's a big deal. And it's great—absolutely fantastic, in fact—that you're getting out of the house again. It just still sounds to me like it's all part of a master plan to get Melody back, and that makes me worry you'll be disappointed if it doesn't work out the way you want it to. And then you'll beat yourself up later."

A tense silence ensued as the waiter delivered salads and refilled their water glasses. Neither made a move to begin eating, and for a moment Allyn felt the whole evening had been a terrible idea. She didn't need unsolicited advice about Melody, least of all from someone who had no clue what it was like to want someone so badly she couldn't go on without her.

"You know what, Allyn? Backspace, erase. Forget everything I just said. It doesn't even matter why you're doing anything. What's important is that it feels right to you." She held out her hand and flicked her fingers. "Give me your hand a minute."

Allyn was surprised but nonetheless complied.

"Something tells me you and I are going to be really good friends. I'm going to start acting like one right now by telling you I support whatever you think is best for you. If you think I'm being hard on you or insensitive about what you're going through, call me on it. All of us need a friend who's going to be on our side no matter what, and I want to be that friend for you."

Those were the kindest words Allyn had heard in a very long time, and she caught herself in time to blink back tears. "Wow, I…thank you."

Bea gave her hand a final squeeze and grinned. "You're welcome. Don't be afraid to ask for what you need. That's how you get it."

* * *

As she waited for the clerk to count out her change, Bea stole a look at Allyn through the window of the gelato shop, where she was waiting outside. The streetlights didn't do justice to the color of her eyes, but the candle on their table had, and all through dinner Bea had resisted the urge to say so. Compliments could be misinterpreted. Flirting, Kit would call it.

Cone in hand, she joined Allyn outside, taking notice of her platform shoes. "You sure you feel like walking in those? We can sit."

"I'm fine. I've been wearing shoes like this since college. Melody's six-one and she's always been self-conscious about it. Whenever we went out, she wanted me to look taller too."

"You're a better person than I am. I wouldn't wear shoes like that for anyone."

"I bet you would if you really loved someone and knew it would make her feel better."

"Eh…" She laughed and shook her head. "You give me too much credit. I'm not breaking my ankles for anybody, thank you."

"You'd let your partner suffer emotional ridicule instead." From her intonation, it was only a playful accusation.

"Not at all. I'm a romantic at heart, but I'd take a different approach, like reminding her over and over that I thought she was perfect, and I'd tell her it was always my dream to marry someone tall."

Allyn twisted her mouth in apparent disbelief but then nodded slowly. "Pretty slick…except it makes me wonder. If you're such a romantic, how come you're single?"

Now that they'd agreed to be friends, Bea knew she needed to tell Allyn about Wendy, and the sooner the better. Her biggest fear—and the reason she rarely shared details of her former life with anyone—was that Allyn would criticize her decision to leave. As far as Bea was concerned, only someone who'd been in her situation had a right to judge.

"I haven't always been single. I was married once too. Legally, just like you."

She took several more steps along the sidewalk before realizing Allyn had stopped.

"Are you serious?"

"Yup. Eight years ago last month, and I've been divorced for the last three." She walked back to where Allyn was standing and guided her to sit on a knee-high brick wall that kept pedestrians from trampling a shrubbery garden. "It's a complicated story and I don't tell it to many people. You sure you want to hear it?"

"Of course."

"Okay, here goes. Wendy and I met when I accidentally tried to cut my hand off with a broken lightbulb. She sewed me up at the walk-in clinic, and the rest, as they say, is history."

"She's a doctor?"

"An ER doctor, originally from Canada. She went to school at the UW and was trying to get her green card. We lived together for about a year and a half, but then after Canada passed their same-sex marriage law, we just decided to run up to Vancouver and get married. I know that probably doesn't sound romantic but it was. We always liked doing things on the spur of the moment. Plus it made her parents' heads explode and that was a bonus."

Allyn was giving her the strangest look.

"They're Chinese. Very traditional. Suffice it to say they had other plans for their only daughter." She finished her gelato and stood so she could pace...nervous energy building up to her big reveal. "Wendy was always so funny about her parents. I accused her more than once of marrying me just to get under their skin, and she never denied it. I didn't care though. We were in love, and I thought we'd be together forever."

"But obviously you weren't."

"No, but we should have been," Bea said wistfully. "We were out hiking with a bunch of friends on Mt. Rainier, and Wendy... she had so much more energy than the rest of us. We were all gasping for breath but she wanted to go just a little higher so we waited for her. I never should have let her go up there by herself, but nobody could stop her when she set her mind to something. After about twenty minutes, she hadn't come back so Kit went looking for her. She'd fallen."

"Oh, my gosh!"

"Broke her neck. I waited with her until they could get a helicopter up there. Longest hour of my life. She could hardly breathe, and we were all freaking out because she kept saying she couldn't feel her arms and legs. They flew her right into surgery."

"And what happened? Please tell me she's all right."

"She survived, but she's completely paralyzed from the neck down. They did a surgery about three months after the accident hoping to get back some movement in her arms, but it made things worse. Now she can't even breathe without a ventilator."

Allyn's brow furrowed and she kept shaking her head. "That's so sad. Where is she?"

"Back in Vancouver with her parents. We Skype all the time—she's got a computer with voice commands. And I go up to see her at least once a month. Yesterday in fact. She divorced me because I couldn't take care of her." It always sounded so harsh when she put it that way, since Wendy's true motives were rooted in love and compassion. "Not really, but sometimes I think about it that way when I feel like beating myself up. She divorced me so I wouldn't *have* to take care of her. She knew how hard it would be, how expensive. She also knew I'd be loyal to her until the day one of us died. Said she felt like she was stealing my life."

"I had no idea. All this time I've been going on about Melody leaving me like it was the worst thing in the world, and you've been through so much more. And poor Wendy. You must have thought…God, I've been such an ass."

"No!" Bea returned to sit on the wall and put her arm around Allyn's shoulder. "I haven't thought anything like that. You have every right to hurt the way you do. At least what Wendy did wasn't deliberate. Besides, this isn't a competition. It's not like there's a shortage of misery and we have to fight over it."

"Was that…a joke?"

"Sure, why not?" She pulled Allyn to her feet. "Come on. I need a little joy after all that. Let's go see Dexter."

* * *

Bea pointed through the windshield at the picture window in her living room. "See, what did I tell you? He watches for me every night."

"What's he going to think when I walk in?"

"He'll go crazy but I'll keep him from jumping on you. Wouldn't want him to mess up your pretty dress."

The moment she'd pulled to the curb on the quiet residential street, Allyn experienced a severe case of house envy. From the outside, Bea's pale yellow bungalow looked like the ideal hideaway—small and simple with privacy hedges on both sides. The front porch light cast a beam into the yard to brighten their path.

"You and Wendy lived here?"

"No, we had an apartment near the medical center because she was on call a lot. I snagged this from the bank a couple of years ago because it was close to my shop."

Allyn heard Dexter scratching at the door, but then it sounded as though he was running around inside the house.

"Brace yourself," Bea said. "He's losing it."

Indeed, the spectacle of him tearing through the house in a circle was hilarious, and she couldn't resist getting in on the action by clapping and yelling to encourage him even more.

When Bea finally turned him out into the backyard, Allyn got her first good look at the house. A center wall with a fireplace separated the cozy living room from the kitchen and dining area on the right, and a narrow hallway on the left led to what appeared to be two bedrooms and a bath.

"Why do you have so many balloons in here?"

"So Dexter won't get on the furniture. He's terrified of them." Bea corralled all but one and tucked them in a closet by the entry. "I always keep one out so I can pop it if he forgets. Works like a charm."

"Poor baby. I bet he has nightmares."

"Don't 'poor baby' that guy. He's spoiled rotten." She gestured toward the couch. "Can I get you something to drink?"

"No thanks. I can't stay long. I have an interview with a client in San Antonio at seven o'clock in the morning. I just wanted to see my little buddy."

Bea let Dexter back inside and he went straight to where Allyn sat and put his head on her knees. "There's no such thing as dog loyalty when someone new comes around. Other than Kit and Marta, you're the only other friend who's ever been here."

"I don't get that. I watched you at the softball game. You get along with everybody. You ought to have lots of friends."

"I used to. After what happened to Wendy, I'm not as...I guess the word's free-wheeling when it comes to friends. I still like people but I keep most of them at arm's length." She sank into a plush armchair perpendicular to the couch and propped her feet on the end of the coffee table. "I went to a cookout once for somebody's birthday and overheard a bunch of people I thought were my friends talking about us. One of them said she'd never leave her girlfriend if something like that happened. In sickness and in health…yada yada. In the first place, I didn't think it was any of her fucking business. In the second place, I was already feeling guilty enough, thank you. It wasn't even my decision. It was what Wendy wanted. If it had been up to me, I'd have moved in with her and her parents in Vancouver. She needed somebody with her all the time—that should have been me. But those people who were supposed to be my friends and didn't know shit were passing judgment on me anyway. Nobody knows what they're going to do until it happens to them. People ought to keep their fucking opinions to themselves."

It was by far the most emotion Bea had ever shown, and it made Allyn even more ashamed that she'd bemoaned her own situation. "I'm not going to pass judgment on you. Well, maybe I am, but my judgment is I believe you did what was best for Wendy, and not only that—she did what was best for you. In my book, love doesn't get any stronger than that."

"I appreciate you saying that. I told you it was a complicated story. Your story is too. The way you hurt…it reminded me a lot of myself."

"Oh, please don't even say that. What Melody did was so trivial compared to what you've been through."

"She turned your whole life upside down. That's not what I'd call trivial."

"No, but at least I know I'm going to be okay eventually."

Hearing those words come out of her mouth was startling. Even more startling was her realization—for the first time— they actually might be true.

CHAPTER TEN

Allyn swiveled from side to side in her executive chair as she studied the résumé displayed on her oversized monitor. Everything in her office was calibrated to her ergonomic specifications. That mattered a lot to someone who spent up to ten hours a day at her desk.

"This all looks good, Katie," she told the woman on the phone, "except I think you need to adjust your salary demands."

"Come on, Allyn. I've got twelve years' experience, half of that with the Big Four. I deserve to be compensated." Katie's husband was taking a new job in Chicago and she needed to relocate.

"I couldn't agree more. The men I place at your level are asking at least ten thousand more and so should you. We might not get it, but we definitely won't get it if we don't ask."

She finalized the résumé and promised to put it in front of half a dozen HR directors within a week. A security programmer with Katie's accounting firm expertise would be snatched up in no time.

Eleven thirty. Allyn removed her Bluetooth earpiece and stood to stretch. She was rigid not only about her work schedule, but also her breaks. Her most productive hours were between six and eleven-ish, after which she'd have lunch, shower and walk down to the Pak & Ship to collect her mail. Then it was back to work until about five.

As she nibbled her salad at the kitchen bar, she caught up with the news of the day on her tablet computer. Bea had sent her a link earlier and she followed it to an article in the *Westside Weekly*, a neighborhood newspaper that covered community events and local sports.

There, in living color, was a picture of her in uniform. The photographer had taken it from somewhere over her shoulder, so her profile was barely recognizable, especially since her cap was pulled low over her eyes. The caption gave her away, however. *Allyn Teague, playing first base for Pak & Ship in the Ladies Recreation League, readies for the next pitch.*

"Oh, my gosh. I made the paper," she said aloud. She grabbed her phone and called Bea.

"Is this Allyn Teague, the world famous softball player?"

"That's insane! Of all the pictures they could have run, why on earth did they pick me? I'm just standing there."

"Are you kidding? Look how cute you are with that sassy blond ponytail. And all crouched over with your little butt sticking out. *That's* why they picked you."

Allyn had to admit it was a decent picture, but she was even more flattered by Bea's characterization. "Cute, huh? I'm supposed to be fierce."

"That too. I'm going to blow it up and make a poster for my store. My logo's plain as day across your back. Do you have any idea how much it would have cost me to buy an ad that big?"

"At least they spelled my name right."

"Wait till you see it on my wall. We're still on for tonight, right?"

"Absolutely. Pick you up at six thirty."

Dinner and a movie two Fridays in a row. Most people would call that dating. Allyn wanted to call it friendship, but it wasn't ordinary despite what she'd been telling herself. It reminded her of high school when her days were organized around passing Reagan Fuller in the hallway between classes and sitting with her at lunch. It was only when she fell in love with Melody in college that she acknowledged her feelings for Reagan for what they'd been—a crush that might have turned into love if her feelings had been reciprocated.

And now she fluttered with that same excitement just from talking on the phone with Bea.

How could she have a crush on someone when she woke up every day wishing she were still married? Granted, her feelings for Melody weren't nearly as all-consuming as they used to be, but that was only because she'd been forced to get on with her life.

What made her connection with Bea unique was how they both seemed to have the same needs and expectations. Bea explained that she'd started dating again a couple of years ago but hadn't developed feelings for anyone. It either happened or it didn't, she said, and there was nothing she could do about it.

Allyn understood that perfectly and agreed with every word. A dozen years had passed since she last played the dating game, but she viscerally recalled feeling anxious about the impression she was making, and the uncomfortable pressure to indulge those who were more interested in her than she was in them. She hadn't worried about any of that with Melody because there was a spark when they met that drove both of them to be together every possible moment. That's how she'd known it was love.

The excitement she felt when Bea called was just like that, a spark that told her Bea was special…but only if she felt it too.

* * *

Bea took a breather after dispensing with the last of six customers who'd walked in within thirty seconds of one another.

"Somebody has a girlfriend," Kit sang softly as she returned to her task of restocking the rack of mailing supplies.

"Oh, for freak's sake. Dexter, get out here and bite her—preferably on the mouth."

"You have to admit, you've seen a lot more of Allyn Teague in the last two weeks than you've seen of anyone else in the last two years."

Bea was momentarily saved by another arrival, a man of about thirty, sharply dressed in a creased suit and tie, who was desperate to get his package to his fiancée overnight in San Francisco. "She celebrates anniversaries for everything. First date, first—" He cleared his throat. "You probably don't need to hear all the details. Let's just say I forgot this particular anniversary last year and she didn't speak to me for a week."

"Hmm…anniversaries for everything," Kit said after the door closed behind him. "It was about two weeks ago you and Allyn went to Summerfest. Got any plans to commemorate that?"

"My only plan for the weekend is to hire a new employee to replace the one I'm about to fire."

"Ouch!"

The ensuing silence left Bea feeling guilty for being so gruff. Kit and Marta had seen her through the most difficult time of her life. "She's picking me up after work and we're going out for dinner and a movie. It's possible we'll do something else tomorrow night or on Sunday, but please don't go setting up a bridal registry just yet."

Kit joined her behind the counter and dragged up a stool. "Now see? That wasn't so hard, was it?"

"It was excruciating."

"Because you're afraid I'm going to tease you about it? Of course I am. I tease you about everything else, so why should this be any different?" Her tone had turned uncharacteristically serious. "I think you're worried somebody might start running off at the mouth. They might say you don't deserve to be happy with another woman, not after the way you went off and left Wendy."

"Stop it, Kit."

"But I happen to know the truth. The person who says that loudest is you. You've been telling yourself for three years that you don't deserve to have another girlfriend…a *real* girlfriend."

There was more truth to Kit's words than she wanted to admit. "It's not that simple."

"It's very simple. You need to get on with your life. Wendy wants you to move on, but you think she's just saying that to be noble. She's not."

Dexter came out of the office and whined, clearly upset by Kit's scolding tone.

"Take it easy, boy. She's only talking to me this way because she's too old and decrepit to physically kick my ass." In her head she'd already conceded that her ass probably needed a good kick, and Kit was the only one she'd ever allow to do it.

"I'm serious, Bea. She talks about it every time Marta and I Skype with her. I know she talks to you too. She always asks if you're seeing somebody, then she gets frustrated and depressed when we give her the same old news over and over. Marta tried to tell her you just hadn't met the right person yet, but Wendy thinks it's more than that. She says you freeze up whenever you think about it, like you're the one who's paralyzed."

"Oh, crap. The last thing I want is for Wendy to get all bent out of shape over me and my nonexistent love life. She has enough to worry about."

"Which is the point, dipshit."

If anyone else had talked to her this way, she would have walked away in a huff. The fact that Kit and Marta had Wendy's confidence forced her to take their opinions seriously.

"Do you have any concept of how hard it is for me to talk to Wendy about this? We were married. She was the one I was supposed to grow old with, and now she's asking me why I don't go out and have sex with other women."

"Because she wants you to know it's okay if you do. She knows the score, Bea. That's why she divorced you. If you're interested in Allyn, go with it."

Allyn interested her far more than anyone she'd met, but there was more than Wendy standing in her way. "There's something about Allyn that's…" It was critical to use the right word and not let Kit extrapolate all the way to the wedding. "I like her a lot. We're just friends—swear to God—but I'd like to date her and see where it goes. I'm just not sure she's emotionally available right now. She's not over Melody yet. She still talks about her a lot, and if we started dating and Melody came back into the picture, she'd drop me like yesterday's fish."

A new flurry of customers put their conversation on hold for several minutes, after which Bea escaped to her office to prepare the bank deposit. The mundane task did little to distract her from worrying that her ambivalence about dating was upsetting Wendy, and she momentarily considered picking up the phone to put both of their minds at ease.

But what would she say? That she was finally interested in someone—a woman who was still pining over her ex-wife?

"Let's get out of here, Dexxie." She clipped his leash in place and led him out past the counter. "We're going to the bank. Then I need to drop Dexter off at home. Call me if you get really busy. Otherwise I'll be back in about an hour." She really needed to hire more help.

Kit followed her to the front door. "Take your time. I've got your back, you know. No matter what you do."

Bea nodded, fully aware she wasn't talking only about minding the store.

* * *

They were the last two people in the theater, and Allyn appreciated that Bea didn't rush her out before the credits rolled. One of her favorite parts—finding out where the film was made—usually came at the very end.

"Whittier, Alaska. I thought so."

"I take it you've been there," Bea said as she stood and stretched, baring several inches of her flat belly as her red cropped shirt crept up from her jeans.

"About three years ago. We flew up to Anchorage with some friends and rented a car to drive up into Denali National Park. Then we cruised from Whittier back to Seattle down the Inland Passage." It was a lovely trip, she recalled nostalgically, though she was none too happy about Melody's idea to spend their entire two-week vacation with Jillian and Tiffany. It irked her even more now to know the three of them had shared a bond that excluded her.

"Wendy and I had reservations for an Alaskan cruise, but she had her accident the month before we were supposed to go."

"That's so sad."

Bea shrugged. "We could probably do it one of these days if she still wanted to. Except I'd have to lock her parents in the basement so I could sneak her out of the house."

Allyn experienced a puzzling wave of jealousy at the thought of Bea taking a trip with her ex-wife that would have them sharing a small cabin, maybe even a bed. Were they really only friends now, or had the divorce been merely a legal formality to disentangle their finances for health care purposes? Bea visited her regularly in Vancouver, but on the other hand had also mentioned going out with—

A horrifying thought entered her head. "Does Wendy know you've dated other women?"

"Yeah, we talk about everything. In fact, she—oh, my God!" Bea clutched Allyn's forearm as her eyes went wide. Panic. "You didn't think I'd cheat on her? I'd never do something like that."

"No, of course you wouldn't. I was just…confused."

"Trust me, Wendy knows everything I do. I think Kit files a report with her every day."

Allyn chuckled awkwardly, since Bea obviously meant that as a joke—one she didn't exactly get. What was Kit telling Wendy about the time Bea was spending with her?

There were too many people milling toward the exit to keep probing about matters so personal, so she used the walk to the car to assemble her thoughts. "I'm sorry about how that came out. I didn't mean to jump to any conclusions or accuse you of anything. The way you talk about Wendy, I guess I don't understand how your relationship works. In my mind, a divorce means it's over, at least for one of you."

"No, a divorce just means you aren't married anymore. It doesn't have to mean your relationship is over. Though ours certainly changed." Bea buckled herself in and swiveled to face her as much as the seat belt would allow. "Wendy and I still love each other very much. But it's not romantic love, not like it used to be. It took me a long time to get there, and it hurt like hell to have her let it go so fast. That's where I was coming from back in January when I said I understood what you were going through."

"I'm so sorry about that. I was an ass."

"No, you weren't. You were right in the middle of the worst thing that ever happened to you. I know exactly what that's like."

Allyn wished they'd saved this conversation for another time. It was too poignant for the car, especially in the dark, since she couldn't see Bea's face.

"If Wendy had her way, I'd meet someone else and start a new life. I seriously think she wants that more than anything."

"I don't get it. How can she feel that way if she still loves you?"

"If you asked her, she'd probably say she wants what's best for me, and that would be for me to have a full life. But then if you asked me, I'd say it's all part of her personal guilt trip. She couldn't bring herself to ask me to take care of her, and she can't stand to think I'll go through life alone. That's the simple answer. It's a lot more complicated than that...there's also the issue of how we would pay for her medical expenses, and the fact that her parents never accepted her being gay. I've always wondered if getting divorced was one of their stipulations, but she'd never tell me if it was."

Allyn snaked slowly through the parking lot in the long line of cars, not minding the snail's pace at which they emptied onto the boulevard. The drive to Bea's house would take only five or six minutes and she wasn't ready for their evening to end, even though it was nearly midnight.

"What does she feel guilty about? It's not like she fell on purpose."

Bea shrugged and shook her head. "You know how it is. We all believe that part about marriage being for better or worse, in sickness and in health...all that. But Wendy says it's different when you're the one who's sick, especially when you know you aren't going to get better."

Her melancholy tone caused a lump to form in the back of

Allyn's throat. "I guess no one ever knows for sure how they'll feel unless it happens to them."

"She told me outright she felt like she couldn't hold up her end of the bargain. It wasn't only that I'd have to take care of her. The hardest part, she said, was she couldn't take care of me either. She couldn't be there for me if I needed her, and that made her feel terrible. Once I saw it from that perspective, it made more sense. I hope I would have done the same thing for her, but that doesn't make it easier to accept."

Under those circumstances, letting go was a profound expression of love for both of them. "That's so sad...but it's beautiful too. She loves you so much."

"Thank you for saying that." Bea sniffed and blinked a few times, and then laughed softly to signal a change in mood. "It sure makes for some interesting conversations. Nothing like getting the third degree from your ex about your last date—especially when you don't exactly want to talk about all the... intimate details. But then she knows you so well that you can't hide anything."

"I'm not having that conversation in a million years, thank you." Allyn had never considered releasing Melody to her new life with Naomi out of a sense of love and wanting her to be happy. Nor was it likely she ever would.

"Oh, come on. Don't you want Melody to know every detail about who you date and what you do?"

"Hardly. I bet she wishes I'd find somebody too so she wouldn't have to feel guilty anymore about what she did. I can't imagine ever being friends with her like you are with Wendy. Maybe a few months ago when I was willing to take whatever little crumb she tossed me as long as it meant I could still be in her life. But now...some days I'm not even sure I could stand to be in the same room with her. After what she did, I don't really care if she feels guilty or not. In fact, I don't even want to know how she feels." The words tumbled out with the usual bitterness. "If that makes me an asshole, so be it."

"No matter how things shake out with you and Melody, nobody in their right mind would think you were the asshole.

She deserves her guilt, every ounce of it. But you don't need to spend your energy on making sure she feels it. You know that old saying about living well being the best revenge. That's what you ought to be doing—living well. Having fun. Enjoying life again."

"That's exactly what I'm trying to do."

"That is so awesome."

"What?" Allyn slowed to a stop in front of Bea's house, peering through the window to see what she was grinning about. It was several seconds before Dexter appeared at the window, so it couldn't have been that. "What's awesome?"

"What you just said. Not even a week ago you were going on about all the things you were willing to do to get your old life back. Apologize…forgive. You were ready to leave Seattle if that's what Melody wanted. Now you don't even want to be friends."

"Oh, my gosh…"

"Don't look now, but I think you're starting to get over Melody Rankin."

It was true her brooding about Melody had dissipated recently. She had other interests now, and new friends who made her feel better than when she stayed home and agonized over what she'd lost. That hadn't been a conscious shift, she realized. At no point did she simply decide not to dwell any longer on how Melody had hurt her.

"I won't say I'm over her entirely," Allyn admitted slowly, "but these last couple of weeks have been a lot more enjoyable with you around." Her feeble acknowledgment didn't do justice to the urge she felt to be with Bea as much as she could, but she couldn't articulate what she hadn't yet given herself permission to feel. Besides, Bea had made it pretty clear she was still struggling to move on from Wendy.

"I'll see your enjoyable and raise you a downright fantastic. Honestly, I thought I had enough to keep me busy with Dexter and the softball league, but hanging out with you has put a whole new spin on how I want to spend my time." Bea smiled sheepishly and raised her eyebrows before looking away. "And on that note, I should stop talking before I say something that gets me in trouble."

Fantastic…a whole new spin. Allyn hoped the dim glow of the dome light was enough to hide the heat rising in her face, telltale proof of the self-consciousness that set in once someone showed her attention. No matter how anxious it made her, she had to hear for certain what Bea was keeping from her. "If there's something else on your mind, you should say it."

Bea opened the car door but made no move to exit. "Mmm…I probably shouldn't. I'd be getting ahead of myself, and ahead of you too since you only started getting over Melody about sixty seconds ago. What I will say is once I get out of the car and start walking away, I'll already be looking forward to the next time I get to see you. That's what I've done ever since we left JoJo's on Wednesday night. Sounds crazy, doesn't it?"

On the contrary, Allyn understood every word. Bea was trying to say—or not to say—that she too felt this attraction, this compulsion to grasp for something even as they questioned whether or not they were ready.

"I don't think it's crazy." Her knee began bouncing uncontrollably, so much that she had to slide back the driver's seat to rest her heel on the floorboard.

"That's not exactly the effect I was hoping for," Bea said with a shaky chuckle. "Obviously you weren't ready to hear that just yet. Maybe we should just pretend I didn't say it."

Pretending wouldn't work, not with Allyn's self-confession that she felt the same way.

"Whatever you do, don't let this freak you out," Bea pleaded. "There's no pressure. I'm not asking you to do anything or say anything or feel anything. I just thought it was better if I told you I was thinking about it. I wouldn't want you to feel creepy if you found out later."

"No, no…I'm glad you told me." No pressure, except what Allyn imposed on herself. She'd never been good at the tap-dance of acknowledging someone's interest or revealing her own. Though it had been twelve years since she last worried about impressing a potential date, she remembered vividly how her self-confidence plummeted the moment she found herself in a flirtatious situation.

"So I guess I'll see you," Bea said, finally exiting the car. "Call me if you want to do something."

"Sure," she squeaked, the word barely audible.

Her social ineptitude bothered her far less than her uncertainty. Bea couldn't have laid out her feelings more plainly. All Allyn had to do was speak up and say she felt something too.

Instead, she'd swallowed her tongue and left Bea to worry that she'd gone too far.

* * *

Bea knelt on the rug so Dexter could share his excitement by licking her face each time he dashed through the room. "Dexxie, your mommy just screwed the pooch."

He stopped abruptly and barked, pounding his front paws on the floor.

"Not literally."

She'd totally misread her friendship with Allyn, and it was clear from Allyn's shocked silence that blurting out her feelings too soon had sent the poor woman into full retreat. No matter how much she pleaded after the fact for Allyn to disregard her words, there was no taking any of them back.

She opened the back door to let Dexter out.

"Screwed...the...pooch," she repeated, knocking her head against the doorjamb in rhythm with her words. Lucky for her, she had loving canine companionship, since she wasn't doing so well with her own species.

Dexter ran around the yard with the same energy he'd shown in the house. The poor guy had spent the whole evening at home alone and now was hyped up to play, but Bea needed to calm him down so she could get ready for bed.

Sleep probably wouldn't come easy tonight, not once she closed her eyes and saw Allyn's leg shaking with terror. A disastrous miscalculation. Despite what she'd said, Allyn wasn't nearly ready to move on from Melody. Bea's premature disclosure probably set her back six months.

"Let's go, Dexxie." She filled his water bowl and rewarded him with a treat, a biscuit with mint and parsley that freshened his breath. "Since you're the only one I get to kiss."

Walking toward her bedroom, she turned out the lights and loosened the buttons on her shirt, wondering if Allyn had noticed she'd gone to the trouble of ironing it. They weren't calling this dating, but Bea was going through all the motions as if it were.

Until tonight she'd been pretty sure Allyn was going through those motions too. She was dressing better than usual, at least compared to how she looked when she came in to pick up her mail, and she even wore makeup to play softball. Why would she do that unless she wanted to be noticed and appreciated?

"I'm so glad you're a boy, Dexxie, because I don't understand women at all."

He watched her every move in the bathroom as she readied for bed, and then followed her into the bedroom. His bed, a large plaid beanbag, was situated in the corner on the floor.

It was only when she went to set the alarm on her cell phone that she remembered she'd muted it during the movie, and she'd missed a text message from Allyn fifteen minutes ago: *I'm ready if you are.*

"Are you kidding me?" She double-checked the time to make sure it wasn't sent before Allyn picked her up for dinner. That would mean something else entirely.

She typed her response: *Does this mean dinner tomorrow night would be a date?*

It was nearly ten minutes before her phone chimed with a reply: *Dinner at my place.*

Funny how Allyn had ignored her question of whether or not it was—

Another chime: *A date.*

Bea flopped onto the bed and kicked her feet in the air, prompting Dexter to rush to her side. "Dexter, old boy, Mommy has a date. And for once, it's with somebody she really wants to be with."

CHAPTER ELEVEN

Picking up bottle of chardonnay...10-15 minutes.

Allyn smiled at Bea's message and set her phone aside. Texting would have made life so much easier back in high school when she first started dating. It gave her time to think up clever ways to answer and to edit her words until they were perfect.

She'd traded several texts with Bea nailing down the details for their evening. Sautéed scallops over angel hair pasta with a salad. Gelato for dessert. A Mariners baseball game in the background.

Bea had worked all day and deserved to relax. They could spend the time talking and getting to know each other better, something they'd missed out on when surrounded by their softball buddies or while sitting through a movie. She knew nothing about Bea's family, or even how she and Wendy had met. What had drawn them together, and were there other girlfriends before?

With embarrassment, she realized Bea had already asked all those questions of her. She knew Allyn was the classic "middle child" from Centralia who wore hand-me-downs and suffered a stricter set of rules because her older sister couldn't handle limits, and whose school accomplishments were ignored because her younger brother was a phenomenal athlete who sucked up all the attention in the house. Bea also had heard how her coming out was her "declaration of independence," a once-and-for-all statement that her parents' dismissive opinion of her no longer mattered.

What did she really know about Bea other than the tragic story of Wendy? Not much, it seemed, and she found that oddly encouraging, since asking questions about her family and how she'd ended up in Ballard running a postal shop was much easier than making up topics for clumsy small talk.

To say nothing of the fact that it was high time she stopped complaining about Melody.

On her last sweep through the apartment, she turned on the bedside lamp...then turned it off...then turned it back on. This being their first actual date, it was ridiculous to debate the point. She had no intention of ending up in the bedroom—despite having put on fresh sheets and spritzing them with honeysuckle. Routine housecleaning. Except the honeysuckle part, which had been a silly afterthought.

Would Bea think the lamp was an invitation? Allyn shuddered at the question and snapped it off again.

She touched her lips with gloss and stepped back to check her look. Gray yoga pants with a dark purple V-necked T-shirt and black flip-flops. Their pact had been for a casual night at home, but Allyn hadn't meant to go overboard on the casual. If Bea showed up in something dressier, she'd feel like a total slob.

No, this was how you got to know someone—let them see who you really are.

A knock sounded, rendering moot any last-minute changes. Allyn opened the door to find Bea dressed in low-slung white shorts and a sleeveless denim shirt, and swinging a bottle of chardonnay.

"Thank God, Allyn! I'm so glad you really meant casual. A lot of people say casual when what they mean is two-inch heels instead of three. I brought an extra outfit just in case you were all dressed up. I would have gone back to the car for something and changed clothes."

Allyn laughed at the irony. "Not thirty seconds ago, I was having the same conversation with myself. Kick off your shoes and let's call this 'barefoot casual.' Then we won't have to worry about what it means next time."

Bea took the corkscrew from her hand and opened the wine. "I hope this is all right. They didn't have much chilled and I wanted to start drinking immediately. It was a day from hell at the shop." She went on to explain that one of her customers had won a drawing for a free set of tires and had her pack and ship all four of them to his daughter in Denver.

When the glasses were poured, Allyn raised hers in a toast. "To…"

"Our first date," Bea answered, not missing a beat. "Thanks for texting me last night. I almost missed it because my phone was off. I slept a lot better than I would have if I'd gone to bed thinking I'd stepped in it."

"I'm sorry it took me so long. It's been years since I've done this."

Bea took both glasses and set them on the counter. "You know what? I'm kind of nervous too, so I think we should get this part over with." She stepped forward and drew Allyn's head down toward hers. A light smile played on her lips before her eyes closed and they kissed.

It lasted no more than three or four seconds, but it was long enough for Allyn to notice a flood of emotions, most of them related to the enormity of what it meant to kiss someone new after a dozen years with the same woman.

"There. That was nice, don't you think?"

Allyn froze in position, pretending for a moment to be in a daze. "I think I liked it."

"Lucky for me. We can do it some more later, but first you have to feed me. I'm starving and dinner smells too good to wait."

"I find it hard to believe you're nervous about anything."

"That's because I practice everything first with Dexter. You're a better kisser, by the way."

"Good to know. I would have told you to bring him along, but I'm not allowed to have pets here. It's in all caps in the lease." She appreciated how easily Bea navigated what could have been an awkward moment, that she'd put it behind them almost immediately. "Take the wine and I'll bring dinner."

Allyn had squeezed a small dinette into the back corner of the living room so she could use the dining area for an office. Since she always ate at the kitchen bar or in front of the TV, tonight marked its first use.

"This looks delicious," Bea said, rubbing her hands together. "I had someone bring a dish of sautéed scallops into my shop once. She wanted to send them to her sister in Utah, and I had to break it to her that we could only ship perishables if they were on ice."

"How did you end up owning a Pak & Ship?" The first of many questions on the road to finding out what made Bea Lawson tick.

"I always wanted to be my own boss, so I went to a franchise fair about eight years ago to check out some ideas. Their representative made a good pitch, and the money was good if I was willing to put in the work. I was, as long as it didn't involve food service. I'd be miserable at that. I've always liked the postal work, even on days like today. The only downside is working six days a week, but that's my own fault for not trusting anyone else to take over." She took her first bite of dinner and closed her eyes. "Mmm...amazing."

"Thank you. There's plenty." Even Allyn ate with more gusto than usual, something she'd done increasingly when eating with Bea. "How long has it been since you had a day off?"

"I get Sundays and all the postal holidays. Other than that, a couple of years. I can't close the store and take a vacation because people have to get to their mailboxes. I'm trying to hire somebody else full-time so Kit and I can have another day off."

"Where would you go if you suddenly found yourself with a week's vacation?"

"Good question. What about you?"

"Oh no, you don't. We always talk about me. I realized this afternoon that I don't know a thing about your family or even where you're from."

"I was raised right here in Seattle, Nathan Hale High School." Bea took a gulp of wine and got up to fetch the bottle from the refrigerator. "Now if we're going to talk about my family, I'll need more to drink. It's just my mother, and she's a real piece of work. She's all about following the Bible when it comes to me being gay, but not where it says you can't get divorced. One of my happiest days was when she married her fourth husband and they moved to Hawaii."

Allyn topped off their glasses. "I guess that means the islands aren't on your vacation list."

"Certainly not those islands. If I had a week off, I'd probably want to visit a city like New York or San Francisco. Maybe New Orleans. I like cities."

"I would have figured you for something in the Great Outdoors, like one of the national parks or something."

"I have plenty of that here. Besides, who wants to be in a sleeping bag when you can have a king-sized bed?"

"Amen to that!" Allyn raised her glass in a another toast. In her mind, she was already envisioning the two of them wandering the streets of Chicago or stretched out in the sun on Miami Beach. She'd never been to either place and wanted new memories with someone other than Melody.

* * *

That kiss was bloody brilliant, if Bea had to say so herself. Both of them were noticeably jittery when she arrived, and the impromptu smooch had settled their nerves like magic.

"I didn't expect you to clean my kitchen," Allyn said as she rearranged the top rack of the dishwasher. "You're supposed to be my guest."

"This is how I make myself feel welcome. Besides, I can't return the invitation unless you like frozen pizza or Chinese takeout."

"Go put your feet up and watch the game. You want another glass of wine? Coffee? Hot tea?"

"I'm good."

The TV area held a captain's chair of butterscotch leather with an ottoman and a love seat. A cozy love seat. Bea opted for the captain's chair.

"Are you…comfortable there?" Allyn asked hesitantly, as though taken aback by her choice. She seated herself at the near end of the love seat.

"It's not bad, but I'd rather sit by you." Bea hopped up and joined her. Batting her eyes with mischief, she added, "I only sat there so you wouldn't. Now you're stuck here with me."

"Sneaky."

"Not usually, but this time? Guilty as charged." She lifted Allyn's fingers to her lips and placed a light kiss on her knuckles. "Was there anything else you wanted to know about my sordid past? I've probably had enough wine to tell you everything."

"That's a tempting offer. Give me a minute to think about it. I don't want to waste it with something trivial."

Bea was a few inches shorter, and when she scooted closer, it practically forced Allyn to drape an arm around her shoulder. "This is very nice," Bea said. "I don't even care if the Mariners lose as long as I get to sit like this."

"And you call yourself a fan." Allyn propped her bare feet on the coffee table and relaxed against her.

"Seriously, I'm not used to this. I'm five-six and I've always been the taller one. Wendy was barely five feet tall, so when we sat together, it was physically impossible for her to put her arm around my shoulder like this. It feels good."

"I'm not used to it either, actually. Melody's six-one, but sitting like this didn't have anything to do with her height. She wasn't what most people would consider butch, except with me. She always liked to be in charge, and she wanted her family and all our friends to see her as the big, strong protector, the one who took care of everything. It never bothered me before, but now…now it makes me feel even worse about what she did. I always trusted her to take care of me."

"Melody Rankin is a sleaze-bucket." Now that they were officially dating, Bea wasn't going to tiptoe around the obvious anymore. She wriggled out of Allyn's embrace and turned to face her. "I'm not all that much into labels and roles. In fact, I can be a different person every day. When I've packed a set of Michelins and polished off half a bottle of wine, I like being held like this. But then tomorrow I might be the one who wants to do the holding. Think you can handle that?"

"Try it and see." Allyn pulled her back to nestle beneath her arm.

As the ballgame played in the background, they compared stories of the strained relationships with their mothers, both conceding the hurt they felt. Neither wanted a complete break with her family, just friendlier terms.

"One of the things that hurt so much when Melody left was losing her whole family. She has two sisters, both of them married with kids. It felt so good to be part of the Rankin clan at Thanksgiving and Christmas. Her family accepted me as much as they did her sisters' husbands—her mom used to say I was special because I was her only daughter-in-law—and I loved being Aunt Allyn to our nieces and nephews. Melody just ripped that away from me."

"Have you been in touch with any of them since she left?"

Allyn shook her head and sniffed, fighting her emotions. "She pretty much ordered me not to. Who knows what she told them? It kills me sometimes to think about this Naomi person just stepping in and taking over my whole life. She has everything that used to be mine."

Bea shifted into a kneeling position on the love seat so she could wrap her arms around Allyn. "See, this is what I meant about not wanting any labels or roles. I want to be able to do this whenever you need it without worrying who's supposed to be the strong one."

"I promised myself I wouldn't go on like this anymore. All I've done since the day you came to my house with Dexter is cry over Melody. Tonight was supposed to be about you, with me listening for a change instead of whining."

The barrage of questions from Allyn suddenly made sense. Bea was touched by the effort to put her feelings aside but it wasn't needed. "I never thought you were whining. If Melody had done that to me, I'd still be yelling about it to anyone who would listen."

"No, you wouldn't. You're not like that."

"Ask Kit how long I went on about Wendy, even after she divorced me."

"That's different. What happened to you and Wendy was so sad for both of you. Melody was just a garden-variety cheater and I'm a garden-variety chump."

Bea squeezed harder. "Remember what we said. This isn't a competition to see who can hide their misery best. If you want an honest relationship with me, you can't pretend to be okay when you aren't. I'm here to listen whenever you need that. We don't have to take turns."

It was then she noticed Allyn's hand caressing her back, the faintest of gestures, but one she relished as a sign they were connecting on a much more intimate plane than earlier. She couldn't resist dropping a kiss on the top of her head before lowering her face to see if Allyn had composed herself.

She had.

"I do want an honest relationship," Allyn said, "but I felt like I was being selfish. Everything can't always be about me."

"Sure it can. I'm still in that obsessive phase where everything you say and do fascinates me." Now that her feelings for Allyn were out in the open, she took a chance on revealing even more, this time with levity. "I'm particularly fascinated by what your hand is doing on the small of my back. Makes me want to slow dance."

The gentle massage stopped abruptly but then started again.

Bea rested her chin on Allyn's head and continued, "Though 'Take Me Out to the Ballgame' leaves a lot to be desired in the romantic ballad department."

"Is that what this is, a romance?"

"I hope so. Don't you?"

After several seconds of silence, it was apparent Allyn wasn't going to answer.

"Did I just freak you out again?"

"No, I want it to be a romance too, which is really amazing considering where my head was just two weeks ago. How did you do that to me so fast?"

"Two possibilities," Bea said, allowing her fingertips to stroke a sliver of skin that bared itself beneath the hem of Allyn's T-shirt. "Either it's my irresistible charm or you fell for my dog. He's my secret weapon."

"It could be both…but I admit I really like Dexter a lot."

Bea chuckled. "I walked into that one."

"But I like you a fair bit too." Allyn buried her face into Bea's neck as if to avoid making eye contact. "You make me feel good again. I wasn't sure that would ever happen."

The bold admission sparked a long silence in which Allyn tightened her hold and Bea responded by cradling her head.

"Both of us have been through a lot, Allyn. We deserve to feel good again."

Bea couldn't deny feeling strong at that moment, nor that her embrace was intended to make Allyn feel safe. What she hadn't expected was a surge of lust, the desire to convey her protectiveness by making sweet, gentle love.

Again she kissed the top of Allyn's head, this time with a loud smack meant to break what felt like an overly serious spell. She was getting ahead of herself again, but this time wouldn't make the mistake of saying so. It would be too easy—and unforgivable—to take advantage of Allyn's vulnerability tonight.

She settled back under Allyn's arm and said, "Looks like the Mariners are going to pull this one out. We should go to a game sometime. They have two more home stands. They might even make the playoffs. What do you think?"

"That could be fun," Allyn said with a squeaky voice that could have been either shyness or relief. She released her grip and drew her knees up, hooking her arms around her ankles. It was an unmistakably defensive posture, leaving Bea to wonder if she was shielding herself from the fear of intimacy or the humiliation of rejection.

CHAPTER TWELVE

Allyn stared at the TV without seeing it. Only moments ago, she'd come close to drawing Bea into her arms and kissing her senseless. Instead, Bea had pulled away and left her wondering just how much influence Wendy still had on her feelings. When she could no longer endure the silence, she made the bold decision to ask.

"Are you afraid of what might happen between us?"

Bea nodded slowly without making eye contact. "I'm afraid I'll do something that freaks you out. I'm thinking I should back off and let you set the pace."

Allyn laughed softly, but not because anything was funny. She was relieved to know she hadn't done anything to push Bea away. "There's only one problem with that. I'm a lot more likely to follow than I am to lead. It's just who I am."

"Okay, then." Bea scooted beside her and adopted the same curled-up posture, though hooking their elbows together. "I'm cool with leading as long as you talk to me."

"Talk about what? I couldn't even answer you in the car last night, and you have no idea how hard it was for me to get up the nerve to send you that text."

"Let's talk about how much I want to kiss you. I mean really kiss. Really, really kiss."

By the deep, sexy timbre of her voice, it was clear Bea meant more than kiss. Allyn found it titillating.

"Normally I wouldn't even talk about it," she went on. "I'd just…do it. But I don't know what you're ready for."

"I'm ready for…who knows? You tell me." Allyn couldn't bring herself to say it, but there was no question she'd follow wherever Bea wanted to go.

"Okay…I enjoy all kinds of kissing and touching…private places, especially with someone I care about. And it so happens I care about you. Seeing as how this is technically our first date, I don't expect us to rush into anything, but that doesn't mean I wouldn't if I had the chance."

Allyn grew more aroused with every word, with every mental image of what it meant to share herself with Bea. Someone who cared about her.

This was what she wanted. She bowed her head until their lips met, and after several seconds dropped her safeguarding posture. Drawing courage from Bea's honesty, her kiss grew more assertive, and soon her mouth exploded with excitement, the nerve endings afire with an almost electrical charge that made her want to reach deeper inside.

Bea too had surrendered to the sensations. Breathing heavily, turning her face from side to side to press their lips together from every angle.

Allyn slid her hands beneath Bea's shirt to stroke her back. Then she deftly loosened the clasp on her bra. Kissing and touching. They both wanted it.

As her physical excitement built, she wrestled barely a moment with the question of how far she wanted to go. She felt no loyalty to Melody, nor to the adolescent morals of sharing her body only inside a committed relationship. It didn't matter that this was only their first real date. This wasn't like the days of her youth when she guarded her virtue against making an immature decision she'd regret.

She flicked her tongue against Bea's teeth and sucked gently on her lips, all the while imagining what those lips would feel like elsewhere. And then her hands were in front, trembling slightly as they worked the buttons on Bea's denim shirt. She pushed it off her shoulders, and Bea shook free of her bra.

Now dressed only in her shorts, Bea made no effort to hide herself, throwing her shoulders back to allow Allyn's gaze. Her breasts were small, with wide pink areolas, pebbled by the cool air and, no doubt, by the anticipation of being touched. She guided Allyn's hand to cover one, inhaling sharply the instant they touched.

"You're lovely," Allyn murmured, gently kneading the soft mound of flesh. "Do you like this?"

"I love it." Bea allowed the gentle massage until it was obvious she was teeming with want. She tugged the hem of Allyn's T-shirt upward. "Let me help you out of this."

Allyn raised her arms and when Bea saw her thin sports bra, she hooked it in her thumbs and pulled both pieces off together.

They kissed again, straining awkwardly to press their chests together on the love seat.

"I want to lie down with you," Bea whispered. "Can we take this to the other room?"

Allyn collected her shirt from the floor and covered her breasts self-consciously as she led the way into the bedroom. One by one she tossed the decorative pillows aside, and then pulled the coverlet to the foot of the bed.

Tonight was about more than welcoming Bea to her bed. She was closing the door on Melody.

* * *

Bea flicked on the bedside lamp and took in the sight of Allyn's half-naked form as she stretched across the bed. Exquisite breasts, not small, not large. Fair in color like the rest of her skin with reddish-brown nipples that stood erect. "I hope you don't mind the lamp. I couldn't stand not being able to see you."

"Whatever you want."

"No, it's whatever we want. No labels, no roles. We're partners in here." She stepped out of her shorts and, clad only in her panties, stretched out atop Allyn so their breasts could finally press together. "Fantasies never stack up to the real thing."

Bea supported herself on one elbow to keep her weight from crushing Allyn and began lavishing attention on her jawline and neck...drawing the tender skin between her lips as though to suck but then nibbling and kissing before moving to a new spot. The area beneath the earlobe was her favorite because she knew Allyn could hear her measured breath and the soft smacking of her lips.

Allyn inhaled deeply and held it, a sign she was concentrating on the sensations. As their bodies rocked slowly from side to side, she pushed at her waistband.

"Let me do that," Bea said. She grasped both sides of her yoga pants and slid them down, careful not to lower the black satin thong. Allyn would have to decide when the time was right for that, though if she changed her mind at this point and retreated, Bea would need a dip in a frozen lake to quiet her desires. "You're absolutely gorgeous. Everything about you."

From the sweet scent emanating from Allyn's thong, Bea wasn't the only one excited.

To her surprise, Allyn then guided her onto her back as she buried her face into the hollow of Bea's breasts. In only a matter of moments, her lips drifted to capture a nipple, causing Bea to hiss with pleasure.

With pillows propping her up, she could see Allyn's bottom rise and fall as her body roiled with sexual energy, but all of that beautiful bare skin was out of arm's reach. That left her long silky hair, which fell through her fingers as Bea caressed her head.

Despite her intent to stay focused solely on the physical sensations, it was impossible to forget she was only the second person with whom Allyn had shared this level of intimacy. She was aching to touch and taste her, but it was up to Allyn to set the pace.

Allyn slid her fingertips under the waistband of Bea's panties. "I want us to be naked."

By the time she'd removed her panties, Allyn had stripped off her thong and was lying on her back with her arms out, inviting Bea to lie on top. It was an interesting shift, as though she'd had second thoughts about taking the lead. Bea wasn't surprised by her wavering and wasn't totally convinced even at this point they'd see this all the way through.

Hovering above her on all fours, she craned her neck for a kiss, and as their mouths slid together, positioned both knees between Allyn's legs to urge them apart. "You and me," she whispered, lowering herself until their pubic curls mingled.

Allyn closed her eyes and moaned at the contact. Within moments, she wrapped her legs around Bea's thighs.

Bea kissed her again, rolling her hips to deepen their pleasure as they slowly ground together. It was more than enough stimulation to make her come, but that wasn't her main goal, or even her goal at all. Their first time happened only once and she selfishly wanted it to be a moment Allyn would never forget.

Her lips started a slow journey downward, stopping to pull a rigid nipple into her mouth.

"Ohhh." Another resonant moan, and Allyn's hands came to rest on her shoulders as though ready to urge her lower when she could no longer stand the wait.

Using her elbows for support, Bea cupped both breasts and pushed them together so she could lavish first one and then the other with barely a turn of the head. Once she'd teased both nipples into hardened peaks, Allyn's hands covered hers and took over the task.

Bea moved lower, inhaling the arousal as she drew closer to its source. She hadn't meant to tease, but the tender skin of Allyn's inner thighs proved too enticing. As she kissed her way upward from the knee, she paused to feel the satiny smoothness against her cheek, causing Allyn to rise in anticipation.

When it seemed Allyn was near the point of frustration, Bea homed in on her prize and swiped her tongue from bottom to top. She was careful not to linger in any one place, not wanting

Allyn to come too soon. For both their sakes, she wanted to prolong the thrill.

The tart wetness was tinged with salt, and Bea slid her tongue in and out in quest for more, eliciting a whimper. Allyn was writhing with excitement that was growing harder to deny.

As she took Allyn's hand, she gently drew her swollen clitoris between her lips and flicked it again and again with her tongue. Then she dipped one fingertip inside, barely enough to notice until she pressed downward in a fluttering motion.

Three…two…

"Ahhhhh!" Allyn's head thrashed from side to side as her legs tightened around Bea's shoulders. "Oh, God…"

Bea relaxed her tongue but held it in place in case another orgasm was lurking nearby. As soon as she felt the legs loosening their grip, she started again.

Allyn lasted about fifteen seconds before her second climax, this one not nearly as intense as the first. That was her limit apparently, since she tugged Bea up to lie beside her. "That was so amazing."

"I'll second that," Bea said, offering her softened lips for a kiss. She nestled into Allyn's arms knowing it would be but a moment before they began again.

Her confessions thus far had brought them to this, but it wasn't the end of the road for Bea. Allyn Teague was the first woman since Wendy who had a chance at capturing her heart.

* * *

Allyn couldn't remember the last time she'd awakened to so much sunlight in her bedroom. It was hours ago that she'd first stirred, when Bea had gotten up to go to the bathroom and returned to snuggle behind her, planting a warm kiss on her bare shoulder. Instead of lying awake contemplating her impulsive decision of the night before, she'd fallen back into an even deeper, dreamless sleep.

She rolled over to face Bea, whose mouth was fixed in a slight smile, though her eyes were still closed. "Are you awake?" she whispered softly, not wanting to rouse her if she weren't.

"My brain is...and maybe a little piece of my left ear. The rest of me is comatose." She draped her leg across Allyn's and wrapped an arm around her waist. "You feeling okay this morning?"

"Very okay." Allyn stretched her neck as far as it would bend and kissed her on the forehead. What she felt was brand new, no longer chained to the painful memories of the last year. She didn't have to think about Melody anymore, not when she could think about her new possibilities with Bea.

"Me too...except for a few muscles I haven't used for a while. Don't laugh at me if I get out of bed and fall down."

Allyn didn't like to dwell on the last time she'd made love, not since she registered it was after Melody had already begun her affair. It sickened her to think anyone could go back and forth between two lovers without remorse.

She had no idea about Bea's last time but recalled her saying some of Wendy's questions about her dates made her uncomfortable. "You've done this before, right? Since Wendy?"

"Yes...and no." Bea propped her head with her hand so they were eye to eye, and ran her fingers gently across Allyn's lower abdomen, tickling the edge of her pubic hair. "I hooked up last year with a woman from Spokane. We hit it off at a wedding reception and spent the night together. But it wasn't like this, Allyn. I didn't have feelings for her, and I didn't wake up on cloud nine the next morning the way I did just now. And I haven't even talked to her since."

"Good. See that you don't." As they exchanged a tender kiss, Allyn was struck by the realization that another loss so soon would be devastating. "I hope you'll stay this way, on cloud nine. I don't think I could handle it if you left, not after last night. I don't do this kind of thing. You're just the second person in my whole life who—"

Bea put a finger over her lips. "Hush...I'm not going anywhere. And I know this is a big deal. It is for me too, but the hard part's over. Neither of us has to be nervous about our feelings anymore. After what we did last night, we ought to be able to say and do anything we want, don't you agree?"

Physical intimacy wasn't the same as expressing emotions, but Bea was right that it should be easier now. "Does it change anything about how you feel?"

"Of course it does. For starters, it means I won't be sharing these kinds of feelings with anyone else, and I definitely won't share this." She cupped Allyn's sex and jiggled it for emphasis. "This is mine and mine is yours. We have something private and special to build on, to see if we want more, and if so, how much. And it also means you're my girlfriend now."

Every word was exactly what she needed to hear, and she pulled Bea into an embrace. "I like being your girlfriend."

"And you're also stepmother to a spoiled rotten, bouncing, slobbering fur ball with occasional bad breath."

"Dexter! Poor baby. He's been by himself all night."

"He's fine. I took the panel out of his dog door in case I got home late…or not at all, as the case may be. One of the great things about dogs is they forgive and forget. Once I get home, it'll be like I never left."

"I wish you could bring him back here, but they'd probably kick me out."

"We could always move the party to my place. I have a nice big bed too, and I could easily spend the entire day in it with you."

"Except if we go to your place, you'll have to feed me."

"There is that." Bea snuggled again into her side and skimmed a fingertip across Allyn's prominent hipbone. "Can I tell you something? Sure I can, because we just agreed we could talk about anything now."

"I can't wait to hear this."

"That day when I saw you at the Pak & Ship, the one you go to now, I was horrified to see how much weight you'd lost. Horrified. Please tell me you aren't still losing."

What once had been a battle for self-control had turned into a visible symbol of her own defeat, not surprising since a part of her had wanted to punish Melody by destroying herself and forcing her to feel responsible. That urge was mostly gone, replaced by a wish to have Melody see her looking better than ever so she'd know what she'd given up. "Believe it or not, I've put back about five pounds from the worst of it. With my luck it'll all come back eventually and I won't have anything to show for my misery. Back to my pudgy old self."

"Your old self was pretty damn cute if you ask me. And yes, I noticed you years ago. Kit gave me hell every single time you walked through the door…she always said I was flirting with you, but I didn't mean to be. I thought you were nice and I wanted us to be friends. Melody too."

It would have been nice to have had someone to turn to after Melody left. "I asked her about it a couple of times. I remember you invited us once to a cookout on Pride weekend and then to a basketball game at the UW. She always had one reason or another why we couldn't go. I never thought much about it when we were still together, but then when she left I discovered that all of our friends were actually just her friends." It was a mess of her own making, she admitted to herself. As she mentally scrolled through all the women she'd met through Bea, those who'd followed the softball team to JoJo's, she acknowledged she was repeating that pattern. Left to her own devices, she'd likely have no friends at all.

"What are you thinking about?" Bea asked.

Allyn hadn't realized she'd gone silent for so long. "Nothing really…us being friends. It should have happened. That was my fault for always letting Melody decide who we'd hang out with. She was leery about meeting new people except through her friends, but she should have tried harder for my sake."

"I would have liked that back then but you know what? I wouldn't change a thing if it meant not being right here, right now."

She rolled toward Bea, pushing her onto her back, and sprawled over her with a knee wedged between her legs. "Has anyone ever told you that you have an uncanny gift for saying the perfect thing?"

Bea smiled up at her, her wide green eyes sparkling behind the jagged strands of dark hair that covered her brow. "The whole truth and nothing but the truth, your honor."

Even more uncanny was how quickly Allyn had come to need those assurances. It hardly seemed possible that only two weeks ago she'd been mired in despair and now she was on the verge of falling in love again.

CHAPTER THIRTEEN

"*Parked in fire lane. Burn some rubber,*" the text read.

Allyn laughed and pounded out her reply. "*With blazing speed.*"

She'd returned home from Bea's house only an hour ago to shower and change for the Labor Day picnic at Woodland Park. She wore a gold top with capped sleeves and brown knee-length pants that sported half a dozen pockets. Leather sandals showed off her cherry-painted toenails, though she was taking along a pair of sneakers in case someone organized a pickup game of softball or volleyball. She finished off her outfit by pulling her ponytail through the back of a beige canvas ball cap.

As promised, Bea was parked next to the building, and she started her car the moment Allyn appeared.

"Wow, I didn't know you were in such a hurry," she said before giving Bea a quick kiss and turning to pet Dexter.

"I have forty pounds of ice melting in my trunk and about a hundred cans of pop. I should have just given Kit money for the ribs and chicken like you did. At least I didn't have to cook anything. My friends know me well enough not to ask."

For dinner the night before, Bea had gone out to her back porch to grill a pair of salmon steaks, which she served atop a fresh salad. "You're not as horrible as you led me to believe. I liked what you made for dinner."

"Enough to eat it every night? I don't have a lot of variety in my skill set."

Allyn's first inclination was to answer that she'd be happy to handle the cooking, but it shocked her how such overt discussion of their division of labor made it sound as though they were setting up permanent housekeeping. Two days together did not a marriage make.

"I can't believe you were only gone for an hour," Bea went on. "I missed you like crazy. I don't know how I'm going to make it through the week after we go back to work."

Unless Bea was willing to start her day by heading home at five thirty in the morning, Allyn's work schedule would make it all but impossible to spend the night together except on the weekends. That was a lot to ask, especially since it meant leaving Dexter on his own. On the other hand, it would be difficult to sit home alone knowing Bea was only ten minutes away.

"I missed you too. We'll have to figure out something." She remembered from her early days with Melody the desperate need for private time together, which had driven them to move out of their college dorm and into an apartment after only a month.

"Right now I don't even want to let you out of my sight. Just don't let me wear out my welcome."

"Not going to happen." Allyn clutched her hand and kissed it, noticing for the first time her aqua Run Seattle T-shirt, which she wore over cuffed denim shorts. "I didn't know you were a runner too."

"I'm not. I just like the color. Reminds me of your eyes." She returned the gesture, raising Allyn's hand to her lips.

"You're quite the flirt. I can't believe I never noticed."

"I'll make sure you notice now." Bea slowed considerably when she entered the park. "Keep an eye out for Kit's truck. She was supposed to get here early to set up."

A rainbow flag fluttered from one of the pavilions where at least two dozen women had already gathered. "There she is. Pretty hard to miss, huh?"

Kit met them at the car to help carry ice and drinks. "About time you got here. Would it be rude to ask what took you so long?"

"Yes, as a matter of fact, it would," Bea said, chucking Kit with her hip as she opened the trunk. "Stand there like a pack mule while I stack these bags in your arms."

"Watch my shoulder."

Despite the warning, Kit didn't appear fazed by her heavy load, nor did Bea, but Allyn's arms trembled when she finally dropped two cases of pop on the picnic table. Then she hurried to brace Marta, who was standing atop a step stool decorating the pavilion with gay-themed streamers. "Thanks, Allyn. Kit promised to help me do this but she's too busy being in charge."

"Good thing somebody is." Melody would never have participated in such a conspicuous display of gayness, but Allyn felt right at home, especially when she noticed most of the women were softball teammates and their partners, the same crowd that gathered at JoJo's after their games. It was nice to feel like one of the gang. Even though she'd met these women through Bea, she felt connected in her own right because she was part of the team.

"Allyn?"

The voice belonged to a familiar face, but it took her a moment to place the woman in this context, since she wasn't part of their usual Wednesday night group. Candace Landini, the girlfriend of a woman who worked with Melody at the university. Short and full-figured, she wore jeans that could have been a size larger and a T-shirt stretched across her ample breasts. Her coloring was dark, consistent with her Italian heritage, and she had a dime-sized mole next to her left eye that distinguished her pretty face. "Candace, how are you?"

"Not too bad considering. How about you?"

Considering what? Allyn was struck by how much calmer she felt talking to Candace, whom she hadn't known very well, versus Jillian, who was clearly Melody's ally. "It's been a tough few months, but things are looking up."

"That's great to hear. I felt really bad for you after what Melody did. Lark and I both were shocked by it. It was so sudden."

"Where is Lark?"

Candace made a small clicking noise with her tongue and shook her head. "We aren't together anymore."

"Oh, no. What happened?"

"I shouldn't say too much for now. Lark has a few things to work on, and if she does, we might get back together one of these days. I don't want to poison her with any of our friends."

"That's really kind. You're a better person than I am."

"No, I'm just a psychotherapist with ten years' experience counseling people about their relationships. I'm trying to take my own advice."

She'd forgotten that about Candace, and it made sense now why she seemed easy to talk to.

"Besides, anyone would find it hard to be nice to someone like Melody after what she did. As far as I'm concerned, you don't have to say a kind word about her ever again."

"Good, because I don't know what that word would be." Until right then, Allyn had no idea she had anyone in her corner from her former life, especially after hearing Melody had brought Naomi back to Seattle to meet her friends.

She filled two party cups with ice and they fished around for cans of diet pop.

Candace said, "Kit told me we'd need chairs so I brought a couple. Want to go sit in the shade?"

With a quick scan of the park, Allyn spotted Bea joking around with Kit as they set up the barbecue grill. "Sure. How do you know Kit?"

"She used to work at my post office. I was in there all the time because I was selling stuff on eBay."

Allyn smiled.

"What's funny?"

"That's kind of how I ended up here too. I used to have a mailbox at the Pak & Ship in Ballard. That's how I got to be friends with Bea Lawson." She nodded toward the grill. "The woman over there with Kit getting ready to set the whole park on fire."

"I know her, at least I know who she is. Kit works for her now."

"Right."

"She's the one whose wife got paralyzed. So sad."

Bea would hate hearing herself described that way, but it was difficult for anyone to forget a marker like that. "They're still good friends. Wendy divorced her, you know, because she wanted her to move on...which is lucky for me, since we've started seeing each other."

Candace strained to lean forward in her sling chair and held up her hand for a slap. "You go, girl! I sometimes tell my clients there's a reason for everything. I don't necessarily believe it, but it makes them feel better. If it's true, then I hope Bea turns out to be the reason you had to go through that hell with Melody."

Allyn didn't want to believe in that kind of fate, not if it meant Wendy was supposed to end up paralyzed. "Oh, look. They're setting up a volleyball net. Do you play?"

"Afraid not. There isn't an athletic bone in this body, but I'm a great cheerleader. I cheer for whoever is winning."

It was tempting to go play, but talking to a friend who knew what she'd been through with Melody was a rare treat, provided Candace didn't try to turn a friendly chat into a therapy session. "Do you still keep up with Lark?"

"Kind of. She keeps up with me if she has anything to talk about. I don't see her though. I'm not going to do that again until I'm sure she's made some big changes."

"Does it bother you when you don't hear from her?" Allyn remembered too well her frustration at never hearing from Melody unless she needed something related to the divorce or sale of the house.

"It bothers me because I worry about her. If she goes a long time without getting in touch, I wonder if it's because she's not dealing with her problems like she promised to, or if she's thrown in the towel and given up on us."

Lark was probably into drinking or drugs, Allyn decided, and she deeply admired Candace's courage to take a stand. "Aren't you afraid she won't come back?"

"Sure, but I was more afraid of staying with her the way things were. Would you want Melody back if you knew she was going to keep cheating on you?"

"Hell, no!" What's more, now that she had Bea, she no longer thought about getting Melody back.

* * *

Bea lunged backward as the coals flared, singeing the hair on her arms. "Down, Sparky!"

Kit tossed her a squirt bottle filled with water. "Here, use this to keep the flames down. You're going to char everything and it'll be raw on the inside."

She never had this trouble with her gas grill. "I warned you not to make me cook."

"Yeah, yeah," Kit grumbled. "So what have you been cooking with Allyn Teague?"

Nonchalance wasn't an option, not once she broke into a grin. "I'd say she definitely knows I'm flirting now, since she's flirting back."

"Do tell."

"We spent the weekend together."

"Hot damn!"

"I'm pretty crazy about her, but I'm not sure she's over Melody yet. With my luck, I'll fall head over heels and then Melody will come back." She looked over toward the trees where Allyn was deep in conversation with a woman Bea didn't know. "Do me a favor. Don't say anything to Wendy just yet. If this comes to anything, I'd like to be the one to tell her."

Kit was grinning as though the happy news were hers. "No problem. I can tell Marta, though, right?"

"Sure. It'll probably leak out soon, so I may have to make an unscheduled run up to Vancouver. I don't know who all Wendy Skypes with or emails these days. It's not like it's a secret or anything, but I don't want her to hear it from somebody else first." She walked around to the other side of the grill so she could keep an eye on Allyn. "Do you know who that woman is that Allyn's talking to?"

"Candace Landini. Used to be a customer of mine at the post office."

"I remember now. She's a therapist of some sort. Came to one of the Huskies games. Her girlfriend is the one with a cool name."

"Lark. They split up not too long ago because Lark's become a compulsive liar. I've never seen anything like it. Marta and I went to their house once for dinner and Lark told us this bizarre story about hiking up into the Hoh River the day before to catch the salmon we were eating. Except Marta ran into Candace that morning at Pike Place and saw her buying it. You should have seen how red her face got when Lark was telling that whopper. She told us later Lark did it all the time, and always about stupid things. Candace got so she never knew when she was telling the truth."

"That would be creepy." Bea nodded in the direction of their chairs. "You don't think I need to be jealous, do you? They've been over there talking a long time."

Kit snatched the water bottle from her hand. "Go on over there and mark your territory. You're too dangerous around a grill anyway."

Bea went first to the pavilion to get Dexter, whose leash was looped around the leg of a picnic table, and also picked up his tennis ball. Then she led him toward the shaded area, smiling with relief as Allyn came to her feet and welcomed her with a quick kiss on the lips.

"I want you to meet a friend of mine, Candace Landini."

Candace jumped up too and held out a hand. "Our exes worked together at the UW. Who knows what they're putting in the water over there?"

Bea appreciated how Allyn's simple display of affection made her ripple of jealousy subside. "I remember you from the Huskies game last year."

"And who is this doll baby?" Candace squatted to greet Dexter.

"Just the sweetest little boy on earth," Allyn replied.

"I was about to take him over to the off-leash area so he could run a little. You guys want to come?"

Several dogs of all sizes roamed the pet area, chasing balls, frisbees and one another. Dexter had never been interested in other dogs, but he wasn't hostile when they came around to sniff.

Bea tossed the ball and he dashed after it. "The hardest part is getting him to drop it so I can throw it again."

Despite her commands, he steadfastly held the ball in his mouth until she pretended to throw another. Then he dropped it and took off.

Candace clapped. "That's so cute. Let me throw it."

Dexter didn't display his usual boundless energy with Candace. Instead, he turned the tables, chasing the ball leisurely and lying down, which forced her to retrieve it from him.

"Smartest dog I ever saw," Bea said to Allyn. "It's cool you ran into Candace. Have you two kept in touch?"

"No, I figured she was like all the others, buddy-buddy with Melody. Turns out she's not. Neither was her girlfriend. They both thought what Melody did was shitty."

"I'd worry about the moral compass of anyone who didn't."

"She's always been nice to me. I'd like to be friends with her. Is that okay?"

"Of course," Bea said, surprised by the fact she felt she had to ask. "You should have all the friends you want, Allyn."

"No, I meant our friend, somebody we'd go out with or have over. Melody never wanted to do anything with people unless they were her friends first."

Because Melody was a selfish bitch, Bea thought. "I'm not like that. I'm happy to hang out with you and Candace if you want me to, but you should have your own friends too. I don't have to be part of everything you do. You probably don't want that with me either."

By the look on Allyn's face, she wasn't happy with that idea.

"What's wrong?"

"The last time I let somebody have her own private life, it didn't work out so well."

"You're borrowing trouble. I'm not going to have the kind of secrets Melody had and neither are you, but we shouldn't let our lives get sucked inside each other. Bad things happen. If anyone knows that, it's us. If it does, it's a whole lot easier when you have friends of your own you can lean on."

"And you're not just saying that because you don't want to be around any of the women I know?"

Bea laughed and moved close enough to cup Allyn's cheek. "Listen, lady. Save yourself all this worrying. Just take me at my word because I'm not going to lie to you. I'm happy to do things with your friends whenever you want me to, but I want you to be your own person too. That's who you were when I met you, and that's who I've started falling in love with."

Allyn's cheeks reddened as a smile spread across her face. "I said that out loud, didn't I?"

"Yes, and you aren't taking it back."

"Oh, I have no intention of taking it back."

Dexter collapsed at her feet, his tongue hanging to the ground. Candace was holding the tennis ball in her fingertips with her arm outstretched so the slobber wouldn't get on her clothes.

"You look like someone who needs a good hand-washing," Bea said, relieving her of the slimy mess. She pointed toward the parking lot. "There's a restroom over there."

Allyn attached Dexter's leash to walk him back as Candace hurried away. "Picnics are fun but I'm ready for this one to be over."

"Why's that?" Bea asked.

"Because I want to take you home and devour you."

"Deflower me?"

"That too."

* * *

At the last second, Allyn slid two fingers into Bea and spread them wide. When the rapid clenching started inside, she flattened her tongue to cover as much of the slickness as she could.

Bea gasped sharply and thrust her hips upward so hard Allyn nearly lost contact. "God, you're so good," she murmured as she eased herself back down to the bed.

"We're good together," Allyn whispered.

In this room they were uninhibited and focused on learning how to please each other. Across three days, their lovemaking had been alternately tender, fun, heartfelt and adventurous. Today it was passionate. Because Bea had confessed to falling in love with her.

Bea Lawson, the cute woman who ran the Pak & Ship. With a perfect smile that set off her beautiful green eyes and thick hair the color of coal. Even-tempered with a sense of humor. Pensive and philosophical. Morally grounded. Sweet.

All those words came so easily to describe her, but she had something else, something intangible. It was the flint that had sparked, that told Allyn to pay attention to her. Now the spark was growing into love.

Now that she had Bea, she could let Melody go.

CHAPTER FOURTEEN

Poor Dexter. Bea had left him at home the night before while she squeezed in a couple of hours after work to be with Allyn. Now she'd dropped him off at home and run off again, this time to her softball game. Too bad Ballard Park didn't allow dogs around the ball fields. He'd be all right though. He was easygoing and forgiving, though not accustomed to spending so much time alone.

A line of customers at closing time kept her in the shop later than usual, and she barely had enough time to change into her softball clothes and get to the park in time to warm up. As she leaned on the trunk of her car to change from her sneakers to her cleats, she spotted Allyn running from the dugout to meet her.

"What took you so long? Kit's been stalling the umpire over her lineup card until she saw you pull in."

Bea answered first with a quick kiss, not caring who saw them together. After holding hands for most of the day at their picnic two days ago, it was hardly a secret they were seeing each other. "Those damn customers. Always bothering me with their business," she joked.

Allyn's bouncing ponytail made her look like a teenager, especially when she snapped her bubblegum, which they all chewed during their games. "I went crazy after you left last night. Took me forever to get to sleep."

"Tell me about it. I had to ride home with the air conditioner on full blast." An hour of making out on the couch had left her in a frenzy.

"You can come back tomorrow for dinner if you want."

Allyn surprised her by taking her hand as they walked toward the dugout, and Bea made note of several people looking their way. She knew lots of the women who hung out at the ball field for the women's league on Wednesday night, and so did Wendy. "About tomorrow...I think I should go up and talk to Wendy about this before somebody else does." She raised their joined hands to indicate what she meant by *this*.

"You're going to drive all the way to Vancouver and back after work? You won't get home till midnight."

Probably closer to one or two, depending on how long she and Wendy talked, but the urgency was growing every day. She could do it during their regular Thursday night Skype session, but that seemed cold and impersonal. "Wendy still has a lot of friends here. One of them could be watching us right now, and I don't want her to hear about us from anyone but me. You understand that, don't you?"

"Of course. I just hate to think of you working all day and driving all night. I wish I could go with you—not to see Wendy. Just to ride in the car and keep you awake."

"I'll have Dexter for that. He's pretty good company." She found an errant ball in the grass behind the dugout. "Let's throw a few. I need to warm up."

After each toss, they took a small step backward, with Allyn tossing grounders and Bea hurling them back as if throwing to first base.

"Candace came out to cheer us on," Allyn said, waving toward the bleachers.

"Is she coming with us to JoJo's?"

Allyn held the ball and stared into the stands, her cheery demeanor fading. "Shit. Guess who's sitting right in front of her."

Bea turned and peered into the distance, recognizing the woman Allyn had run into at their first game. "Is that Melody's friend?"

"Jillian and her wife Tiffany. What the hell are they doing here?"

It wasn't unusual for players to hang around and watch other teams, but Jillian's team wasn't playing tonight. Most likely they had come to watch Allyn, a realization that made Bea feel both protective and possessive. Turning her back to the bleachers, she walked toward Allyn. "Are they looking this way?"

"Yeah."

"Good." She rose up on her tiptoes and planted a kiss on Allyn's lips. "I sure hope they saw that."

* * *

Allyn counted out seventeen dollars and added it to the pile in the center of the table. Over Bea's and Marta's objections, she gladly shared the cost of two pitchers of beer she didn't help drink. That's what it meant to be part of a team, and tonight was special because they'd won their final game of the season.

Most of the women had gone already, but she was stretching out every moment with Bea, knowing they wouldn't see each other again until the weekend.

Bea held up the small plaque that commemorated the season and thanked Pak & Ship for sponsoring the team. "After such a miserable start, I can't believe we finished the season tied for third."

"I finished undefeated," Allyn added haughtily.

"Something tells me they're going to miss us here at JoJo's," Kit said, flipping through the stack of cash. "We should get up a team for the volleyball league. That starts in about three weeks."

"Let me know what the sponsor's fee is. I'm game," Bea said, looking toward Allyn for her response.

"Me too. I haven't played in forever though. I might not be good enough."

Marta laughed and slapped the table as she stood. "That didn't stop any of you from playing softball."

On that disparaging note, they filed out to the parking lot. Bea hung back until the others left and followed Allyn to her car. "You weren't upset about me kissing you in front of Jillian and Tiffany, were you?"

As the game had worn on, Allyn worried about the ramifications, especially when she noticed Jillian and Tiffany taking photos, which they would likely send to Melody. The more she thought about it, the more unsettled it made her, so she'd kept her distance from Bea for the rest of the game. "No, but I didn't like that we were putting on a show for their benefit. You can kiss me anytime you want when you really mean it."

"I did mean it, but I got a little carried away. I figured they'd run back to Melody and I wanted to rub her nose in it. I won't do anything like that again if it bothers you."

"It's okay. I didn't mind it when you did it, but when I saw them taking pictures of you over on third base, it made me wish we hadn't. Melody doesn't need to know my business."

"You're right. I'm sorry."

The solemn look on Bea's face made her feel guilty for coming down too hard. "It's not that big a deal. We haven't done anything wrong."

Bea checked around to be sure no one was watching. Then she tugged on Allyn's neck for another kiss. "You're such a sweetheart."

The words melted her inside and she pulled Bea into a bear hug. "What I am is lucky. You came into my life right when I needed you most."

"I need you just as much, Allyn."

Even after all the hours they'd spent making love, this felt like their sweetest moment yet. "I'll miss you tomorrow night. Be safe."

They turned in opposite directions coming out of the parking lot, leaving Allyn to face her feelings alone. She understood now what Bea had meant when she said she started looking forward to their next time together the moment she walked away. The weekend couldn't come soon enough.

Seven years ago, she and Melody had privately laughed at Jillian, who'd just met Tiffany and was frantic to be with her every minute of every day. It was silly, or so they thought, for someone to be so crazy over a woman she'd known only a week or two.

And now she was fighting the urge to turn the car around and follow Bea home.

* * *

Dexter had slept most of the way in the passenger seat, oblivious to her nervousness about breaking the news to Wendy. His annoyance over her recent absences was unmistakable in his cool demeanor. He'd greeted her at the door the night before, but couldn't be bothered to run through the house no matter how much she coaxed him.

"Almost there, baby." It was nearly nine o'clock, and she envied him his nap.

The Huangs weren't happy about her impromptu visit, but they accommodated it for Wendy's sake. Joseph Huang answered the door with his usual air of detachment and cast a scornful look at Dexter.

"I wiped his feet," she said, holding up the cloth she carried in her car for just that purpose. Wendy had made it clear to her parents that she enjoyed seeing Dexter, but Bea still felt obliged to be a considerate guest.

He stood aside to let her enter. "Wendy is already in bed, but I believe she's still awake."

"Thank you."

Bea held Dexter close to her side as she walked past him into what once was a formal living room but had been converted for Wendy because the house lacked a bedroom on the ground floor. She was situated in a poorly disguised hospital bed, its head tipped at an angle to make the respirator's work easier. A bedside lamp was the only light in the room.

"Hey, sweetie." Bea leaned over to kiss her while Dexter put his paws on the edge of the bed.

"Can't wait to hear this." The respirator puffed for another breath. "Must be important for you to come so late."

"Yeah, I had to work all day. Your dad wasn't exactly thrilled to see me. I considered letting Dexter pee on his leg."

"Turn off the monitor."

"Oh, shit!" She'd forgotten the Huangs left a baby monitor in Wendy's room at night while they were sleeping upstairs. "Oh, well…it's not as if they used to like me and now they won't."

"You met somebody."

Bea sighed and smiled weakly. "I guess some big mouth got to you before I could. I was afraid of that."

"Nobody told me. It was the only reason I could think of… why you'd come all this way on a weeknight."

She took Wendy's hand and raised it to her lips, hoping she could see the love even if she couldn't feel it. "Yeah, I met somebody, and I think she might be special enough that I should come up here and tell you about her before someone else beat me to it."

Even after the last two years of Wendy imploring her to find someone else, Bea hardly expected a joyous reaction if and when she finally did. To her, it marked the definitive end to their romantic relationship, perhaps more than the accident because it meant giving her heart to another woman.

"I'm happy for you."

"I can tell by the way you're jumping up and down." Bea knew she had questions, and it would be easier to tell the whole story rather than force her to ask for details. "Her name is Allyn Teague. I told you a little about her before. She used to be one of my regulars, but she and her wife split up last year and she moved up to Broadview. I ran into her about a month ago and we went out—just friends, that's all. But then we hit it off, and I knew I needed to tell you because it has a certain feel to it. The kind that makes me think it might turn into something serious one of these days."

"What makes it feel that way?"

Bea laughed softly and shook her head. Though she knew Wendy didn't mean any of her questions as a challenge, they forced her to articulate things that hadn't yet taken form. "I could tell you all the little things. She's fun, she's sweet. I think she's very pretty. But the main thing is something I can't even put my finger on. We clicked."

"That's the best part." Wendy closed her eyes and smiled. "Tell me more."

"For starters, she's about a foot taller than you are. I never appreciated how much your neck must have hurt from looking up all the time."

"I always liked looking up to you…in more ways than one."

The idea that Wendy, who'd graduated near the top of her class in medical school, could look up to someone whose greatest accomplishment was owning a postal franchise, never failed to amaze her. Wendy said her success came easier because she had parents who pushed her and paid her way through school, while Bea had been forced to make it on her own.

"Allyn works at home. She's a headhunter for tech companies. Oh, and she's left-handed like you. Plays first base on our softball team."

"Do you have a picture?"

"As a matter of fact…" She scrolled through her smartphone to the download from the newspaper's website. "You can't really see her face though. This was in the paper."

Wendy studied it for a moment before pronouncing, "Nice butt."

Bea chuckled awkwardly at the absurdity, remembering how she'd thought the same thing.

"Would I like her?"

"I think so. Dexter does." She described the circumstances of Allyn's divorce and how she'd struggled to get back on her feet. "Bottom line is we're just a couple of rejects who happened to find each other."

"You're not a reject." Wendy said more with her eyes than most people did with their speech, and at that moment, she was showing love and sorrow so deep it made Bea want to cry. "I want you to be happy, Bea."

"I know, honey. If you tell me right now there's a chance for you and me to be happy together, I'll end this with Allyn tomorrow. We can still find a way to be together."

"I love you, but what I really want…is for you to stop thinking that way." An unusually scolding tone for Wendy. "Choose to be with someone else."

After years of pleading her case, Bea would have been shocked by any other response. But she'd never asked when the answer meant so much. "I don't know for sure this is going to work out. There's always the chance her old girlfriend will come back one of these days and she'll leave me on the side of the road."

"Or maybe she'll pick you. I know I would. Will I get to meet her?"

"I hope so. We need a little time to see where it's all going." She also had to be sure Allyn could handle the depth of her feelings for Wendy without feeling threatened, and Bea had to know for certain Allyn was over Melody for good. "One thing's for sure. We're not going to rush into anything."

"When will you come back?"

"A week from Sunday, I guess. Same as usual." She nodded toward the baby monitor. "Assuming your folks let me. Can't believe I did that."

"It was funny."

"I'll never be out of your life, Wendy. Even if I fall madly in love with someone and get married again. No matter who it is, she has to understand that."

This was where Wendy sometimes retorted that she might not want that once Bea moved on. Now faced with the real possibility, she wasn't so flippant. "So I'm stuck with you."

"That's right."

Dexter, who'd been sitting quietly at their feet, stood up on the edge of the bed and whimpered.

"I think he's telling you it's time to go," Wendy rasped.

"Probably a good idea. It's been a long day." She clutched Wendy's hand again and kissed her goodbye. "I love you, you know. If I'm lucky enough in this lifetime for lightning to strike me twice, I'll have you to thank for both of them."

CHAPTER FIFTEEN

"I wish I had your willpower," Candace said, pointing to Allyn's plate, which she'd barely touched. "First you order a salad in a place that has the best hamburgers in Seattle, then you hardly eat any of it."

"Bea's taking me out for dinner tonight," Allyn said. Besides that, she'd picked up another four pounds in the last couple of weeks and was finding some of her new clothes snug.

"Where are you going?"

"She won't say but she told me to dress up. My guess is Bastille because we drove past there last week and I said I wanted to try it sometime."

"Oh, Lark and I went there last year for our anniversary. Try the short ribs. They'll melt in your mouth."

Fine dining wasn't their usual fare, but Bea said it was time to go someplace fancy so they wouldn't take their relationship for granted. It was special and they deserved to treat it that way once in a while.

The best part of their date would come afterward. Even though Bea had to work on Saturday, Allyn didn't, so she planned to spend the night at Bea's house. It wasn't until she started staying over on the weekends that she realized how much she missed the comfort of sleeping with someone, of knowing all through the night that she wasn't alone.

Candace pushed her sandwich basket aside, leaving her fries untouched. "Lark called last Monday and asked me to meet her at JoJo's for a beer. I have to admit I was tempted. I wish I could see her again."

"Why didn't you?"

"I get the feeling we're at a turning point. She wants to come back but I have to hold the line on getting her to face up to what she needs to do. It's not easy though, not for either of us. I went from living with somebody and having my whole life wrapped up in hers to being totally by myself. You know exactly how miserable that is."

"Boy, do I ever."

"The hardest part is knowing I could put a stop to it"—she snapped her fingers—"just like that whenever I wanted to. All I'd have to do is say the word and Lark would come back."

Allyn, having gotten the lowdown on Lark's compulsive lying from Bea, decided not to mention it unless Candace brought it up. She didn't blame her one bit for breaking up under those circumstances. "And you say I have willpower? If I'd had that chance with Melody, I would've caved a million times just to make the hurt stop."

"It does hurt but she needs to know I'm serious," Candace said as she wiped mustard from her fingers. "I've never shut the door on her all the way though. I suppose I'd have to if I knew she wasn't ever going to change."

"I left the door open for Melody for a long time. Then one day I met Bea. My feelings for Melody just…poof." She flipped her hands casually as if tossing powder. "I didn't close it. It closed itself."

"You're so lucky, Allyn. A lot of people in your situation latch onto the first person coming down the pike just because they need to be with somebody who makes them feel better. In your case, that first person turned out to be a keeper. Bea's so nice, and she's cute too. I watched her at the ballpark the other night. It's obvious how much people like her. That's a good sign."

No matter how many compliments Candace paid to Bea, Allyn still heard a measure of doubt in her choice of words. It was probably therapist-speak, designed to make people question their decisions. "You think it's possible the only reason I'm seeing Bea is because she makes me feel better?"

Candace's face softened. "It's as good a reason as any. Anyone who's been through a bad breakup will welcome a port in the storm. That's only natural. Your port turned out to be a place you really wanted to be. That's what makes you lucky."

Once Candace qualified her remarks, Allyn dropped her internal defenses enough to acknowledge to herself that part of Bea's appeal in the beginning was making her feel wanted again after Melody's devastating rejection. She'd reveled in the attention, but her feelings changed dramatically the moment she learned about Wendy. It forced her to acknowledge that their new relationship wasn't only about Bea helping her move past Melody. Whether it was conscious or not on Bea's part, Allyn was serving a similar purpose—giving Bea a chance for happiness again after years of grief over the accident.

Allyn still thought about Melody more than she wanted, and though she rarely made comparisons aloud to Bea, she made them to herself. Bea's scorecard looked pretty good. She told Candace, "I'm not sure it even matters what brought us together. It feels real to me. I'm happy again. That's worth everything."

* * *

Grady Halloran, a fifty-three-year-old victim of downsizing from a bank merger, sat across from Bea's desk, warily allowing Dexter to sniff his outstretched hand. With his graying hair and glasses, and a soft deep voice, he gave off a gentle vibe. "I haven't been around dogs much. Both of my daughters were allergic."

"He comes to work with me every day. Would that be a problem?"

"No, he seems pretty laid back."

More laid back than usual, Bea thought. Dexter wasn't accustomed to sharing her with anyone, and though he clearly liked Allyn, he seemed to miss getting all of Bea's attention. She'd have to take back all those accolades she'd given dogs for not holding a grudge.

Since she had little experience in conducting interviews and a poor track record on hiring decisions, she'd gotten help from Allyn to prepare a list of questions. Grady had already made a good impression by showing up on time for his interview and dressing neatly. Older workers understood how much these small details mattered. She hadn't expected the swarm of applications from mature workers for an entry-level retail job, but mergers and takeovers had left a lot of older workers in the lurch. She found his application compelling, particularly his years of customer service experience. "What is it about this job that interests you?"

"Many things. It's full-time so it'll keep me out of trouble. My wife isn't used to having me under her feet, so if you don't hire me, maybe you can hire her instead."

She smiled and scribbled a note about his sense of humor.

"I like working with the public. I don't know much about the postal business, but it seems like it would be easy to learn. Let's see…what else? I live over on Seventeenth Avenue, so it's convenient to get here. You won't have to worry about me not showing up if it snows."

"It's not a lot of money for somebody with your salary history." But it was a damn good wage for entry-level retail, she thought, designed to attract an employee she could trust to work independently.

"I don't expect a banker's salary. To be honest, I got a nice buyout when they bounced me out, so money's not a major concern. I just want to be productive…something to keep me in the habit of working till I'm ready to retire for good."

Grady was the third person she'd talked to about the job, and by far the most appealing. Only one hurdle left, but it was a biggie. "Grady, you've worked a long time. I'm sure you know how important it is for everyone to feel comfortable with their co-workers, and with the atmosphere of their workplace. We're a gay-friendly shop because I happen to be gay and so is my assistant manager, the woman out there at the counter. If that sort of thing bothers you, this might not be the best place for you."

He huffed and waved off her concerns. "I saw that equal rights sticker on your door when I came in. It's the same one my nephew has on his bumper, and I love him to death."

He probably couldn't have answered any of her questions better, and she smiled and extended her hand. "The hours are nine to six with a lunch hour, Thursdays off. How soon can you start?"

"You're not going to check my references?"

"You worked in the same place for twenty-six years. That's reference enough for me."

"Tomorrow then." Grady grinned, tentatively brushing the top of Dexter's head as he stood. "Is it okay with you if I bring him a treat?"

"If it's okay with you to have a new best friend."

Grady could turn out to be her best hire ever. Next to Kit, that is.

She followed him out of the office and introduced them to one another, and while they were chatting, she retreated to call Allyn. "Thanks to all your help, I just hired somebody I might actually trust to run the place with Kit if I take a vacation. Where would you like to go?"

"San Francisco. How soon can we leave?"

"I have to train him first, then install a webcam so I can watch the store from anywhere in the world."

Allyn huffed. "Doesn't sound like much of a vacation."

"Hey, it's progress. How's your day going?"

"I had lunch with Candace. That was…interesting. It's never an ordinary discussion when you're talking to a therapist."

"Did she psychoanalyze you?"

"Not exactly, but she has a unique perspective on practically everything. I'll tell you about it tonight. I'll be waiting at your house when you get home."

Bea made a silly kissing noise before hanging up, and then sat on the floor and tugged Dexter's head into her lap. On tap this weekend was a tricky conversation about how depressed he'd become since they'd started spending so much time together, after which Bea would propose they try to plan more things where they could take him along. It would probably sound selfish, but his well-being was important to her.

Good thing she'd never had children.

* * *

Allyn had cooled her heels while Bea showered and changed, but the result was definitely worth the wait. Who would have guessed Bea Lawson had a little black dress tucked away for special occasions? It was long-sleeved with a straight neckline that dipped in a V down her back, and it tapered from her waist to just above her knees.

"I've worn it to both weddings and funerals. And now I can add 'out with a sexy date' to my list. That's what I call versatile."

"Is it really your only dress?"

"Yes, but please don't let them bury me in it. I'm saving my Griffey Junior Mariners jersey for that."

Once they reached Bastille, Bea guided her onto the bench seat behind the table for two. Allyn was glad she'd made a quick run to Nordstrom for her dress, a turquoise wrap that flared from her waist. Heads had turned as they walked through Bastille, making her feel both pretty and proud.

"Thank you for coming out with me," Bea said seriously, clutching her hand across the table. "Not just tonight. After what you've been through this last year, I know how hard it must have been for you to take a chance on me—on anybody for that matter—but I'm really glad you did. You have no idea what a difference being with you has made for me. I wake up happy every day, and there were lots of days I thought I'd never be happy again."

"Same here." Allyn loved that Bea never let go of her hand, not even as the waiter took their order. The whole evening so far could have been a script for a romance movie. Pretty clothes, candlelight dinner, tender caresses. "Is there a special reason for Bastille tonight? Not that you need one. You can bring me to this place and tell me how happy you are anytime you like."

"It's always special when I'm with you. I mean that. But I realized the other day that nearly every time we go out, it's for brats, burgers or beer. I thought it was time I showed you that I know how to treat a beautiful lady."

"You certainly do." In eleven years together, she could count on one hand the number of times Melody had taken her out like this when it wasn't a birthday or anniversary. Melody's main excuse was being tired from a whole day at work—as though Allyn's ten-hour workdays were nothing—and she took for granted the fact that a gourmet dinner magically appeared on her table every night. "I like this. I don't need it every day, or even every week, but I like it."

The waiter returned with a bottle of red wine and Bea performed the tasting ritual with impressive aplomb.

"Wendy and I got a bad bottle once. It tasted like rancid vinegar. They took it back, of course, but it put us off wine for a while."

Allyn envied Bea for how she spoke so openly about her life with Wendy. It wasn't only the warmth and respect she obviously felt for her former wife, but also the ease with which she dropped references from their past into ordinary conversations. Allyn couldn't talk about Melody that way because every single memory came through a prism of bitterness.

"Something wrong?" Bea asked.

"No, no. I was thinking about how nice it is that you're able to talk about things you did with Wendy. I don't know if I'll ever get there with Melody."

"Does it bother you when I do that? I can try not to if you want. I can see how it would be annoying."

"It's not annoying. It's just…" She sighed and took a sip of wine so she could formulate her words before saying something that might sound insensitive. "I can't help but make comparisons. You and Wendy versus Melody and me. I wish I could talk about our good times the way you talk about yours, but I can't because I know how the story ends. My pleasant memories are tainted."

There was another comparison that bothered her even more, how she stacked up against Wendy in Bea's eyes. How did anyone stack up against a quadriplegic saint who'd been to medical school?

"Our past is part of us, Allyn. What Melody did was awful, but it didn't wipe out your whole life with her. It took me three years to talk about Wendy without crying. You'll get there too one of these days."

"Candace said something today...in fact, she's brought it up more than once. I get the feeling she's trying to tell me something without actually saying it. She swore she wasn't talking about us, but you know what they say about when the shoe fits."

The waiter interrupted with their meal, braised short ribs for Allyn and Dungeness crab cakes for Bea, served on white square plates with brightly colored sauces drizzled around the edges.

Allyn went on, "She was talking about how some people who've been hurt by somebody latch onto a new person with a death grip just because it feels so good to make the pain stop. She says practically anything feels better after you've been through a breakup where the other person made you feel worthless, but it means your new feelings might not be real. They're just a Band-Aid till you get over the other. She didn't come right out and say that about you and me, but I read between the lines."

"Let's hope she doesn't charge her clients a lot of money to warn them about being on the rebound. That's Romance 101. Everybody knows it."

Not everyone. Allyn had never been on the rebound before.

"Nothing against Candace, but I'll take that with a big grain of salt," Bea continued. "Don't get me wrong. She's nice and I'm sure she knows what she's talking about, but she's still a therapist. Her business is dealing with people's problems. I bet she tries to figure out the underlying issues in everyone she meets. When you're always analyzing stuff, it's easy to forget that sometimes a cigar is just a cigar."

"What do cigars have to do with anything?"

"I don't know. It's a Freud thing. It means not everything is a symbol of something else. I like being with you because of you, not because deep down I miss Wendy and I'm using you to plug the gap. I hope you feel the same way about me, but I can see how Melody muddies the waters. If Candace is right, though, no one could ever have another real relationship. I'm not willing to accept that."

Allyn didn't need to understand the psychology to know what she wanted, and that included all the wonderful moments she'd shared with Bea. It wasn't only their lovemaking or being romanced at a nice restaurant. It was Bea holding her hand or texting her in the middle of the day just to say hi. She'd missed having someone care about her, but it mattered that it was someone as sweet as Bea. "It's true you make me feel good. I can't help comparing that to how miserable I was before."

"You know what I say to that? Hallelujah! We can't help where we are or what we've been through, but it makes zero sense to question how we feel just because some people think the timing's off. If you're worried about things moving too fast, all you have to do is say so. We can slow it down. One night a week, two…whatever. I'm not going to get all frantic about it. 'Oh, Allyn might break up with me if I don't *latch on* to her.' You're what, thirty-three years old? And I'll be thirty-six two weeks from tomorrow." She cupped her hand around her mouth and whispered loudly, "Which just happens to be the same day as the Mariners' last home game. Hint, hint."

Allyn laughed. "I get the message."

Bea set her fork down, leaving half her dinner untouched. "The point is, we have lots of time to work this out. Days, months, years…whatever our timeline turns out to be. In the meantime, there's nothing wrong with living for today. You make me happy today. I hope I do the same for you."

"You do." It was a simple philosophy, and Allyn appreciated that Bea seemed to be trying to downplay her worries about the authenticity of their feelings for one another. She was troubled however by her casual regard for their future, as though it would work out or it wouldn't, and the only factor was time. Relationships didn't happen on their own. They took effort.

* * *

As soon as Grady got up to speed, Bea planned to start taking Saturdays off once in a while so she wouldn't have to leave Allyn in bed. It was all she could do not to wake her to make love before heading out.

Keeping her voice low, she scratched Dexter behind the ears. "What's wrong with you, Dexxie?" He'd barely touched his breakfast, the third day in a row. It seemed he was stuck in a pouting mood no matter how hard she tried to show him extra attention. His last appointment with the veterinarian was only five months ago, but clearly he needed to go again.

As she finished her coffee, she reread the note she'd been working on for the last hour. In their dinner conversation the night before, she'd meant to convey that she didn't share Candace's doubts about their future, but as she lay awake after lovemaking, she played her own words over in her head until it struck her that she'd left something very important unsaid.

Good morning, sweetheart. I woke up early and watched you sleep. You're so beautiful. I hated to leave you.

I couldn't stop thinking about our talk last night because there's something important I forgot to say. It's true my life is better now that you're in it. I know I said we should live for today and enjoy what we have, but it doesn't mean I don't care about tomorrow. I hope what we have keeps growing, and we'll be so happy we'll never want it to end. We both know that won't happen by itself, so I'm giving you my promise I'll work for it. I'm crazy about you.

Hallmark will never hire me because I'm terrible with words. I just wanted you to know you don't have to worry about me comparing my other life to the one I have now. It's all about you. Only you.
XOXOX Bea

CHAPTER SIXTEEN

Allyn turned up the volume on her earpiece as the gardeners blew grass from the sidewalk below her window. Her client on the other end of the call seemed oblivious to the racket.

"You don't have to sell me on this, Roy. It's a great position, exactly what Josh is looking for. He liked everyone he met and he liked Dallas. He just can't accept it at that salary. His wife's a teacher, and she'll have to take a seven thousand-dollar pay cut to move to Texas."

Roy's business was tech security, so she'd dealt with him many times before. He was the company's vice president and had the authority to negotiate salaries. After an extended silence, he groaned, a sign he was either ready to cave to Josh's demands or give up on him altogether.

"Look, Roy. We've been doing this a long time. You know I'm not just trying to jack you up here. I don't get paid at all if I don't place him, so I want this deal done too. Josh is perfect for this job. You know it as well as I do. I'm willing to make your case for you, but if you really want him, you've got to give me something."

She patiently tapped her pen against her palm until he blurted out a new number—his final offer. After a quick call to Josh, she called Roy back to convey his acceptance. Two more satisfied clients. If she could get the paperwork signed by tomorrow, it would be her best quarter ever for commissions.

With so many elements of her life coming together at once, she felt like celebrating. A quick check of her pantry yielded a bottle of pinot noir, a nice complement to chicken parmesan, which needed to go in the oven in half an hour.

She smiled and picked up the card on her counter, reading it again for what had to be the hundredth time. Once she memorized it, it would go in a special box she'd started for mementos with Bea.

After a long talk on Sunday about letting their relationship evolve on its own time, they'd agreed to spend weekends at Bea's house so they could be with Dexter, and to see each other during the week only on Wednesday. That meant dinner together tonight, but starting next week Wednesdays were volleyball night, to be followed by going with the gang to JoJo's. "Unlimited calls and texts," Bea had said in a chirpy ad voice. It was a good plan, one that gave them enough time together without suffocating each other, and it meshed with their work schedules.

Back at her desk, she prepared her invoice for Roy, discounting it five percent to show her appreciation for his willingness to negotiate with Josh. He would remember that gesture the next time he had a position to fill.

Within five seconds of sending it off, a new email landed in her inbox. It was from an unfamiliar Gmail address but she recognized the handle as one Melody had used for her old Flickr account.

Hey stranger. Heard you were playing softball. Kicking ass and taking names. Jillian sent some pics—you look great! Down to 97 today in Tucson. The locals call that a cold snap. Hope you're doing well. Drop me a note whenever. M.

With her hands shaking, Allyn read it over and over, studying each line. She'd found a Yahoo account under the same name in the CC line of an email from their realtor and assumed

Melody had created it to chat with Naomi. It occurred to her that Naomi might not know about this one.

What did Melody want from her? Her casual tone was peculiar considering the last note she'd sent was a bitter tirade about their divorce settlement that ended just short of *Fuck off*. Surely she didn't expect Allyn to forget that hurtful attack. Something had changed that made Melody want to be friends again, and the only thing Allyn could think of was her learning about Bea. Jillian must have told her about them holding hands and sharing a kiss at the ballpark, and now Melody felt "safe" to be friends, "safe" from worrying that Allyn would beg her to come back, "safe" from having to listen to stories of how she had ruined Allyn's life.

Then again, Melody wasn't to be trusted. She probably needed something and this was her way of greasing the skids before she asked. Was there an unsigned paper that fell through the cracks, an overlooked account they hadn't divided, an old password to access a website?

Allyn was disgusted by her own excitement, even though it was fleeting and offset by anger and suspicion. No matter what had motivated Melody to reach out, Allyn had sole control over how she responded.

Her impulse was to answer that she didn't give a shit how hot it got in Tucson, and to leave her the fuck alone. That particular note would never get written without her polishing off two glasses of the pinot noir that sat on her counter. She disliked confrontation as much as the next person, even with someone who deserved it.

The better strategy might be to ignore the note altogether, dishing out to Melody the same frustration and angst she'd felt when her calls and emails had gone unanswered. It could never be as cold or cruel as what she'd experienced, but it would spare her getting sucked into a power game where Melody was the one doling out morsels of kindness and civility as long as it suited her.

The riskiest response of all was the one she contemplated most seriously—letting go of her resentment and answering in the spirit of friendship. That was her deeper truth. No matter how much Melody had hurt her, she'd never stopped believing in the basic decency of a woman she'd loved enough to marry. That she could write a friendly note like this one was proof she was a good person, and that Allyn hadn't been such an awful judge of character after all. Now Melody was handing her the chance to demonstrate that she too was caring and compassionate, someone who could forgive and wish the best for a person she once had loved.

Hi to you too. Softball was fun but the season's over. Used muscles I forgot I had. Cool and wet here—

Vapid nonsense. She deleted the words and flickered her fingers above the keys.

Hope it cools off in AZ for fall. Take care.

Cordial enough but impersonal. A terse response such as that would probably end their exchange.

Sounds miserable. Any plans to escape the heat? Take care.

She doctored the note some more, re-adding the bit about the muscles she used playing softball. It was friendly without being overly familiar, and by asking a question, she admittedly was inviting more dialogue.

Her cell phone chimed to announce a text from Bea: *Leaving shop now.*

Time had gotten away from her. Bea was due in a matter of minutes and she hadn't even started dinner, which would take at least an hour from start to finish. Chicken parmesan would have to wait for another night. Stir-fry was quicker. She could toss in the vegetables she'd planned to steam and serve it over rice.

What would Bea think of her note from Melody? A purely rhetorical question, since she had no intention of telling her about it, at least not right away. She wouldn't want to keep it secret if she and Melody mended their friendship enough to trade emails every now and then, but for now, she wanted the freedom to decide for herself what course to take without anyone questioning her judgment.

She saved the note to her draft folder so she could think about it later. Waiting a day or two would downplay her eagerness and let Melody know she had more important things to do than sit on the edge of her seat and wait for a reply.

* * *

Exuberant. That's what Bea thought of the energy with which Allyn greeted her, and she was surprised by a kiss that was as passionate as any they'd shared.

"Wow, someone had a good day."

"I sure did. I placed a client today…it was a perfect match and they both wanted it, but we had to work out the compensation. It's a huge commission, and that's why"—she handed Bea a bottle of wine and corkscrew—"we have to celebrate."

"I'll celebrate anything that makes you kiss me like that."

Throughout dinner, Allyn was curiously animated, laughing louder than usual and voicing uncharacteristic excitement over every detail Bea shared about Grady's first few days at the shop. In their early days of dating, she would have chalked it up to nervousness, but there was no obvious reason for this level of giddiness.

"Anything else interesting happen today?" she asked.

"No, what makes you ask?"

"Nothing, really. I'm just not used to seeing you so excited about your work. Too bad Dexter couldn't be here with us. He could use a little excitement. He's been down in the dumps lately. We have an appointment at the vet tomorrow. I half expect him to say Dexter's mad at me for not getting enough attention."

"Maybe you should go home and be with him," Allyn said sharply.

Bea was shocked by her sudden change in demeanor. "I didn't mean—"

"I just closed one of my biggest deals ever. If I can't be excited about that without getting the third degree, maybe you ought to just go home to your dog." She stood abruptly and began clearing the table.

Allyn's reaction was downright bizarre.

"I wasn't giving you the third degree," Bea said calmly. She'd done nothing a reasonable person could construe as offensive or uncaring. On the contrary, she'd been thrilled at Allyn's news and happy to share in her celebration. "Did I do something wrong?"

"No." Allyn ferried the dishes into the kitchen and dropped them in the sink so carelessly it was a miracle they didn't break. "I'm probably just anxious about it because the papers haven't been signed yet. One of them could still back out and I'd be screwed out of a commission."

"That would make anyone anxious." Though it shouldn't cause her to fly off the handle. Something else was bothering her, but Bea didn't want to press the issue for fear of making it worse. Allyn would come around in her own time. "You're probably right. I should go. That'll give you a chance to relax… soak in the tub, read a book."

"You don't have to go, Bea. I shouldn't have reacted that way."

"No, it's okay. I really am worried about Dex. I need to make sure he knows he's my guy. We can get together again on…Friday?"

"Friday. Definitely. Another movie?"

"Pick whichever one you want." She stretched across the counter to give Allyn a kiss—more like a friendly peck on the lips—and stopped at the door to blow another kiss across the room. "I'm proud of you for closing that deal."

As Bea drove home, she replayed in her head as many bits of their conversation as she could recall. Nothing jumped out that might have set Allyn off. Sometimes people's actions came down to idiosyncrasies that couldn't be explained, little quirks that stirred unpleasant memories or just plain old rubbed them the wrong way.

As she pulled into her driveway, the living room curtains parted and her sweet baby boy appeared. No matter how bad her day had gone, she could always count on Dexter to make it better.

* * *

Dr. Kyle Schaefer, bespectacled and dressed in blue scrubs with red high-top sneakers, squatted to coax a cowering Dexter from underneath the stainless steel exam table. "What's the matter, fella? You aren't afraid of me today, are you?"

"Let me see if I can get him out," Bea offered. She was surprised by Dexter's shrinking demeanor since he usually greeted everyone with gusto, even those who sometimes poked him with needles. A gentle tug on his collar brought him out, and it took all her strength to hoist him onto the table.

Though he lowered himself with his legs stretched out front, he appeared poised to bolt at any second.

"Tell me what's been going on," Kyle said.

"He's not eating very well, but he's drinking a lot. You saw his record. He's down six pounds since May. And lately he doesn't seem to have any energy."

"Anything changed? New food? Pest control service? New plants in the house?"

"No, same everything. I was worried it might be psychological. I started seeing someone recently so I'm not home every night like I used to be. But it's not like I'm gone a whole lot. I take him with me whenever I can, and both of us give him a lot of attention."

Kyle checked his ears and teeth, and paid special attention to his eyes. Next he listened to his heart and lungs. "Are you jealous, buddy?"

Dexter responded with a thump of his tail, and he rolled onto his back when Kyle began to palpitate his tummy.

"What do you think's going on, Kyle?"

"I don't think it's attitude, but I won't totally rule it out. His glands are a little swollen." He took her hand and tucked it under Dexter's jaw. "Feel that? That's probably what's interfering with his eating."

There was definitely a bump, but rubbing it didn't seem to bother him. "That isn't a tumor, is it?"

"I doubt it. It could be an infection." His frown was unmistakable as he ran his hand along Dexter's flank.

"Is something else wrong?"

"Hard to say without some tests. I'd like to draw some blood and send it off." He touched a button to summon a technician. "It's possible he's gotten into something—bad water, rotten food—and now he's got a bacterial infection. There's no evidence of fleas or ticks. That's the usual culprit, but it could also be an allergy of some sort."

"Ha! You mean like my new girlfriend. Wouldn't that be ironic?"

"It's happened."

"What sort of treatment would we be looking at if it's an infection?"

"A course of antibiotics should do it. If it's an allergy, we can treat it with prednisone. The main thing we want to rule out is lymphoma."

"Lymphoma? Isn't that…cancer?" Her pulse quickened with fear and she instinctively cradled Dexter's head as though to cover his ears.

The technician appeared and escorted Dexter into the back.

Kyle washed his hands and leaned against the sink with his arms folded. "It's not uncommon for his breed, but we don't see it much in young dogs like Dexter."

"And even if it is, you can treat it, right? We caught it early."

"Let's cross that bridge if we get there. We'll know in a day or two."

A day or two was forever to wait for news like that.

CHAPTER SEVENTEEN

"You should have called me yesterday, Bea." Allyn tossed her purse on the chair and sat beside Dexter on the couch, which apparently wasn't off limits to him anymore.

"I didn't want to worry you till I knew something for sure, but they didn't get the blood work back today. And Kyle said the lab's closed on Saturdays so it'll be Monday before I hear anything."

"You must be going crazy."

"Pretty much." Bea sat at the other end of the couch, still wearing her khaki pants and Pak & Ship shirt. By her drawn face, she was very worried. "You won't care if we skip the movie tonight, will you? I really don't feel much like going out."

"I don't care at all. We'll call for some burgers at JoJo's and I'll run get them. Tonight's all about Dexter."

Bea stretched out a hand and tugged Allyn toward her, and they kissed with Dexter in the middle. "You're sweet. I appreciate it."

Allyn didn't feel sweet at all. What she felt was guilty, not only for the shabby way she'd treated Bea two nights before, but for wallowing in her own selfish game with Melody while Bea was frantic over Dexter. Even worse, she'd returned Bea's honesty with secrecy, which she was determined to fix.

She returned from JoJo's to find Bea still on the couch with Dexter's head in her lap.

"He might be sick, but he sure looks happy."

"Doesn't he though? I guess my plan to keep him off the furniture is pretty well shot."

Allyn spread their bounty on the coffee table and pulled up an armchair. "I got an extra hamburger patty in case he wants it."

"He's going to be so spoiled, but that's all right." Bea broke off a few small pieces of meat and fed him. "I don't want to give him too much. He's been getting sick right after he eats."

"It's awful how they left you hanging all weekend. How they left *us* hanging."

"I'm sorry," Bea said solemnly. "You don't have to stay the whole time. I'm not going to be very good company."

"Of course I have to stay." It horrified her to realize Bea thought she could leave at a time like this. "You want me to, don't you?"

"Yes, I…I don't know why I said that. I don't want you to leave."

"I know why. Because I was a brat the other night when you said that about Dexter not getting enough attention. I wouldn't blame you if you didn't want me here. I was totally out of line."

"I was being a jerk too. It was a special night for you and I should have done more to recognize that. We're all guilty of being self-centered sometimes."

Allyn couldn't let her take any of the blame, not when she knew the real reason for her gruff behavior. She wrapped her dinner in paper and pushed it away, leaning on the edge of her chair to rest a hand on Bea's leg. "Look at me. It was not your fault. I had something else on my mind and I didn't tell you about it because I was trying to sort it out by myself. I was afraid if I told you, you'd try to tell me what to do."

Bea pushed her food away also, and with a frown that bordered on irritation, asked, "What in the world are you talking about?"

With a weighty sigh, she slumped back in her chair and rubbed her face with both hands. "Right before you got to my house, I got an email from Melody. It wasn't anything…just a note about how she'd heard I was playing softball and how hot it was in Tucson. She wanted me to keep in touch."

"Humph! I hope you told her to go piss up a rope."

Allyn pinched the bridge of her nose. "I didn't tell her anything. I haven't answered it yet."

"Yet? You're actually thinking about responding to the person who shit all over you and didn't care how much it hurt?"

"This is why I didn't tell you, Bea. I know all these things you're saying, but part of me wishes we could be friends or something. At least not enemies. I don't like hating her. I don't like *me* when all I feel is anger and hostility. It takes so much energy. I knew if I told you, I'd be opening the door for you to make all those arguments, and I'd feel bad if I didn't listen. I didn't want to keep secrets…I just wanted to be in control of what to do."

It was several long seconds before Bea finally spoke, her words also punctuated with a deep sigh. "I get where you're coming from. I'm just angry at her because she's coming back around to mess with you. After the way she hurt you, I was hoping she'd crawl under a rock and stay there."

"Part of me wanted that too, but her note made it seem like there was a window for something more civil. It's stressful to always worry about running into her friends. In a way, I'm dreading volleyball because Jillian will probably be there. Who knows how many others? I don't want to be some shrinking violet every time I run into those people."

"You shouldn't be. You didn't do anything wrong. Anyone who thinks otherwise has a screw or two loose, and you shouldn't care what they think."

Though Bea pretended for a moment to give all her attention to Dexter, Allyn knew the discussion wasn't over. "I haven't answered her yet. If you'd rather I didn't—"

"It has to be your decision. I can't tell you on one hand to go out and make friends with people like Candace so you can be independent, and then turn around and try to bully you into doing something because it's what I want." She reached over to grasp Allyn's hand and gave her a scolding look. "But I don't like you keeping secrets from me, especially not something like that. I don't need to know every little thing you do, but I want you to feel like you can trust me when it really matters. I'll try harder not to always put my two cents in, and I'll take your side no matter what you feel you have to do."

Allyn had been right to worry about Bea's reaction, but wrong not to realize the best solution was to talk out their differences. Honesty mattered a lot to Bea. After the way Melody had treated her, it should have mattered more to Allyn too. And now that she had Bea's unconditional support, she truly was free to answer Melody any way she wanted.

Unfortunately, she was no closer to knowing what that was.

* * *

Dressed for bed in panties and a tank top, Bea knelt next to Dexter's beanbag in the corner of the room to settle him down for the night with a tummy rub. She was encouraged that he'd shown some spark when she turned him out to the backyard. His romp didn't last long, but she was delighted to see him chase his ball again. She hoped on Monday Kyle would prescribe something to knock out what was a simple infection and get him back to his old self.

It wasn't only Dexter she had to worry about. Now she also had Melody back in the picture, her biggest fear since she first realized she had feelings for Allyn.

Allyn joined her from the bathroom wearing a long-sleeved satin nightshirt. After their talk about Melody, she'd pushed her way onto the couch and taken over the TV remote control.

Three hours of giggling and cuddling through a *Golden Girls* marathon was the perfect antidote to their doldrums.

Bea tumbled into bed beside her. "That was a great idea you had to chill out and watch something on TV that didn't require emotional investment."

"And what about now?" Allyn asked as she tracked a finger around the neckline of her tank top. "Do you have any emotions you might be interested in investing with me?"

"I do." She guided Allyn's hand beneath the elastic of her panties and closed her eyes. "Let's start with trust."

Allyn slid her body on top and they kissed, a deep, slow kiss that grew more heated until they were trading breaths. All the while her hand continued its languid strokes across the triangle of hair, gradually pushing Bea's panties to her knees until she rid herself of them.

Cool air enveloped her as Allyn pulled away to strip off her nightshirt before peeling the tank top over Bea's head and tossing it toward the foot of the bed. Then she pulled up the blanket and drew her long smooth body alongside.

"You're mine tonight, Bea." She snaked one arm underneath and with the other began a firm massage. Thigh, hip, side, breast and back again while nibbling not so gently on an earlobe.

Each time Allyn's hand wandered across her hip, Bea surged upward hoping it would find her. By the time it did, she was dripping with want, and Allyn buried two fingers inside her, then three. "Oh, yes," she hissed.

Bea opened her eyes to find Allyn deep in concentration, her brow furrowed and twitching in tempo with the hand that moved in and out. She could picture her folds pinching together with each plunge, relentlessly teasing her climax. She wanted to come.

The sliver of space between them allowed her to slip her hand to where it joined Allyn's. Just the pressure of her fingertip was enough as Allyn supplied the motion with her steady thrusts.

"Oh, that's it...you're making me come."

Her gasp was covered by Allyn's mouth, and her chest nearly crushed with a mighty hug. As she throbbed around the fingers inside her, she wrapped a leg over Allyn's hip and tightened their clutch. In that moment, they were sharing so much more than their physical selves, and she felt a desperate urge to cling to Allyn for the strength she'd need to get through the next few days. That's all she could ask for now.

* * *

A car door closed and the engine started. Daylight crept through the blinds…eight fifteen by the digital clock. Allyn was alone in Bea's bed. It was luxury to sleep in on Saturday, especially after starting her Friday at five thirty and ending it well past midnight. She would have enjoyed an even longer slumber had she been in her own apartment.

She wasn't uncomfortable alone at Bea's house by any means. She had the run of the place, and even though it wasn't a rambling ranch or a towering Victorian, it had a cozy back porch with a glider where she could enjoy her morning coffee and catch up with the world on her tablet computer.

After a quick shower, she dumped the contents of her overnight bag onto the bed in the second bedroom. Though technically it was still summer, the weather was turning more toward fall, her favorite season, and she had several errands to run. She liked herself in tight jeans and knew Bea would approve. Her first stop should be at the Pak & Ship to show off a little.

The coffeemaker was set to start with the touch of a button, and when she opened the cabinet for a mug, she was greeted by another envelope containing a handwritten card:

Trust.
Warmth.
Passion.
Pleasure.
Euphoria.
Desperation.
Security.
Trust.
XOXOX Bea

She carried it outside to the porch and read it again, remembering their lovemaking from the night before and imagining Bea as she gave herself over to these emotions. Of all these, it was desperation that was the most vivid. She'd felt it herself, holding Bea tightly as she came down from her climax, not wanting to let her fall.

The strongest though, the one that permeated everything between them, was trust. Bea wanted Allyn to trust her. Even more, to know she *was* trusted.

She opened her tablet, scrolled to Melody's email—and deleted it.

CHAPTER EIGHTEEN

"I'm so sorry, Bea. I'm afraid we're dealing with the worst-case scenario," Kyle said.

Her hands were shaking so hard she nearly dropped the phone. With tears flooding her eyes, she sank to the floor to hold her poor, sweet Dexter. "So what do we do?"

"The good news is that most dogs respond well to chemotherapy. We can probably get this into remission for a few months and make him feel pretty good."

She knew the rest from all the information she'd downloaded last week. After six or nine months of remission, the cancer would return. The long-term prognosis was always grim.

"There's another option, especially if you have financial concerns. It's perfectly all right to skip the chemo and go with palliative care. Make him comfortable and let nature happen. Sometimes that's the right choice."

"No! He's just three years old. He deserves a lot longer."

"Dexter's age could definitely work in his favor with the chemo. We should get him in here and set him up with a plan as soon as possible. You got time this afternoon?"

She made the appointment for two, but couldn't compose herself enough to pick up the phone again and talk to anyone else, not even Allyn. It was all she could do to hold it together alongside Grady while they tended to a steady stream of customers that kept them busy until Kit arrived at eleven.

"What's wrong, Bea?"

She explained Kyle's call and her plans to start Dexter on a sixteen-week regimen of chemotherapy. "Think you guys can handle the shop for a while? I'm going to sit back here with my boy. Call me if you get busy."

After nearly losing it while sharing the news with Kit, Bea dreaded the call to Allyn. Dexter seemed to sense her anguish, and he growled playfully before laying his head in her lap.

"It's not fair, Dexxie." If his disease progressed according to averages, he had about a year, but much of that could be normal. With medication, he'd recover his appetite and energy, even tear through the house again when she walked in.

If she ever left him home alone again, that is.

* * *

Allyn's heart broke at the sight of Bea's swollen face and red-rimmed eyes. She too wanted to cry, but it wouldn't do for both of them to come unglued. "You should have called me earlier, sweetheart. I'd have gone with you to the vet's office."

"I know. It was just one of those things I had to do by myself." Bea sat on the top step of the back porch watching Dexter sniff the bushes in the backyard. "It was kind of like what you said the other night about getting the note from Melody. I knew I'd have a decision to make when I got there, and I didn't want to listen to anybody else telling me what to do."

"What kind of decision?"

"Some people skip the treatment because all it does is postpone the inevitable. It's going to come back eventually and Dexter's last couple of months will probably be just as hard on him as if I let him go now."

Dexter climbed the steps into Bea's arms and licked her face.

"Judging from how he's acting right now, I don't think either one of you is ready for that."

"I know I'm not. I just want to do the right thing by him. Kyle says chemo for dogs isn't as bad as it is for humans. There aren't as many side effects and he should start feeling better right away."

"I don't see that as a tough decision at all. You get a few more months with him, maybe a year. That's a win for all of us." It saddened her to think Bea had chosen to go alone to the vet. "I would have supported you no matter what you decided. I hope you know that."

"I do...but I wouldn't have blamed you for having doubts, since I have a well-deserved reputation for giving up when things get tough."

"That's bullshit! Anyone who says that about you is an asshole. That includes you, so knock it off."

Bea finally cracked a smile, though a sheepish one. "Yes, ma'am."

Allyn sat next to her on the top step. "Speaking of assholes...I deleted Melody's note without answering it."

"You didn't have to do that for me."

"I did it for me. Thanks to you, I've finally gotten most of that negative energy out of my life. I don't need to invite it back in. We've got Dexter to focus on now."

"You're so sweet." Bea leaned over for a kiss, and laughed as Dexter inserted himself between them. "It's my weekend to go to Vancouver. I guess I'll have to break the news to Wendy. It'll be hard on her too. She loves him."

"I...can go with you...if you want," Allyn offered hesitantly. A meeting between her and Wendy was bound to happen eventually. "Ever since you said you wanted me to meet her one of these days, I've been worrying about how awkward it would be. Having this weekend be mostly about Dexter might make it easier on everybody."

"That's not a bad idea." Bea grew quiet as she scratched Dexter's chest and ears, and after nearly a minute sniffed loudly, a sign she was fighting back tears. "I may not be much of a girlfriend over the next few months. I'll try, but right now I have a feeling I'm going to be selfish. It's all about Dexter for me. If you want to go out and do stuff with Candace, it'll be okay."

"Don't go planning my calendar," Allyn said, wrapping her arm around Bea's shoulder. "I know who the top dog is, and I'm fine with that. As a matter of fact, he's my top dog too."

"You're unbelievable. What did I do to deserve you?"

"You were just being you, and the you I know isn't selfish at all."

"I'll try my best to make that true, Allyn. I promise one day I'll show you what you mean to me."

Allyn placed a kiss on her temple. Even if Bea gave all her attention to the ailing Dexter for now, she'd never think of it as selfish. Selfish had another meaning, one set by Melody. It only came to light when she realized how much she'd bent to accommodate her wants and needs. Melody had taken advantage. Bea would never do that.

"I'll wait for that day," she whispered to Bea. "But it's my time now to show you what you mean to me. Don't be afraid to tell me what you need."

"This could last for a year," Bea said. "Are you sure you can put up with me for that long?"

"If it lasts a year, it'll mean two things. You'll have Dexter that long, and you'll have me that long. That sounds like a good year in my book."

Bea tipped her head so it rested on Allyn's shoulder. "You know what I thought about last night? I tried to imagine us twelve years from now. If we get to twelve years, Melody will be a footnote. I'll be the one who was with you the longest, and maybe I'll get to show you what forever really means."

It was a sweet thought, but Allyn reminded herself that Bea's emotions were on overload.

"I'm not saying I want to run out tomorrow and get married or anything like that. When I think about all the relationships I've been in, there was a point where I'd stop and ask myself if it could turn out to be the real deal. There were only two times where the answer was yes, and you're one of them."

"Whew!" She drew a deep dizzying breath and fanned herself with her hand. When she opened her eyes, Bea had turned to face her, wearing the purest, most honest smile she'd ever seen.

"I love you, Allyn."

For several seconds she could only nod. Then she pulled Bea's face toward hers, and in the instant before their lips met, murmured, "I love you too."

* * *

Seattle Parks and Recreation had a longstanding prohibition against bringing dogs to ballparks, but nowhere in their rules did they mention community centers like the one in Ballard. If anything, they were dog-friendly, so the volleyball team anointed Dexter its official mascot. He sat courtside on a leash alternately held by Marta and Candace, and enjoyed attention from everyone on the team as they rotated in and out of play.

Bea could look at him without crying now. Allyn had helped her see past the heartbreak of his certain decline to focus on making him feel like the King of Ballard for as long as he could hold the crown.

A shrill whistle signaled the start of their match as the referee climbed the stand to take her seat above the net.

Team Pak & Ship, wearing the same green T-shirts they'd worn for softball, huddled together for some last words from Coach Kit, who once again enjoyed the game vicariously from the sidelines while complaining about her shoulder. "Forget bump-set-spike. We're not that good. Just send it back over the net and make them make mistakes. On three."

They piled their hands in the center and broke in unison on three, with Bea in the center on the back row and Allyn waiting to serve.

Bea studied the lineup on the other side of the net, which included Jillian on the back row. That meant she and Allyn would eventually square off across from one another at the net. "Sorry you were blindsided," she muttered to Allyn. "I had no idea we were playing Hawthorne Medical Supply until we got here."

"Doesn't matter," Allyn mumbled. "I just want to win."

Her motivation was on full display, and so too her better-than-average volleyball prowess, which she'd downplayed even more than her softball skills. The moment Bea realized Allyn was eager for the kill shot, she scrambled all over the court to make the perfect set. One point after another, Allyn used every inch of her frame to rise up and hammer the ball into the opposite court so forcefully that no one from the other team dared to go up for a block.

They won the first game 15-4, and huddled at the sideline during the break for Kit's instructions. "Something tells me we're going to have a very good season."

Allyn grinned sheepishly. "I forgot to mention my dorm was the campus champ for three years."

"I'm moving you and Bea to the front row to start. Let's keep it going. On three."

The second game was more competitive, with their opponents scoring eight points in a row while Allyn was rotated out on the sideline. Once she got back in and worked her way to the front row with Bea, they wrapped up the win.

Marta handed over Dexter's leash to Bea. "Guess you'll be skipping JoJo's."

"I called her this afternoon. She said it was fine to bring him as long as we stayed out on the patio."

Bea loosened her kneepads so they dropped to her ankles and slid a Seattle Storm hoodie over her head. As teams for the second game took the court and squeezed them out, she looked around for Allyn and was surprised to see her talking to Jillian. On the off-chance she'd been cornered against her will, Bea made her way over just in time to see Jillian hand her an envelope and walk away.

"Everything okay?" she asked.

"Hmm…that was weird. She just gave me a note from Melody."

Weird wasn't the word Bea would have chosen. Ballsy… obnoxious. "What does it say?"

"I have no idea," Allyn answered, shoving it into her small backpack.

"Aren't you going to read it?" She wanted it read right there so she would know what it said, but then realized how invasive and untrusting that sounded. "I'll take Dexter on out and meet you at the car."

Two or three tense minutes passed as she imagined Melody's self-serving pitch for friendship, no doubt an effort to win her absolution from her sins. Though Allyn had deleted her first message, it was obvious that had been difficult, and her resolve probably would wither under a persistent campaign.

"It's just her new phone number," Allyn said as she tossed her bag into the car. Her tone was flat—not even a hint of how she felt about it. "I guess that means she expects me to call."

"I hope you told Jillian you weren't interested."

"I didn't tell her anything. It's none of her business."

"An even better answer."

"What do you want to bet Naomi doesn't know about her new cell phone? That's how it started when she was with me."

Bea bit her lip to keep from saying more, remembering her promise not to always put in her two cents. She wanted Allyn to ignore Melody forever.

"Do you think I should call her and get this over with?"

"Hell, no." She finished strapping Dexter into his harness and started the car, feeling guilty for her outburst. "Let me have another crack at that. You should do whatever your head tells you to do. I don't trust her as far as I can throw her, but I understand how you might feel like you have unfinished business. It's got to be really tempting to try one more time to leave things in a better place."

The operative word being *leave*.

"I don't really trust her either, but it might not be such a bad thing to talk to her. If she's up to something I'll know it and I can tell her to fuck off."

"How come she hasn't called you?"

"She doesn't have my number. We used to have the same cell phone plan but I had to get my own because the old one was in her name. I don't list it on my website, or all those people I work with who are desperate for a job would be calling me all hours of the night." She put her hand on Bea's leg as they pulled out of the lot. "Don't worry about this, Bea. Whatever she's selling, I'm not buying it."

* * *

Allyn slogged into the kitchen and poked at the start button on her coffeemaker. Sandwiches and beer at JoJo's had gone on longer than usual the night before, with everyone reliving the glory of their surprisingly easy victory. According to Kit, the Pak & Ship girls got their share of victories but had never contended for a championship—until now. Bea was already looking ahead to displaying the trophy in her shop.

Fortunately for Allyn, she had nothing scheduled until a call with Roy in Dallas at eight thirty Pacific Time. Until then she'd do what she did every single morning—scour her list of three hundred plus company websites and message boards for news of job openings in the tech industry. To compete in this business, she also had to stay on top of promotions and retirements that might trigger the need for replacements, and business news about contracts and grants that might result in hiring. Even if she had no calls or résumés to sort, her methodical inventory could keep her busy all day.

She'd placed enough successful hires over the last ten years that she could count on most of her HR contacts to send her job announcements as they became available, and that typically meant finding a handful in her inbox every morning. Along with the usual spate of notices was a second message from Melody, one that came via the contact page on her employment services website.

This one began *Dear Allyn.* More direct than the previous *Hey stranger.*

I sent you a note last week, but I wasn't sure if you still used that email address, so I hope it's okay to contact you through your website. I've been thinking a lot about everything that happened last year. I really wish we could talk because I have so many things to tell you. Will you call me?

"Everything that happened?" Allyn said aloud. Leave it to Melody to call her deliberate betrayal something that merely "happened," as though she hadn't meticulously planned it down to the last detail.

And now she wanted to talk about it, which raised the question of why, and to what end. She wanted something. Even if it were only forgiveness, there had to be a burning reason for the urgent flurry of emails and the phone number she'd passed through Jillian. Perhaps Naomi's religious upbringing had them contemplating all the commandments they'd broken.

It didn't matter what Melody wanted, because Allyn knew what she wanted. She was finally feeling good about herself again—thanks to Bea—and she didn't need Melody back in her life to mess that up.

Melody, I received your note but I decided not to respond. It's best for me if we just let it go. I've gotten on with my life and I'm happy again.

She studied the last sentence, reveling proudly in its truth before deciding she didn't want to share anything with Melody about her new life. She struck it, finishing her note with *best for me if we go our separate ways*, and sent it without even a cursory sign-off.

CHAPTER NINETEEN

"Tell me again not to be nervous," Allyn said.

"No need." Bea had noticed an uptick in her fidgeting since they entered the outskirts of Vancouver. "Wendy doesn't bite, not even metaphorically."

"And she definitely knows I'm coming, right?"

"She not only knows, she's excited about it. But it may not totally seem that way because she's upset about Dexter."

"You told her already? I thought you wanted to do that in person."

"I did at first but I changed my mind, so we Skyped about it the other night. We always Skype on Thursday and she could tell there was something wrong. I didn't want us to walk in and have her be all happy and excited about meeting you and then hit her with the bad news. I know she's going to cry." Her voice cracked as she thought about it, but she took a deep breath and continued. "It's good you're going to be there because that'll make all of us feel better."

"Just don't let me do something stupid, like sit on her oxygen line."

As nervous as Allyn was, Bea had the feeling she wasn't being entirely facetious. "You'll be fine."

"Seriously, what's the protocol? I can't shake her hand or pat her on the arm because she won't feel it."

"No, but she can see you do it, so it has the same effect of making her feel good. I do that kind of stuff all the time. Probably the hardest thing for people to wrap their heads around is that Wendy is just like everyone else except for the obvious. She has friends, spends a lot of time on her computer, laughs at all the same crazy shit as the rest of us. It's only her physical challenges that set her apart, and she understands better than anyone how uncomfortable people can be about that. Just be honest about it."

"What does that even mean?"

"It means don't try to pretend you don't notice any of it because that'll come off as fake." If Allyn's growing restlessness was any indication, Bea was only making it worse. "Look, here's what to expect. She'll probably be in the sunroom in her chair. Most of her catheters and tubes are hidden except for the ventilator hose. She needs that to talk, so be sure you give her enough time to finish what she's saying. Whatever you do, don't try to finish her sentences. I learned that the hard way."

"Now you're scaring me."

"Relax and be yourself. You're adorable, and Wendy knows how I feel about you. You already have a head start. She's primed to like you."

As they pulled into the circular driveway, Bea was disappointed to see the Huang's Lexus SUV parked alongside the van they used to transport Wendy. Today would have been a good day for them to take a drive somewhere.

After walking Dexter out by the curb and wiping his feet, they rang the doorbell.

Krystal barely acknowledged Bea's introduction of Allyn, overcoming her usual fear to cautiously greet Dexter with a scratch of his head. Apparently she'd gotten the sad news.

"Is everything okay?" Bea asked, gesturing toward the family car. "I was hoping they'd be gone."

"They came home right after church and went upstairs." Krystal cupped a hand by her mouth and snickered. "I think they wanted a peek at your friend. Wendy's in the sunroom."

Dexter tugged at his leash as they ambled through to the back of the house.

"Look who it is, Dexxie," Bea said, dropping his leash so he could hurry closer. "Hi, sweetie."

With her hand on the small of Allyn's back, she watched with delight as Wendy showered him with more than her usual sweet-talking affection. Losing Dexter would hit all of them hard.

Wendy's normal attire was a comfortable tank top with a long-sleeved flannel shirt on top, but today she wore a pale yellow cashmere pullover with a collar that nearly covered her ventilator tube. Her long dark hair had been styled in buoyant curls, and she wore a hint of eye shadow.

It was only then Bea realized with amusement that Allyn too had taken extra care to look nice for today's visit, wearing slacks instead of jeans with an expensive-looking cable-knit sweater. The two women were preening for one another.

She made the introductions and listened as they made small talk. Over the course of a couple of minutes, Allyn visibly relaxed and seated herself in a high-backed wicker chair directly across from Wendy.

"There are things you need to know about Bea," Wendy rasped. "Her dirty tricks."

"Do tell. Wait, let me get a pen. I don't want to miss any."

"Oh, no," Bea said, holding her head for dramatic effect. "I can't believe I didn't see this coming."

"I'll email you all of them…she always hides the last piece of chocolate."

"Oh, that's mean," Allyn said, sneering in Bea's direction. "I already noticed her knack for leaving two sheets on the toilet paper roll so she won't have to change it. What else?"

The list grew as Wendy and Allyn bonded over her imperfections, and before long they were talking like the best of pals.

"…but I never expected to find myself playing softball or volleyball again. Bea can be very persuasive."

"Tell me about it," Wendy replied, smiling as she turned her head toward Bea. "Just don't ever let her…talk you into going rock climbing."

"What a horrible thing to say!" Bea made a show of raising Wendy's hand so she could see her smack it. "Just for that, I'm going to take my dog and go home."

"Take your dog and go outside."

Not very subtle. Wendy obviously wanted her to get lost so she and Allyn could talk alone. They seemed to be hitting it off, and Allyn showed no signs of alarm.

She took a tennis ball from her bag and started toward the back door. "You heard the lady, Dexxie. Time for us to put on a show."

Even though he didn't have his usual energy, she could build in some rest periods that would let them stay outside a while. What she wouldn't give to hear every word inside.

* * *

At Wendy's urging, Allyn dragged the wicker chair alongside the wheelchair so they could watch Dexter chase the ball. In only a few short minutes, Wendy's personable charm had dispelled her worries about making a good impression. Allyn's initial reaction to seeing her motionless in her elaborate chair was sorrow, but it very soon gave way to profound respect.

It was easy to see why Bea had been drawn to her. In the first place, she was pretty—head-turning pretty—with dark hair and eyes and delicate facial features. But Allyn suspected their connection had begun with Wendy's wicked sense of humor, which seemed a perfect match for Bea's. From the way they played off one another, it was an essential element of their relationship.

Wendy started, "They're cute together…I love to watch them play."

"Dexter's a sweetheart. I remember the first time I saw him at the Pak & Ship. I expected him to be ferocious but he came up to me wanting his chin scratched." She was touched to see Wendy blinking back tears. "It'll be hard on Bea to lose him."

"You need to make sure she gets another dog. She…"

This was one of those times Bea was talking about, where Wendy had more to say but had to gather her breath.

"She'll say she doesn't want one…she'll think it's disloyal." Short, halting sentences. "But you have to convince her."

Allyn suddenly understood they weren't talking only about Dexter. "We have to give her a little time. Everybody needs to grieve before they're ready for the next step. Otherwise they'll always be looking backward."

"I know, but she's got so much to give…just don't let her waste it."

"I don't intend to."

Wendy's misty eyes were now a steady stream of tears, and Allyn wiped them away with a tissue.

"Thanks. If Bea catches me crying…I'll tell her you hurt my feelings. You called me lazy."

"Wow, that's low. Have you always had this evil streak, or is it a wheelchair thing?"

"Got to keep my sense of humor."

Allyn choked back an unexpected sob and walked swiftly to the window as she regained her composure. Such an awful tragedy.

"You'll get used to it," Wendy said softly.

"I just can't fathom how you and Bea got through the past few years. She loves you so much."

"I love her too…but I need for you to love her now… because I can't…not the way she deserves."

She turned back and took Wendy's hand, holding it to her chest the way Bea had done. "I do love her, even more now that I understand what you've both been through. I thought it would be really weird to come here and meet you. I was nervous as hell. All I could think about was how I'd measure up to you in Bea's eyes…and whether she'd be disappointed once she saw us both together."

"I was nervous too. I wanted you to like me…so Bea could still come see me."

Still holding her hand, Allyn looked toward the door where Bea was wiping Dexter's feet so they could come back in. She turned back to find Wendy's eyes shining with fresh tears. "I think you're an amazing woman, and I want us all to be friends."

Dexter clicked across the hardwood floor and collapsed on the rug by the wicker chair.

"We're both worn out," Bea said. Frowning as she came closer and noticed their faces, she added her hand to Allyn's, the one that held Wendy's. "Is everything all right?"

"Allyn said I was lazy."

* * *

Bea cocked her ear at the sound of footsteps on the stairs, followed by the voices of the Huangs as they walked through the foyer to the kitchen. She checked her watch and grimaced. "It's four o'clock already. Guess we ought to hit the road."

Allyn stood and stretched. "I probably should stop by the little girls' room. Bea would pull over if Dexter needed to go, but not for me."

When she left the room, Bea stepped closer to Wendy and gave her a questioning look. "Well?"

"She gets my vote."

"How's that for surreal? My ex-wife is voting on who might be my next one."

"Someone has to watch out for you."

"You've never stopped doing that, Wendy. All this time I thought we were divorced. Turns out you've still got your hooks in me."

"So you finally figured that out." Wendy closed her eyes and smiled. "I want to see lots of Dexter. Come as often as you can."

"I'm sure The Doctors will love that."

"Isn't that half the fun?"

The Huangs had grown more accommodating of late, so it would be interesting to see how they reacted to Bea having a new girlfriend. Perhaps it would bolster their hopes that their daughter's lesbian phase was over. "This isn't a done deal, you know. Her ex-wife has started coming back around. If she wants to kiss and make up, I have no idea what Allyn will do."

"She loves you. Can't imagine why."

"You just can't help yourself, can you?" Bea rolled her eyes and chuckled. "I have to admit this feels pretty good. We like the same things. More important, we respect the same things, and that's a better place to start. But first we need to get past that rebound window and make sure we're not just a couple of desperate rejects."

"Desperate rejects need love too."

"There's another test she'll have to pass though." Bea glanced up when they heard the bathroom door open, and she lowered her head to whisper, "She has to vote on you too, and if she says no...then I guess I can't come visit anymore."

"But you'll still send her and Dexter. Right?"

It was impossible to out-wisecrack someone as whip-smart as Wendy.

Outside after they'd said their goodbyes, Allyn took the lead in getting Dexter strapped into the backseat, and kicked off the ride home with an extended silence that had Bea ready to burst.

"So?" Bea demanded.

"So?"

She pounded the steering wheel with frustration. "You're killing me. What did you think? Did you like Wendy? What did you talk about when I was outside with Dexter? Are you freaking out?"

"Maybe that last part a little."

Bea's heart sank. Judging by the way they'd laughed and talked all day, she was sure they'd hit it off. Now it appeared it was all an act on Allyn's part—a good one, because she hadn't seemed anxious at all after the first few minutes. "I don't get it. By the time we left, you guys were practically best friends. What's freaking you out?"

"I'm worried because I just started a new relationship with a woman I love. Now I've met someone I like even better. What am I going to tell her?"

"You did—" Bea played the words over in her head before glancing sideways to see Allyn covering her mouth to suppress a laugh. "Oh, my God! I left you alone with her for ten minutes. Ten minutes! And now you're acting just like her. Everything you say from now on, I'll be waiting for a punchline."

"How's this for a punchline? I adore her."

"Are you being serious now?"

"Yes, and I also adore you even more for the way you've stood beside her." She put her hand on Bea's shoulder. "And don't even try to say you haven't. You're the number one person in her life."

"Both of you will be the death of me." She took Allyn's hand and brought it to her lips. "She adores you too. What did you guys talk about?"

"Dexter, mostly. She's worried this is going to break your heart."

"Because it will."

"Yeah, it'll be tough. But you two…you've already lived through your worst nightmare, and next time you'll have me beside you too."

The overwhelming sadness of losing Dexter was a dark cloud on the horizon, but there was no denying it would be easier to face with Allyn by her side.

CHAPTER TWENTY

Allyn paced the thin carpet that marked the line between her dining area and living room as she reviewed the job announcement for the benefit of the woman on the phone. "It's an executive position, vice president for technology at a major pharmaceutical company located in the Southeast. I was hoping you might know of someone in your business network who's looking for an opportunity to make an upward career move."

It was her go-to strategy for recruitment, calling qualified candidates and asking for recommendations. Everyone knew how the game was played, and after three or four such calls, she'd reach someone who was ready to jump ship.

"I, uh…" the woman said hesitantly. "I actually do have someone in mind, but I can't discuss her right now. I'm sure I'll need some more information to pass on. Is there a number where I could reach you around noon tomorrow?"

Allyn smiled to herself and rattled off her number. Anyone interested in changing jobs needed to be discreet, and Celia Drummond was definitely due for a promotion. She'd paid her dues for five years in tech security at a hospital supply company where her boss would likely hold the top job for another eight or ten years. She couldn't guarantee Celia this particular job, but a thirty-eight-year-old, mobile African-American with her skill set should be easy to place.

It was volleyball night, which meant dinner afterward at JoJo's. She wouldn't last that long without a snack. Nothing too heavy, just a stick of low-fat string cheese with celery stalks. Her weight had leveled off in the last couple of weeks, thanks to her new pre-lunch ritual of thirty minutes on the treadmill in the apartment complex's fitness facility. She had the room to herself at that time of day, and the time passed quickly while she read through the news on her tablet.

Already dressed in warm-up pants and her Pak & Ship T-shirt, she stepped back from the large mirror in her dining room-cum-office and sucked in her tummy, twisting from side to side to check her figure. All those extra pounds she'd accumulated in her years with Melody were the result of her sedentary lifestyle, and she wouldn't let that happen again. With Bea and her friends active in the recreation leagues, keeping fit would be fun. This was her new life and she was loving it.

Another hour of working the phones and she could call it a day. As she adjusted her headset, she was startled by a knock at the door. Middle of the afternoon...broad daylight. It never occurred to her to check through the peephole.

"Hi, Allyn."

"Melody." The utterance was all she could manage. Her ex-wife in the flesh, holding a bouquet of wildflowers wrapped in cellophane. An irrepressible thrill surged through her, an excitement her conscious self would have denied at all costs.

It was shocking to see Melody for more reasons than one. She'd never told her where she was moving, and all her mail went to the Pak & Ship mailbox. How could Melody have known where to find her?

"I would have called first but I didn't have your number. May I come in?"

Still speechless, she stepped aside, looking her up and down for a visible sign that Melody had suffered from their parting. She was darkly tanned, and the Arizona sun had left white creases around her eyes and neck. Her hair was shorter, a precision cut around her ears that bore more than a passing resemblance to the one Naomi had sported in her web photo. Not particularly flattering for someone as tall and round-shouldered as Melody, but Allyn saw past the tiny flaws to appreciate a smile she thought she'd never see again.

"You look really amazing, Allyn."

She smoothed her T-shirt self-consciously, feeling dowdy and underdressed compared to Melody's crisp white shirt and creased slacks.

"These are yours," Melody said, holding out the flowers. "It's not much. I happened to drive by a vendor at a stoplight and remembered how much you liked them."

Allyn set them aside on her kitchen counter. She'd gotten rid of so many things when she scaled down that she doubted she even had a vase to put them in. "How did you know where I lived?"

"Sandy had this address from when she sent over the closing papers on the house."

Of course, Sandy Valiant, their realtor. She'd asked for a physical address because Allyn needed to sign for the package.

"I can't stay long. I just wanted to stop by and say hi." She looked around the apartment, craning her neck toward the bedroom. "Nice place. You like it here?"

"Very much. It's perfect." In truth, Allyn had almost no opinion about her apartment, other than its functionality as a place to work and sleep. Her faux enthusiasm was a reflexive response, a defense mechanism to demonstrate she had survived their breakup and was thriving in her new life.

Melody stepped into the TV area, clearly expecting an invitation to be seated.

Allyn mindlessly held out a hand toward the love seat, choosing to sit on the ottoman, which she dragged across the carpet to put some distance between them. "What are you doing in Seattle? Is your family all right?"

"Yeah, they're fine. I just came up for a quick visit and thought maybe we could…" Her voice trailed off and she leaned forward, resting her elbows on her knees as she pressed her palms together and stared down at the floor. "I'm just going to come out and say this, Allyn. I've been trying to get in touch with you because I can't stop thinking about how horrible things ended for us, how awful you must have felt. It's been eating at me for months. It's gotten so bad I can't stand it. I just needed to tell you I was sorry for everything you went through."

Words failed her, thoughts failed her. She'd always hoped for an apology someday—and she intensely wanted this one to be sincere—but her instincts kept her from accepting it at face value. It would devastate her if Melody had contrived this visit to take advantage of her vulnerabilities once again.

"I've missed talking to you," she went on, her voice subdued and even conciliatory. "I heard you were playing softball. Jillian said you looked like you were having a really good time. It made me wish we'd found a way to stay friends. I know it was hard for you…it was hard for me too. Everything was so stressful back then, people pulling me in different directions. I just wanted to make it stop, you know?"

"You could have stopped it if you'd just let me help." How could Melody not have known she needed only to step back from the brink and put her faith in Allyn instead of running to Naomi? They could have overcome anything together.

"Not really. No matter what I did, it was all coming apart. Work especially. You have no idea what that was like back in January. That new guy they brought in last fall, Keith Johnson. He was on my case all the time. I had to get out of there."

Allyn listened intently for anything that might shed light on how their life together had come undone. The problems at work were a new revelation, but they weren't enough to explain how Melody had gotten involved with another woman.

"Anyway, Johnson's gone now. He got kicked over to admin at the business school and they promoted Gladys Martinez. You remember her. I always liked her and she liked me, so when I heard she was heading up the department, I called to see about getting my job back at the UW. That's why I wanted to talk to you. We didn't leave things in a very good place, so I thought

I ought to give you a heads-up that I might be coming back to Seattle."

Lovely. Perhaps she and Naomi would buy another house in Redwood Heights.

"It's a free country. You should do whatever you want." She winced inwardly at her flippant tone. This was their chance to salvage at least a friendship from eleven years together, and a huge opportunity to heal the greatest hurt she'd ever known. "Seattle's been your home for a long time. I can see why you'd want to be here."

"Exactly. But the sticking point was you and me. After I left, we were so…at each other's throats. It was awful. It tore me up to know you felt that way." She shook her head and smiled weakly. "I certainly own my part of that."

It was gracious of Melody finally to admit fault, and Allyn was moved to do the same. "I'm really sorry things got so vicious over the settlement. None of that was my idea. You know how attorneys are. Everything's about money and winning. They don't have a personal stake in how it makes people feel."

"Kim was the same way. We should have just worked it out by ourselves. Who knows? If we'd waited a while and let the dust settle, there might not have been anything to work out."

Allyn put her hand over her chest to still the flutter. Countless nights she'd lain awake imagining the day Melody might return and admit she was wrong about everything. Was this finally that day?

Melody abruptly slapped her knees and stood, and Allyn felt a rise of panic. There were far too many things she still didn't understand, and she was desperate to hear more. "You're leaving?"

"Yeah, I'm staying with Jillian and Tiffany. They wanted to get a bite to eat before the volleyball game tonight." She gestured toward Allyn's outfit. "Jillian said you guys have the first game. They play at seven thirty. Maybe we'll come early and cheer you on."

"How long will you be in Seattle?"

"Till Sunday. Want to have dinner tomorrow night? We could go to Bastille. You always wanted to try that."

"Sure, I guess." Bea wouldn't like it, but she'd understand. This was an opportunity to move beyond the acrimony of the past year so she and Melody could enjoy the kind of warm, respectful relationship Bea had with Wendy.

At the door, Melody turned and held out her arms, a gesture Allyn was powerless to resist. "I've missed you, Allyn."

Their silent hug lasted nearly a minute as a storm of conflicting emotions swirled through Allyn's head. There were too many unresolved issues for this to be the long-sought closure to her heartache, but she couldn't deny how good it felt to forget all the pain for just this moment and enjoy the comfort of Melody's arms around her. It was clear time hadn't completely healed her wounds.

* * *

Bea had turned Dexter over to Marta and was at the end of the bench with Allyn, far enough, she hoped, to be out of earshot. Their teammates didn't deserve to be dragged into dyke drama, and that's what this was. Through gritted teeth, she asked, "What do you mean she just showed up out of the blue? How did she even know where you lived?"

"She got my address from Sandy, our realtor."

"You should sue her for breach of privacy. What if Melody had been a murdering stalker? She would have led her right to your door."

"I'm not going to sue anyone."

Bea was so agitated she wanted to stomp around the gym floor. It didn't help matters that Allyn was acting like it was no big deal. "I can't believe this doesn't even bother you. You sent her a note that said you didn't want to talk to her anymore, and what does she do? She shows up at your house uninvited. What part of *fuck off* did she not understand?"

"I never told her to fuck off. I just said it was best for me if we went our separate ways."

"That's my point!" Bea said, waving her hands wildly. She squeezed her eyes shut and tilted her head back, determined to get a grip on her anger. No matter what Melody had done, none of it warranted bullying Allyn about her response. "Sweetheart, I'm just upset that she didn't respect what you said. I don't get people who think they can take whatever they want. That's what she did by coming to your apartment. Who does she think she is to decide she knows better than you what's best for you?"

Allyn looked past her toward the entrance. "Don't turn around. She's coming in now with Jillian and Tiffany. She told me she might."

"Un-fucking-believable."

"Please don't make a big deal out of this. I didn't want to see her again, but when she showed up it turned out all right. I didn't get upset and neither did she. We just talked a little." She waved over Bea's shoulder to someone up in the stands. "They see us. You can turn around if you want."

"Can I flip her a bird?" Despite her snippy reply, she twisted sideways to look in their direction.

Allyn gripped her shirt so she couldn't leave. "Don't be this way, especially right now. I don't want to give them the satisfaction of seeing us argue about it."

She was right, of course, on every level. It would be the height of stupidity for her to throw a hissy fit with Melody watching, and the height of paranoia to assume a casual chat with her ex meant Allyn was leaving her. It was also the height of hypocrisy to browbeat Allyn over something she clearly wanted to do.

"I will do my best to not be this way," she proclaimed, adding a broad grin she didn't feel at all. "You do whatever you think is best for you, and I'll support you. Is that better?"

Allyn cocked her head dubiously. "Are you being sincere?"

"I'm trying to be. I'm definitely not going to make a scene in front of Melody. I want her to look down here and think you're happy."

"I am happy."

"Then you should smile too."

* * *

By the time she reached Bea's house, Allyn was fuming. She sat in her car debating whether to drive off or walk up to the porch and pound on the door. Never had she expected such childish petulance from Bea.

Their volleyball match was hard-fought, going down to the wire in the third game, but they'd prevailed when Bea sent over a serve with topspin that proved too hot to handle. Hand slaps all around, and shouts for whoever got to JoJo's first to pull a couple of tables together. It was only upon arriving on the patio that she learned from Marta that Bea had gone home without having the decency to tell her.

The urge to confront her won out and she stomped up to the porch, where she tried to calm herself again before knocking on the door. After several minutes and numerous knocks, she used her key and found Bea in the glider on the back porch watching Dexter play in the backyard.

"Do you feel better now that you've taken your ball and gone home?"

"Actually, I feel like shit. Why did you wait till we were leaving to tell me you were having dinner with Melody tomorrow night? That should have been the first thing out of your mouth."

"Because…" She sat down next to Bea and put a hand on her leg when she started to get up. "I knew what you'd say and I didn't want to hear it."

"I distinctly remember both of us saying we wanted an honest relationship. Honest means we both say it and we both hear it."

"It's not like I was planning to sneak around and meet her. I just waited because I was afraid you'd make a scene with everybody looking at us." She shivered against the cool night and scooted closer to warm her side. "I don't know why it bothers you so much that I finally have a chance to sit down with Melody and have a civil conversation. You and Wendy are so good to each other, and she's so happy for you. Can't you see how I'd want that from Melody after spending eleven years of my life with her?"

"Don't compare Wendy to Melody. Wendy didn't lie to me. She didn't suck the life out of me and then run off to be with somebody else. The reason I respect her so much is because she earned it. Can you honestly say that about Melody?"

"No, and I never said I respected her. But I want to understand her. There has to be an explanation for what she did, something I could have fixed before it went all to hell. If I don't know what it was, how will I ever be able to trust my feelings for someone else?" Someone else being Bea.

"You want an explanation? She's selfish. She's weak. She's a lowlife. Did she even have the decency to apologize for what she did?"

"Yes." Allyn strained to recall her exact words. She was sorry for the things Allyn had gone through…though she hadn't specifically accepted the blame for being the one who put her through them. "There were extenuating circumstances at work I didn't know about, a new boss that stressed her out and made her want to get out of Seattle as fast as she could."

Bea took off her jacket and wrapped it around Allyn's shoulders. "Her boss didn't make her sleep with Naomi."

"I know." With growing desolation, she acknowledged that Bea was largely right. Melody had done some awful things, and to this day had not taken responsibility. "I want to hear her say she's sorry for everything."

"She might never do that. Some people don't have the capacity to admit they're ever wrong. They come up with excuses for why it's not their fault. Her boss, her stress. It wouldn't surprise me if she let you feel like you were partly to blame."

In fact, she had, Allyn realized. Melody had been very explicit about owning "her part" in their conflict, and Allyn had followed immediately with an apology for her attorney's aggressive demands. "I can't argue with anything you've said, but I need to give her a chance to make it right. If she doesn't, I'm no worse off…unless it upsets you so much that it causes problems for us."

Bea tapped her foot against the floor to make the glider slide gently backward. Once she had it swinging in a steady gait, she took Allyn's hand and squeezed it hard. "I'm sorry for going off without saying goodnight. I don't know Melody but I know she hurt you. I can't forgive her for that. If it were up to me, I'd rather you didn't have anything to do with her. But I understand why you want to, and I was wrong for throwing a tantrum about it. Do whatever you have to do for yourself, and I'll…gnash my teeth in private."

"Gnash your teeth? What does that even mean? I want to see it."

Bea contorted her face into a monster smile. "Gnash, gnash, gnash."

"Oh, you should definitely do that in private." Allyn was relieved to have the tiff behind them, and especially to understand Bea's motives were rooted not in jealousy or an attempt to control her, but in concern that Melody might use the opportunity to saddle her with blame. "You don't have to worry about Melody taking advantage of me again. She wants to move back to Seattle and she's worried I'll make it hard on her with our friends. What she doesn't realize is I don't care what she does, and I care even less about any of her friends. But if I run into her somewhere, I don't want to feel like I have to hide."

"I'm not worried," Bea said. She whistled for Dexter, who joined them on the porch. "While you're out there having dinner with a scummy scalawag, I'll be at home getting unconditional love from the most loyal friend anyone could have."

"Now you're making me jealous."

CHAPTER TWENTY-ONE

Bea sat on the floor beneath the exam table cradling Dexter's head in her lap. It felt as though they'd been waiting all day, but it was only an hour. She was grateful they'd been able to work her in.

A pair of legs appeared through the back door and Kyle Schaefer peeked underneath the table. "Everybody okay down there?"

"Kyle!" Just seeing him filled her with relief. "He's been throwing up all day. Trina said he had a temperature."

He raised and lowered his glasses several times as he studied the chart. "Two treatments…that's about when the side effects kick in. It's not unusual for dogs on chemo to experience vomiting and diarrhea."

"It just started today." She tugged Dexter out and lifted him onto the table. "He'd been doing a lot better. He even had some of his old energy back."

"This is a pattern we see pretty often. The drugs are doing their job but they also open him up to infections, sometimes from his own bacteria. I can give him something to make him feel better." As he talked, he performed a cursory exam. "If he's still throwing up when you come in on Monday for chemo, we'll switch out his drugs."

It broke her heart to see Dexter so glum. His wide amber eyes seemed to be pleading for help. "Are you sure I'm doing the right thing, Kyle? I don't want him to suffer. If putting him through this means he's going to be sick all the time, I'll—" She couldn't bring herself to say it.

"I promise you're doing the right thing, Bea. He'll get past this. Once he does, you probably won't even be able to tell he's sick." He pressed the button by the back door. "We'll get him some fluids today so he doesn't get dehydrated. I can give him a shot for the nausea."

"Sorry, boy. More needles today." She nuzzled his snout until the technician appeared and took him away.

The waiting room was overrun with owners and their pets, all jockeying for positions to keep the animal hostilities to a minimum. The people blended into the background, obscured by the dogs and cats who brought them there.

As Bea squeezed onto a bench between a golden retriever on a leash and a silver tabby in a cloth carrier, one of the exam rooms opened. Out walked an older couple in tears, the reason achingly obvious to everyone, since they were without a pet.

A knot formed in her throat and she bowed her head to give them as much privacy as she could in their grief. She'd been there before—with both Chloe and Fletcher—and she'd be there again.

She texted Kit, who was minding the shop with Grady, and asked them to close up at six without her. The Mariners were playing in Toronto, a four o'clock start on the West Coast, and she wanted nothing more than to curl up on the couch with her best friend.

Between Dexter and the Mariners, she might be able to keep her eye off the clock while Allyn was having dinner tonight with her ex-wife.

* * *

Melody steered her compact rental car between two others at the curb of Chada Thai, a small restaurant in a strip mall not far from Allyn's apartment. "This is a dumpy hole-in-the-wall," she complained. "I thought you were dying to go to Bastille."

Bastille was special because Bea had taken her there. "Forget how it looks. The food here is fantastic."

They were both a bit overdressed for a neighborhood spot where the locals showed up in jeans and T-shirts. Melody wore a houndstooth pantsuit with a black shirt, while Allyn fell back on the slacks-and-sweater outfit she'd worn to Wendy's house in Vancouver.

Melody declined the first two tables offered by the hostess because they were too close to other patrons, and insisted on sitting at a corner table for four. She'd always been forceful about her preferences, and Allyn had to admit they got better service as a result.

They ordered white wine to start and Melody offered a toast. "Let's drink to my very good news. Gladys is pushing through the paperwork to have me come back to the UW, maybe as soon as two or three weeks. I should know something definitive by the middle of next week."

Allyn raised her glass and even managed a smile, which was purely a social reflex. The news didn't exactly make her happy for myriad reasons. Her life didn't need the complication of seeing Melody out and about with Naomi, and she wasn't even certain she wanted a friendship if it meant hearing more about her wonderful new life. She was surprised to feel resentment. Why should people like Melody get everything they wanted? Did the higher-ups at the UW know how shamefully she'd behaved last year, or had she snowed them all into thinking her move to Tucson was solely because of her old boss?

"Which leads me to another announcement. Sad news in a way, but these things happen." She took a sip of wine and made a dramatic show of turning her head so she could give Allyn a sidelong look, as though anxious about her reaction. "When I get back to Tucson, I'll be breaking up with Naomi. She won't be moving to Seattle with me."

Allyn leaned back and drew her hands beneath the tablecloth so Melody wouldn't notice they'd begun to shake. It was too much to think about all at once. Having her close again, her mistake behind her.

"There are things you can't know about people until you live together," she went on. "Never—and I mean never—get involved with someone you work with. That's got bad news written all over it. In the first place, when you start having problems, there's nowhere to go to get away from it."

Her satisfaction with Melody's unhappiness should have come with a measure of guilt, but it didn't. On the contrary, it felt good to know her angst about the two of them cozy and in love in Tucson all this time was for naught.

"The other thing...the really big thing...is that she has no concept of how much work you have to put into a relationship to make it go. It takes sacrifice and dedication, and you have to be grown up about it. She just expects everything to magically fall into place."

Every word was a validation of what Allyn had known all along. Melody's fling with Naomi was based on the flimsiest of emotions—lust, self-indulgence, the excitement of doing something illicit—and it was always destined to fail. The whole fiasco was never more than a cheap affair.

"Anyone who goes into a full-blown relationship as fast as Naomi and I did deserves all the shit that comes with it. The best we can do at this point is cut our losses." She rubbed her hands together lightly to twirl the stem of her wineglass, a gesture that seemed designed to let her avoid eye contact. "Anyway, I'm sure you didn't come to hear my sad story. Jillian said she thought you were seeing somebody. Bea Lawson?"

Allyn nodded. She'd anticipated Bea's name coming up but had no intention of sharing any details, especially none that divulged the depth of their feelings. "We've been seeing each other a few weeks. She's the one who got me into the recreation leagues. I hadn't played since college...forgot how much fun it was."

"Yeah, I was glad to hear you were out making friends. I asked about you all the time but nobody ever saw you anymore. It's like you dropped off the face of the earth."

"I needed to take a few steps back." For months after their breakup, she'd wanted to demonstrate how badly she'd been hurt—the weight loss, the isolation—but now that her suffering was over, the stronger message was that she'd survived. "I still keep up with Candace Landini. Remember her?"

"Candace…Candace and Lark. What a mess that was."

"What do you know about it?"

"Not a lot, except Candace is out there spreading a bunch of lies about Lark. I hope you aren't buying into any of that crap."

"What kind of lies?"

"Oh, you know. Things like accusing Lark of stealing money from her, when in fact, Lark says she was turning over her whole paycheck every week and Candace was doling out a few dollars here and there like it was a kid's allowance. Then Candace told everybody she was using drugs and going to work high. Lark's cousin died of an overdose, so Candace is just saying that because she knows how much it hurts."

"That doesn't sound like her at all."

"Trust me, it is. Whatever she told you is probably a lie. I've known Lark forever, and she wouldn't be saying this stuff if it weren't true."

On the contrary, Lark constantly said things that weren't true, at least according to Kit and Bea. "Candace never told me anything about why they'd broken up. She didn't want me to get down on Lark because she was hoping they'd be able to work things out."

"I don't see how that's going to happen. Too much damage done."

Allyn hoped she was wrong, but if Lark was still lying compulsively, it was probably for the best they didn't get back together. Candace could avoid even more heartbreak ahead.

"So what's going on with you and Bea? Are you guys serious?"

"We aren't getting married anytime soon, if that's what you're asking."

"But you're already talking about the M-word?" Melody's voice was unmistakably shaky.

"That's not exactly what I said."

The waiter interrupted with their dinner, and she seized the opportunity to divert the discussion away from Bea toward the safer topic of Thai food. She didn't want Melody to know how far her feelings for Bea had gone, and Bea wouldn't want her to know anything at all.

The food conversation relaxed them both, and before long they returned to one of their old familiar habits—tasting samples from one another's plate.

"Now you know why I suggested this place. I leave it to the experts when it comes to food like this. It's not like I'm ever going to fix pad Thai at home."

"No, but you sure are a great cook. I miss that."

"Good! Serves you right." Though her tone was haughty, her smile let Melody know she was teasing, and their lingering tension continued to fade with the candid acknowledgment of the elephant in the room.

"I know, but now I have to eat cereal for dinner. You're supposed to feel sympathy."

"You're lucky you still have your teeth. If I could have gotten them in the divorce, I would have."

"You sure got everything else." Melody chuckled and shook her head. "God, Allyn. Your laugh just kills me. I've missed that more than anything."

"You're the one who chose not to hear it anymore." Her manner shifted markedly to one just shy of hostility. All night Melody had artfully dodged responsibility for her actions. Always talking in generalities. People have problems. Relationships take sacrifice. "For that matter, we've now spent at least two hours together and you have yet to apologize for what you put me through."

"I'm sorry. I plead temporary insanity…a midlife crisis. I don't know what it was. I was wrong. Okay?"

Even in the dim restaurant lighting, Allyn could see her face turning red. The words struck her as sincere, but they sorely lacked thoughtful remorse, as if Melody wanted to skate by on the smallest possible expression of regret. Allyn deserved more than a hat tip for the worst heartache she'd ever known.

"You hurt me so bad, Melody. There were some days I actually wanted to die, and if I hadn't been so gutless, I would have. So you don't get to just toss off an 'I'm sorry, I was wrong' and ask me if that's enough."

Melody had the decency to hang her head. "I didn't mean for that to sound frivolous. Ever since I got the call to interview at the UW, all I could think about was seeing you again. I just needed something, any old excuse to get back here."

Allyn was wary—Melody had proven her skills at deception—but she wanted to believe the words were sincere. The confident bluster Melody had displayed earlier was gone, and her lip quivered slightly as she spoke.

"What I did to you was horrible. I think about it all the time, and it makes me sick. Anything I say is going to sound like an excuse, so I won't insult you. I have no excuse. I saw something shiny and I wanted it. Once I developed feelings for Naomi—they weren't what I thought. It just took me a while to realize that. Anyway, I convinced myself staying with you would hurt you more than if I left."

All this time Allyn had wanted an explanation and there wasn't one. Melody had cheated. End of story. "I could have forgiven that. What really hurt was how you turned your back on me after you left. I couldn't understand how someone who said she loved me could be so cruel."

"That was Naomi. She couldn't stand it when I talked to you. She was jealous and afraid I'd change my mind." She pushed her plate aside and nursed the last inch of wine. "But I shouldn't blame it on her. It was my fault. I'm the one who let her push me into cutting everyone off. She didn't even like it when I talked about my family."

The mention of her family caused a fresh wave of pain. Allyn hadn't seen them, hadn't spoken with them at all since Melody left.

There was no clear next step. Forgiveness didn't come in an hour, not after all she'd been through. "I'm not really interested in what went on between you and Naomi. The only thing I care about is why you did what you did to me, and at this point I'm not even sure I care about that."

The waiter collected their plates and brought the check, and Allyn quickly fished the bills from her wallet to cover half. Saying yes to the invitation didn't make this a date.

"I know I have a long way to go before you'll know how sorry I really am, Allyn. I hope you'll give me the time to do that. You were right when you said eleven years is a long time to just throw away."

It was, and it served no purpose to erase those years as if they'd never happened.

"That's probably enough heavy talk for one night," Melody said. "We don't have to iron out everything right now. I just wanted to have dinner so we could talk it out a little, so I could tell you how I feel."

"It's a good start," Allyn admitted as they walked outside. "I'd like to have something to show for the time we spent together."

Melody held the passenger door while she got in. Once she'd navigated the tight confines of the small parking lot, she asked, "Remember who has a birthday this Saturday?"

Bea Lawson, but Melody couldn't possibly know about that. Allyn had a pair of tickets to the Mariners game in her purse.

"Our nephew, Hunter. He'll be eight. We're having a party for him at Mom's house. You should come. Everyone will be there, and they'll go crazy to see you. Mom, especially."

Her heart soared at the thought of seeing the Rankins again. Losing all of them so suddenly without even a chance to say goodbye had caused nearly as much pain as the divorce. She couldn't imagine what Melody must have told them. Surely not that she'd had an affair with Naomi, or that she'd planned her escape to Tucson for months while Allyn thought she was working.

"What do they know about us?"

"None of the particulars, but they know I moved in with Naomi when I got to Tucson, so my guess is they figured it out. They've all met her, and Hunter told her his Aunt Allyn was prettier."

She'd love to see Hunter again. The oldest of the nieces and nephews, he was the one she knew best. She also loved Melody's sisters, Jessica and Elizabeth, as if they were her own. But none were as precious to her as Mom, the name Sheryl Rankin had insisted she use. The Mom she wished she'd had.

"What time is the party?"

Melody's face lit up. "About two. I could pick you up around one."

Olympia was an hour away. "I can only stay a couple of hours max. We have Mariners tickets."

"So now you're a baseball fan too. Just full of surprises."

"Two hours—that's it."

"That works for me too. I need to get back to Jillian and Tiffany's so I can pack. I have to be at the airport on Sunday at seven thirty in the morning."

They pulled into the parking lot at the apartment complex, and when it became clear Melody was looking for a space, Allyn unbuckled her seat belt. "You can just let me out here."

"At least let me walk you the door."

"It's okay. I do it all the time." She didn't care how curt that sounded. Melody needed to see that she was independent now, and needed not to expect an emotional hug like the one they'd shared yesterday. On the heels of her marginal apology, another hug might say too much.

* * *

"Who's that, Dexxie? Who's that?"

The pitch of her voice excited him, and his ears went up as he turned his attention to the front door.

Bea welcomed Allyn with a kiss and stepped aside as she darted across the living room to Dexter. "You didn't have to come but I'm glad you did."

"I thought we settled this last time. You're supposed to call me when something like this happens."

"There wasn't anything you could do. Besides, I knew you had plans tonight with Melody and I didn't want you to think I was trying to screw them up." Though it had crossed her mind more than once. With immense satisfaction, she eyed the overnight bag Allyn had dropped in the entryway. They'd never spent a weeknight together because of Allyn's early start at work. "He's better now. Kyle gave him a shot for his stomach."

Allyn was on her knees in front of the couch nuzzling and sweet-talking Dexter, who clearly enjoyed the attention. "You know I would have canceled. This is more important."

That was a remarkable concession considering her dinner with Melody was something she'd felt she had to do. "How did it go tonight?"

"I finally got my apology, such as it was. It was like pulling teeth. She had the nerve to complain to me about Naomi. Can you believe it?"

"What a narcissist."

Allyn sighed and patted the couch beside her. "There's more."

The rest of the story wasn't entirely surprising, since Bea had entertained it all day as a worst-case scenario for how their meeting would turn out—Melody returning to Seattle without Naomi, obviously eager to reestablish her relationship with Allyn.

"And let me guess the rest. She wants to be your girlfriend again."

"She didn't go that far but it wouldn't surprise me if that's the next thing on her checklist. She's very methodical that way. First this, then that. She's laying her plans just like she did when she moved to Tucson. But it's not going to happen. If she thinks a few minutes of mea culpas and hanging her head are enough to make me forget all the misery she put me through, she's in for a rude awakening. Seriously, like she can make up for turning my whole life upside down with just a few piddly words. It just goes to show you how self-centered she really is."

Bea took pleasure in all the harsh invective toward Melody, but would have preferred hearing she was the reason Allyn was no longer interested in her old life.

"I did promise to see her again though. I hope you won't be mad."

The party plans with the Rankins sounded even more threatening than another date, given the wistful way Allyn described her anticipation at seeing her former in-laws. She knew from her own longing over her sour relationship with the Huangs how much a substitute family could mean to someone who never felt welcome in her own.

"But I told her we were going to the ballgame and I had to get back here by the time you got off work."

So Allyn had mentioned her after all. That revelation was comforting, and she snuggled closer so she was nearly in Allyn's lap. "About that...I know I hinted—okay, *strongly* hinted—that I'd like to go to the Mariners game for my birthday, but if you haven't bought the tickets yet, I might rather watch it from here on TV. I hate to leave Dexxie alone that long, you know?"

"A night right here on the couch with you and Dexter sounds perfect. I'll even cook dinner for you. Just tell me what you want." She nudged Bea out of her lap. "Except right now it's past my bedtime. I hope it's okay I brought my bag. I wanted to be with you guys tonight."

"I love that. We want to be with you too."

After the night she'd had with Melody, perhaps Allyn needed assurance too. It was hard hearing how she'd responded to Melody's overtures, but they had to go through this. Otherwise, she'd never be able to trust that Allyn's old life was truly behind her.

CHAPTER TWENTY-TWO

As the capitol dome came into view, Allyn found herself in the throes of nostalgia. She and Melody had made this trip over a hundred times, most notably for happy gatherings such as this one today. Even as she remembered the sad occasions, like when her father-in-law died and Jessica's husband Will had his heart scare, the overarching feeling was that of belonging. She could hardly wait to see everyone again.

"Mom's making you a hummingbird cake," Melody said.

"The best cake ever." Her mouth watered at the memory. "But it's Hunter's birthday. I'm sure he would have preferred chocolate."

"There's a whole other cake for Hunter. The hummingbird's just for you. Mom was so excited when I told her you were coming."

Allyn wished they could have gotten there earlier. Melody kept her cooling her heels for forty-five minutes because a couple of her friends had stopped by Jillian and Tiffany's. Now she'd have barely an hour to visit before it was time to turn around and go home.

Melody patted her leg as they wound through the neighborhood. "Look familiar?"

She could scarcely breathe when they turned onto the Rankins' street with its towering conifers and well-kept lawns. Several cars she recognized as belonging to her in-laws were lined up on the street in front of the split-level home, leaving the driveway free for scooters and tricycles, plus a small jump ramp for Hunter's skateboard.

They collected the packages from the backseat, presents for Hunter plus a few others Allyn had picked up that morning for the younger children. After all, she had missed nearly a year's worth of birthdays.

As they approached the house, Sheryl Rankin appeared on the porch wearing an apron that proclaimed her the World's Greatest Grandma. She was tall like Melody, with the same dark hair and eyes, but her shoulders were thrown back proudly. She walked right past her daughter to greet Allyn with a hug.

The reunion proved more than Allyn could handle and she let out a sob.

"You shouldn't have stayed away so long."

"Uh, Mom...hello. It's your daughter. I'm over here."

Sheryl finally let go and gave an easy hug to Melody. "I can see you any old time."

The scene inside was just as sweet. Allyn worked her way through the sisters in the living room, her brothers-in-law at the bar in the kitchen, and finished by surprising the children in the family room.

It saddened her when three-year-old Isabella no longer recognized her and ran to hide behind Jessica's legs.

"Give her five minutes and she'll be in your lap," Jessica said. "You won't be able to get rid of her."

"Who'd want to? She's precious."

Jessica and Elizabeth followed Allyn into the family room to talk while she sat on the floor and played with cars, dolls, tablet games and action figures with their children. They were impressed with her new figure, and she nearly burst out laughing when Elizabeth asked her how she did it.

"I stopped eating." It sounded flippant, but that's exactly what she'd done.

"We're really glad you're back," Jessica whispered. "That Naomi…" She turned her thumb upside down and shook her head.

Elizabeth gave her sister a scolding look. "She was nice enough but she wasn't you. We didn't know what to think because you just disappeared. The only thing Melody ever told us was she had this job in Tucson and you weren't going with her."

"I asked her why not and she said it was none of our business," Jessica added.

Clearly they were fishing for details, but it wasn't Allyn's place to share the ugly story.

"Hey, Allyn." Melody appeared and took the tablet from her hands, plopping onto the floor next to Isabella. "Mom says it's her turn to talk to you. She's in the kitchen."

Glad for the chance to visit one-on-one with Sheryl, she followed the smell of her spaghetti sauce. That too had her mouth watering but she wouldn't be able to stay for dinner.

Sheryl ran the men out and directed Allyn to sit at the bar, where she poured two glasses of sparkling cider. Then she stirred her sauce and shook her wooden spoon at Allyn. "I heard everybody telling you how great you looked, but don't you listen to them. You're too skinny, and I'm going to fix that starting today."

"Everything smells so good, Mom, but I'm afraid I can't stay." She glanced at the clock on the stove, noting with regret how much time had passed while she played with the children. Only twenty-five minutes before it was time to go. "I explained to Melody when she told me about Hunter's party that I'd already made plans for tonight, so we'll have to get to back to Seattle soon."

"Don't think for a minute I'm going to let you walk out of here without eating. I'll put the water on for the pasta right now."

Allyn drew an uneasy breath. She couldn't very well insist on leaving just as dinner was ready, but an extra half hour would cut it very close. Besides the hour drive back home—and that was assuming they didn't hit traffic—she needed to pick up the cupcakes she'd ordered for Bea's birthday and set them up with candles before she got home. Instead of making dinner, they could have a pizza delivered.

With her back to Allyn, Sheryl filled an enormous pot with water. "Nobody ever tells me anything, but I know you and Melody had quite the rough patch last year. I hope all that's over."

A rough patch. She understood why Melody had hidden the reason for their breakup—to avoid telling everyone she was a lying cheater. At least she hadn't blamed it on Allyn.

"It's been a hard year, Mom. I'm sure you'll be glad if she gets her job back at the UW. She'll be close again."

"A mother likes to be able to pull her flock in. You're part of that flock too, you know. We've missed you a lot."

"I've missed you too."

"You're always welcome here, whether Melody's with you or not."

The temptation to visit had struck her more than once, but she couldn't bring herself to come between Melody and her family. Even if they'd known about the affair with Naomi, they might have circled the family wagons over the punitive divorce settlement.

"You guys better not be talking about me," Melody said, snatching her mother's glass of cider. "Hunter wants to show his grandma his new karaoke set from Aunt Allyn."

Allyn was annoyed by the interruption, especially since they'd have the drive home to talk.

When Sheryl left, Melody pulled her barstool close, effectively trapping Allyn against the wall. "My family is your family, Allyn. You know that, don't you?"

"I love them. I've missed them so much."

"You don't have to miss them anymore. You can be part of this family again if that's what you want. Just let me back into your life. I don't expect you to forgive me all at once. Just give me a chance. I promise I'll earn your trust again. All you have to do is say yes."

Allyn had been dreaming of such a vow since the day Melody walked out. With just one three-letter word, she could start on the road to recovering their love, their life together, and she could have this wonderful family as her own again.

But it wasn't that simple. No matter her capacity to forgive or how much she longed to have her old life back, things were different now. She'd fallen in love with Bea. "I can't tell you that, Melody."

Melody held up both hands as if to back off. "I'm not asking you to tell me anything today. I know I screwed up, but you'll always be a part of me, and I'll be a part of you. I know you know that. I plan to spend the rest of my life proving how much I love you."

"And I would spend the rest of mine wondering what you were doing in your office, where you were going on your business trips, how many email accounts you had."

"That's all in the past. You have to believe me."

"Why should I? Does Naomi know you contacted me? Does she have any idea we went to dinner the other night, or that I'm here with you and your family?"

The blank look on Melody's face said it all.

"If you aren't being honest with her, why should I expect you to be honest with me?"

Melody reached for her hand. "Look, the other night I said I wasn't going to offer any excuses, but the bottom line is I left you because I was too fucking ashamed of myself to stay. I could never have looked you in the eye again. In eleven years, I never had a secret from you. Not one. I don't know why this was different, but after I met her in Washington, I had to rationalize it, and the way I did that was to convince myself I was in love with her."

Deep down, Allyn had told herself the very same thing— that Melody had known in her heart that her feelings for Naomi weren't real.

"I was too proud to admit I made a mistake."

"I told you over and over I'd forgive you."

"I know, but I couldn't forgive myself. I did such a horrible thing, not just to you, but to myself. The more you pulled at me, the more desperate I got. I laid it on you because I was too much of a coward to take responsibility for myself." Gone was the cockiness she'd displayed at the restaurant, replaced now by frantic uncertainty.

"How could I possibly know it wouldn't happen again?"

"Because I've put my hand on the stove and now I know how much it burns. I'm not ever going to do it again, Allyn. I swear."

The moment was so intense, they hadn't even noticed the lid on the pot rattling loudly as the water came to a boil.

Sheryl hustled back in to add the pasta, shattering the tension and giving Allyn a chance to break free from her position against the wall.

"We'll be ready to eat in twelve minutes. You two set the table."

As was the family practice, they set a plate at the head of the table for John Rankin, who was with them in spirit at every meal. Allyn took her usual seat between Melody and Hunter, and clasped their hands as Elizabeth's husband Daniel said grace. Melody used the opportunity to entwine their fingers, and when the prayer was finished, held on for several more conspicuous seconds. Allyn resisted pulling her hand away, imagining just for a moment giving in to what Melody asked of her. She could have all this again. The warmth and laughter of a loving family. A partner who had strayed, only to discover she could never find real love with anyone else.

All she had to do was say yes.

An hour disappeared while they ate spaghetti and birthday cake, and Allyn finally insisted it was time to leave. The entire clan followed them to the door where she savored hugs with Sheryl and the sisters. There was nothing like the feeling of family.

Elizabeth gave Hunter a nudge. "Somebody better go thank Aunt Allyn for his birthday present again."

She squatted down to catch him, loving the feel of his small arms around her neck.

"Are you coming back to see me?" he asked.

"I sure hope so, Hunter."

"If she really hopes so, then that means yes," Melody proclaimed proudly.

* * *

"And the Oscar goes to…" Bea practiced her most gracious smile in the mirror. After storming off on Wednesday night, she had little choice but to make good on her promise not to behave childishly again. Never mind that it was her birthday and her girlfriend was late, having spent most of the day with her ex-wife.

Her ex-wife who, probably at this very minute, was on her knees begging to be taken back.

Though Allyn hadn't admitted it, there was no question she was at a critical crossroads amidst this flurry of contact from Melody. Nostalgia was a powerful drug, one that managed to amplify the good memories and emotions while tempering the bad ones. She had little doubt Melody and her family were tugging at Allyn's heartstrings, and that she was basking in the warmth of a family life that had made her happy for so many years.

Bea didn't have the antidote to that, nor could she offer a surrogate family to replace the one Allyn had lost. All she had going for her was the future, but only if Allyn was willing to give up her past.

Dexter had moved from his favorite perch on the couch to stretch out in front of the hearth. With nighttime temperatures falling, it was cool enough to turn on the gas log fireplace. Not only did it take the chill off, it also provided a cozy, restful ambience. One might even call it romantic.

Too bad Allyn wasn't here to enjoy it. Had she been anywhere besides with Melody… Bea was mature enough to recognize her jealousy, but there was also the matter of wounded pride that Allyn hadn't hurried back to be with her. Melody was sure to be gloating at commanding most of her day, especially if she knew it was Bea's birthday.

It was a good thing she'd changed her mind about going to the ballpark to celebrate, since the game was already underway and Allyn probably wasn't even back in town yet. Her only word had been a text over an hour ago that she was running late. No explanation of why or how much longer. Just running late. Bea hadn't even bothered to answer, certainly not to say it was okay.

A bark from Dexter preceded the doorbell, and Bea grabbed the money she'd laid out to pay for the Chinese food delivery. So much for the chicken parmesan Allyn had promised to cook. That was twice she'd promised and failed to deliver—both times because of Melody.

Moments after the deliveryman vacated the space in front of the house, Allyn pulled in.

"And the Oscar goes to…" She mumbled it again. It was nearly dark, but not so dark that she couldn't see Allyn dressed in skinny jeans with boots, and a fitted black blazer with the sleeves pushed up. A burgundy scarf looped around her collar and hung to her waist. The look was smoking hot, and it riled her that she'd worn it for Melody.

"I'm so sorry, Bea." She was carrying an elegantly wrapped gift, larger than a book but not by much.

"I ordered Chinese. It just got here so it's still hot."

Allyn set down her package and practically yanked Bea into an embrace. "Dinner can wait. I have to wish a happy birthday to someone I'm crazy about."

The kiss that followed was stunning for its strength, as Allyn drew her tighter than ever and crushed her lips with authority.

"Okay, then," Bea said, shaking her head as if to clear cobwebs. "Being late isn't all that big a deal."

"Happy birthday." Allyn handed her the box. "I wasn't sure what to get you, but when I saw this I knew it was exactly what you needed."

Bea carefully peeled off the silver bow and paper to find a high-end digital camera. Very expensive, she guessed. "Holy wow!"

"I heard you complaining at JoJo's last week about the camera on your phone. I wanted you to be sure you got some good photos of Dexter."

"Awww, thank you." The thought of chronicling Dexter's final months made her eyes cloud with tears. She'd never forgive herself if she wasted the opportunity to memorialize him in pictures, and it was touching Allyn had thought to see that she did. "I'm sure I'll be thanking you again and again. This is wonderful. Way better than a baseball game." Or half a baseball game, in this case.

"It has a really fast shutter speed and a zoom lens. Plus there's this little flap on the side that you can open and take video. I don't know a thing about photography, but I told the saleswoman how Dexter ran in circles through the house, and this is the one she recommended. Oh, and it's got an autofocus, so you just point and shoot. Hold the button down and it'll take three pictures in a row."

Bea didn't know much about photography either, but she knew expensive cameras took better photos than cheap ones. Allyn had dropped a pretty penny on this one to be sure she got good memories of Dexter. "This is so sweet."

"Speaking of sweet, stay right here." She left and returned from her car with a massive layer cake wrapped in cellophane. "I was going to pick up some cupcakes at Trader Joe's, but then I got hung up at the Rankins' because they were all sitting down to dinner and..." She shook her head, as if to indicate that being late hadn't been her idea. "Anyway, Melody's mom surprised me with this. It's a hummingbird cake. The very best cake you've ever tasted."

"And I didn't even tell her it was my birthday," Bea said dryly. She wasn't a traditionalist who needed an elaborate cake with candles to commemorate her special day, but if she happened to get one, she preferred it not be a hand-me-down from her girlfriend's former mother-in-law.

"I know it's not technically a birthday cake, but it's delicious and she baked it just for me. We can't let it go to waste. I don't need to eat the whole thing by myself. I'd rather share it with you than anyone."

Bea took a deep breath to swallow her objections and followed her into the kitchen, where she doled out rice with sweet and sour pork. "Let's eat in the living room in front of the fire."

"I'm not hungry, but you go ahead. Just a glass of water for me."

So not only was she late for dinner, she'd already eaten too.

Once Allyn removed her jacket and scarf and got settled on the couch, Bea muted the sound on the TV and turned off the lamps so they could enjoy the fireplace as they kept an eye on the game. She needed help to quell her annoyance and allow Allyn to turn the evening into something resembling a celebration.

Using chopsticks, she scooped a clump of sticky rice and dragged it through the orange sauce. With her mouth full, she asked in the most cheerful voice she could muster, "So how was your day?"

"My day was…it was really nice."

Bea would rather have heard it was miserable, that Melody was obnoxious and she was never going back again.

"I didn't realize how much I missed everyone until I saw them again, and I could tell they were all glad to see me. It wasn't awkward or anything. In fact, I got the feeling they were trying to apologize to me for Melody, you know?"

"Did they say that?"

"Not in so many words, but they all acted like they were ticked off at her. Mom said—I mean Melody's mom, Sheryl. She always wanted me to call her Mom too. Anyway, she told me she never knew exactly what happened between us, but I was welcome to come back whenever I wanted with or without Melody. I think her sisters figured everything out because they knew she moved to Tucson to be with Naomi."

Okay, she could probably deal with Allyn going off to visit her former in-laws every now and then. After all, Allyn accepted the importance of her trips to see Wendy. "If it makes you feel good to keep in touch with them, you should do it. It sounds like they really missed you."

"From the sound of it, they didn't care much for Naomi."

"They probably won't like anyone who isn't you. Just wait till Melody starts seeing somebody else. That's bound to happen one of these days."

Allyn set her water glass on the coffee table and looked at her somberly. "She wants me back."

The words landed with a thud. A long silence followed until Bea finally muttered, "Can't say I didn't see that coming." The very fact that Allyn hadn't adamantly dismissed it out of hand was all the proof she needed—Melody was a legitimate threat.

It also explained the intensity of their kiss when Allyn arrived. She was probably feeling guilty. Not only about being late, but about being disloyal. Now she wondered how much encouragement Allyn had given Melody to pursue a reconciliation.

"We don't have to talk about this today, Bea. It's your birthday."

"Fuck," she said under her breath, but it was more than loud enough for Allyn to hear. "Eat, drink and be merry, for tomorrow I'm cutting your heart out."

"I didn't say that."

"What else didn't you say?" The urge to withdraw was overpowering, and she shoved her food aside and slid to the far end of the couch, instinctively putting a protective distance around herself.

"I didn't say yes, if that's what you're asking," she answered sharply. "I don't trust her anymore. But at least she finally told me the truth about why she walked out. She knew from the very beginning that she'd screwed up. She left because she couldn't face me—or herself. She couldn't deal with the shame anymore. That doesn't explain why she had to be such an asshole about it. It was just a defense mechanism, I guess. We all do that out of self-preservation. Plus Naomi was pressuring her to cut things off."

It didn't take a genius to read between that particular set of lines—Allyn hadn't told her no. She not only accepted Melody's explanation, but now was making excuses for her.

Allyn squeezed her eyes shut and grasped her head with both hands. "I know you want this to be cut and dried, but it's more complicated than that. One thing I can promise is I'm not going to rush back to her just because she finally took her head out of her ass. I'm not the same pathetic, wailing, deer-in-the-headlights housewife I was a few months ago, and I owe that to you. I'm my own person now. I don't need her validation anymore to feel good about myself."

Bea retreated farther, crawling onto the floor to sit beside Dexter. "What does it mean when you say you aren't going to rush back? That you'll go back gradually?"

"Don't put words in my mouth."

"It's not the words in your mouth that bother me, Allyn." Her voice rose with anger and frustration. "It's the words you're not saying. Did you happen to tell Melody you were in love with me?"

"She knows about us."

"That's not what I asked." From the sound of it, Allyn hadn't given Melody the whole picture. The question was why. It was reasonable to want to protect their privacy—Allyn had been adamant all along that she didn't want Melody to know her business. A more cynical reason was that she was trying to maintain an aura of availability.

The family visit had done exactly what Bea feared it would—triggered a longing for the old days. With Melody hammering her to get back together, it was only a matter of time before she gave in. This had been Bea's worst nightmare all along and now it was coming to pass. "Look, if you're seriously trying to decide between her and me, let me make this simple. She's got all the game pieces, and all I have going for me is the fact that I haven't hurt you. Also the fact that I won't. I'm a better person than that."

"This isn't a game of you against Melody. I'm not asking you to compete with her. I want you to give me enough credit to make a decision about what's right for me."

"That's it? That's all you want from me? No reminders that I love you?" *Or that you said the same to me?*

"You've already given me the one thing I want most—your honesty. You have no idea how much that means."

There was nothing honest about trying to act as though Allyn's wavering on Melody didn't hurt. Nor could she step back and pretend to be mature and supportive while she tumbled aimlessly in limbo. No matter how much Allyn downplayed the threat of Melody, Bea knew she was walking on a wire where if she said or did the wrong thing, there would be no safety net. Allyn would use it as justification to leave her.

After more than a minute of strained silence, she pulled Dexter's head into her lap for comfort. Her comfort, not his. As he lolled beneath her loving caress, she was struck by her sense of inevitability about losing him, and how similar that was to her feelings about Allyn.

"Here's some honesty for you, Allyn. I have a bad feeling about this. I don't blame you for how you feel...there's a lot at stake and you have more to think about than I do. You have a right to decide what kind of life you want—not for me, not for Melody—for you. But while you're doing that, we should back off. Dexter needs me now, and I don't want to spend another night like tonight wondering where you are and what you're doing." Her words were honest, but the calm, rational delivery was indeed Oscar-worthy.

She wanted Allyn to fight her, to say she'd already made up her mind, and it wasn't Melody she wanted.

Instead, Allyn nodded as she pushed herself up from the couch. "I understand. I'm sorry I ruined your birthday."

"My birthday doesn't matter. It's just another day."

Allyn looped her scarf loosely around her neck and slung her jacket over her arm. "I'll call you in a couple of days...if that's okay."

"It's fine." Bea struggled to her feet and went into the kitchen, returning with the cake. "Under the circumstances, I think you should take this."

* * *

Blinded by her own tears, Allyn mindlessly navigated the route to her apartment. Bea's words had scorched her. For the first time, she knew the guilt and shame Melody must have felt under the weight of her allegations. Lies of omission were still lies, and that's what she'd done to Bea.

She also understood why Melody had danced around the reason for her leaving until Allyn finally forced her to admit there was someone else. It was easier not to say. Easier for the one keeping secrets.

The kiss she'd shared with Melody hadn't been her idea but she'd let it happen. It didn't matter that she'd gone completely slack, returning neither the physical nor emotional sensations. She should have pushed her away forcefully, if not for Bea, then for her own sense of pride. No matter what kind of epiphany Melody had finally had, she couldn't erase her betrayal and cruelty with a few words of remorse.

Had Melody ever cried like this over what she'd done? Or had she merely sighed with relief that it was over?

It wasn't over with Bea.

And yet she couldn't bring herself to let go of Melody once and for all. Their years together were the happiest of her life, and now she had a chance to reclaim them. What would Bea do if she could have Wendy again?

Before climbing the stairs to her apartment, she took a side trip to the trash bin and dumped the hummingbird cake. What an insensitive gesture that had been. Yet she'd rationalized it so perfectly with pragmatism, ignoring how it might have made Bea feel. Something Melody would have done.

Bea deserved a better apology than the cursory one she'd given when she walked in the door, but Allyn couldn't face her again until she'd answered the question of why she'd allowed Melody to kiss her. If she secretly wanted it to happen again, it meant she'd chosen Melody over Bea.

CHAPTER TWENTY-THREE

Bea rarely used her desk anymore, opting to spread her papers on the office floor so she could be close to Dexter. With each passing day, he grew more like his old self, pouncing on her to play and covering her face with slobbery kisses. He didn't seem to notice Allyn's absence. No dashing to the window when a car went down the street, no circuits through the house to see if she was hiding in one of the other rooms. On the contrary, he seemed to sense that Bea was out of sorts and stuck beside her like glue.

Out of sorts was a mild way of putting how she'd felt since Saturday night. Four days of walking around like a zombie and four nights of fitful sleep. Allyn would appreciate the irony.

Bea didn't expect hers to last as long as Allyn's had. It wasn't as though they'd been married, or even committed to one another. They had only ten weeks of history, barely enough to honestly call it love. No wonder it had crumbled so quickly when Melody returned waving hearts and flowers.

As of right now, it sure felt as if it had crumbled. Allyn said she'd call in a couple of days but she hadn't. Obviously, she'd accepted Bea's surrender and felt no need to beat a dead horse. By petulantly taking herself out of the picture, Bea had given her the perfect exit strategy, one she could rationalize as what Bea wanted.

For the third time since sitting down she lost her place matching the inventory sheet to her order form. If she didn't get her mind on her work, she'd end up with a whole truckload of packing tape and no boxes to wrap.

"Hey, boss." Kit darkened her doorway and stooped to pet Dexter. "Is it okay with you if I cut out a little early? Grady's got the counter and I need to go put some air in our practice balls before the match."

"Sure, go ahead. Speaking of volleyball...I think I'm going to bail tonight. I've got a headache that won't quit."

"Bullshit."

"What do you mean bullshit? Are you inside my head now?" Kit could be infuriating when she went into her know-it-all routine.

"You've been in a shitty mood all week. Something's going on with you and Allyn."

"Something that's none of your business."

Kit joined her on the floor and traded kisses with Dexter. "I saw Melody at the game last week, so I take it she's back in town."

Bea should have known better than to think Kit would take "none of your business" for an answer. "Not yet, but it's just a matter of time. She came into town to talk with someone at the UW about getting her job back, then she showed up on Allyn's doorstep. Allyn went with her last weekend to visit her family and got caught up in all the old memories. Now Melody wants her back, and all of a sudden she's developed amnesia about all the shit she dragged her through last year."

"So that's it? You guys are done?"

"Who the hell knows? I have to let her try again if that's what she wants, or live with the fact that she'll pine away for

Melody and resent me for the rest of her life. I want her to be happy. I just hoped it would be with me."

"If she goes back to that conniving bitch, she's fucked in the head." The coarse words sounded even more vicious coming from someone as physically imposing as Kit. "But you might as well come to the game tonight and get your mind off it. I just got a text from her about five minutes ago, and she's not going to be there."

"That figures. I don't even get the satisfaction of sulking."

She could hardly fault Allyn for bailing on volleyball since she'd been prepared to do the same. From the way they both were acting, they were finished.

But not from the way Bea was feeling.

* * *

Allyn checked the clock and shut down her employer contacts file. Since Monday she'd dreaded the end of her workday knowing she'd spend the hours before bedtime sitting in the dark brooding, much like when Melody left. Only now she was brooding over how she'd treated Bea. It felt nearly as bad as being on the receiving end, except it wasn't over. She still had a chance to make things right.

"That stupid cake." Could she have been more thoughtless? As though it wasn't enough that she'd shown up over two hours late on her birthday. As though she hadn't spent those two hours entertaining pleas to come back to her ex-wife. As though they hadn't kissed.

All afternoon she'd waffled on whether or not she could face Bea at the volleyball match. The women on the team were Bea's longtime friends, and she'd already come between them last week when she caused her to skip the gathering at JoJo's. What if she went and their teammates picked up on the rift?

She should have kept her promise and called earlier in the week. With every day that passed it grew harder to know what to say. Bea would want an answer and she still didn't have one.

The decision should have been obvious—Melody had destroyed her. Yet she couldn't bring herself to close the door once and for all, not when she had a chance to turn back the clock and pretend the whole tragedy had never happened. That future was there for the taking, since the job at the UW had come through and Melody was already plotting her move back to Seattle in only two weeks.

There was another reason she couldn't talk to Bea right now. The very idea she would consider returning to Melody was humiliating. Bea would say all the right things about how she had to listen to her heart and do what was best for her, but on the inside, she would judge her. Everyone would. She'd be like a battered wife returning to her abuser.

Her cell phone chimed and she knew who it was without looking. Melody had badgered her relentlessly until she gave out her number and knew she stopped work at five sharp.

"Hello," she said flatly, not bothering with the social nuance of faking cheer in her voice.

"Hey…is this a bad time?"

"No, it's okay. I've been dealing with a stubborn client." It shocked her how easily the lie rolled off her tongue.

"I'm sorry. If you want to rant, I'll listen."

This was the new Melody, oozing sympathy and compassion. Actually, it was the old Melody, the woman who used to call her from the car on the way home from work because she couldn't wait to ask about her day. Allyn couldn't remember when she'd stopped doing that.

"It wasn't that bad really. In fact, I had a pretty good day." Two placements and four new clients, thanks to the work habits she'd developed to keep herself busy after Melody left. They were paying big dividends, something she hadn't seen back in the day when she was structuring her work schedule around taking care of the domestic chores while Melody was at her office. Now she was on pace for a six-figure income, her best year ever.

"The reason I called…I've been looking at some apartments online. I thought maybe you could give me some advice."

Melody went on to describe a rental, an upscale complex less than half a mile away that Allyn had ruled out as too expensive. Unless her new job came with a whopping raise, she was over her head.

Jeremy's advice after the divorce that she cut expenses was out of concern that her standard of living would drop considerably without Melody's income, but in fact the opposite had occurred—at least for her. Melody, on the other hand, was probably dead broke, unless Naomi had supported her for the last nine months and allowed her to bank her salary. Money didn't matter much where love was concerned, but it had a way of asserting itself when things went south. Allyn had no inclination to help her out financially, even though she'd gotten the lion's share of the profit from the sale of their home. Melody had dug that hole for herself with poor decisions, and she'd have to climb out of it on her own.

She caught the tail end of Melody's list of amenities and could hear in her voice that she was excited about it. "I looked at that place last year. It's nice but it was too rich for my blood."

"It's higher than most, but it's the only decent place I could find in that part of town that lets me do a month-to-month lease. I don't want to be locked into a whole year."

In other words, she was already counting on them getting another place together soon. "I assumed you'd want to live near the university. You always complained about the traffic."

"I want to live near you, Allyn. I know it's too soon for you to let me move in—and your place is probably too small anyway—but I want to be close enough that I can see you every day…so we can have dinner, hang out, watch TV. That's what it's going to take for me to prove that I'm the person you married."

It would be so easy to say yes. Everything would fall back into place and her life would be so tidy. She couldn't help yearning for what they'd once had, especially when she mentally scrolled through her memories of the times when they'd been close. The cards and photos she'd packed away in her closet told their story. Their love had been real. Deep. Passionate. So why couldn't she do it?

Lingering anger and distrust. Sure, but Allyn felt certain she could make those go away once she decided to recommit. Something stronger was stopping her.

"Anyway, I'll be coming back up again on Friday. I'm flying in late and I guess I'll stay with Jillian & Tiff." A few seconds passed, a transparent pause to see if Allyn would make her a better offer. "We're supposed to look at this place on Saturday, maybe a few others. With any luck, I'll be able to pick one and get started with this grueling process again. Want to come along?"

Tagging along on a rental tour with Jillian and Tiffany was the last thing she wanted to do. She didn't even want them as friends, not after they'd chosen sides. It was weird to think she might forgive Melody's betrayal but not theirs. She had nothing to gain from having them back in her life.

She didn't particularly want to see Melody either, not right now. After a swarm of emails and phone calls since the weekend, all of them filled with apologies and promises, she needed time to process where she was. Melody had already leaped ahead, but she was taking a lot for granted.

The other looming issue was Bea acting as if she didn't care one way or the other. She had a right to be angry, but not so angry that she was willing to throw it all away. That couldn't be real love.

Or maybe Allyn was asking for too much compassion from someone who didn't have it to spare right now. Bea was heartbroken over Dexter and didn't need the aggravation of Allyn's ambivalence over how to handle Melody's return. No one wanted to feel like a consolation prize.

* * *

Bea knew they'd have a hard time winning without Allyn spiking from the front row, but she never expected to get slaughtered. It didn't help that everything she touched sailed out of bounds because she hit it too hard, unable to rein in her aggression.

She fished a twenty-dollar bill from the bottom of her gym bag and handed it to Kit. "Here, buy a couple of pitchers of beer on me. I'm going to head on home with Dexter."

"Come on, it wasn't that bad."

They both knew that wasn't true, but her lousy play wasn't the reason she was cutting out. She'd gotten a text from Allyn asking her to call. No matter what she had to say, Bea wanted to hear it without sharing her reaction with the whole team.

In a Hollywood romance, she'd have found Allyn on her doorstep tearfully proclaiming her love and renouncing Melody for all time. No such luck, though. She'd have to make do with a phone call.

Bea turned Dexter out into the backyard and twisted off the top of a Heineken. Celebration or consolation. A good lager was suitable for either.

Allyn answered on the second ring. "Hey, thanks for calling me back."

"I usually do everything a pretty lady asks." She cringed at how cheesy that sounded. "I know…that was a dorky thing to say."

"It was sweet, just like you. How was the game?"

"Without our Tower of Terror on the front line, we got our asses kicked."

"Sorry about that. I wasn't sure where we stood and I was afraid it would make the others uncomfortable."

If she'd called two days ago like she promised, she would have known exactly where Bea stood—she wanted it back the way it was before Melody showed up again. The more important question was where did Allyn stand. Bea's anxiety rose with every second that passed without Allyn saying why she wanted to talk.

Bea decided against telling her she would have skipped the game too had Kit not told her about the message. "We missed you…and I miss you."

"I miss you too. I still feel really bad about Saturday. I should have at least called you—no, I should have gotten there on time like I said. And the cake…"

"Forget it, seriously." Just the same, she appreciated the apology.

"I wanted to call earlier but I wasn't sure you really wanted me to. I thought a lot about what you said and you're right. It's not a competition, but if it were, Melody wouldn't deserve to win. Not after everything she did."

Bea's heart would have soared with hope but there was something about Allyn's choice of words that gave her pause. "So if it's not a competition, what is it?"

"I don't know. I'm afraid I'm going to screw around and lose everything. Melody keeps pressuring me, and I feel like you are too."

"Me? What am I doing?"

"Nothing specific. I just feel like deep down you don't want to give me time to think about it."

On the contrary, she was sure if Allyn took the time to really look at it, she'd realize she'd never be happy again with Melody. "Whatever gave you that idea? I never said you had to decide anything right now."

"You might as well have. You told me you had a bad feeling about it, and you didn't even want to see me unless I made up my mind right that minute."

"No, what I told you was that I was going to back off while you figured out what you wanted to do. I don't want to be left dangling while you go back and forth between us."

"That's not how it sounded to me. You acted like you didn't even care. As soon as I said Melody wanted me back, you practically pushed me out the door. It's like you were insulted that I'd even think about it."

That was true, Bea conceded, except she wasn't insulted. She was hurt, and she knew she'd never measure up against Melody. "I told you I loved you."

"You have a funny way of showing it."

"Listen to yourself, Allyn. You're doing to me exactly what she did to you—trying to make this my fault. It's like you just want an excuse to cross me off your list so you won't feel guilty about running back to her. If you really cared about me in the first place, you would have told her to get lost already. No way am I going to sit home and wring my hands over what you're going to decide. 'Pick me, pick me!' Fuck that. Save us all the trouble and pick Melody. You can justify it later by saying you had no choice."

She ended the call and slammed her phone on the table before letting out a frustrated scream so loud her neighbors had to have heard. After four quick breaths, she felt dizzy and went out to sit on the glider, where Dexter joined her to lie at her feet.

Tears sprang to her eyes as he thumped his tail and looked at her mournfully. He was the only creature on this earth she could truly count on to love her no matter what, and he was leaving her too.

CHAPTER TWENTY-FOUR

Bea breathed a sigh of relief to find the circular driveway empty but for the van. Today's visit would be hard enough without the added stress of knowing the Huangs were upstairs pacing and waiting for her to leave.

For the last two weeks she'd artfully dodged questions about Allyn, hoping it would all blow over and Allyn would realize going back to Melody was a big mistake. Wendy would pick up on her sullen mood and drag all the details out, after which they'd both probably have a good cry. At least Dexter was feeling great.

Krystal showed her into the sunroom where she dropped the leash and allowed Dexter to race across the room. It was always fun to watch their reunion as he stood on his hind legs and licked her face while she cooed about what a sweet boy he was.

"I should hold on to him a little longer so I can kiss you before he does. It's like licking his food bowl." After a peck on the lips she clutched Wendy's hand to her chest. "How are you feeling?"

"How should I know?" they both answered simultaneously, laughing at their familiar schtick.

"We went out yesterday," Wendy said. "Drove up to Altamont. Had lunch at The Beach House."

"We should go out too sometime. It would be fun to drive out to Mountain Forest or up to the Observatory. Better yet, you could come with me to Seattle for a few days." She'd thought about this before, even going so far as to find where she could rent a hospital bed to set up in the living room. With Grady up to speed, she could take time off work.

"I'd like to see your house for real."

"We could have a big cookout over at Kit's and get the whole gang to come out. Think we could get The Doctors to agree to that?"

Wendy snorted. "Sure, why don't you ask them?"

"I'm serious. Krystal can come along so they won't have to worry about me forgetting to set your parking brake."

"Maybe I should ask them instead. I can cry. Want to see?"

"Oh, please. You've been pulling that one for eight years. No one falls for it anymore." She tugged the wicker chair closer, making sure to stay in Wendy's sight line. Then she kicked off her clogs and crossed her feet in Wendy's lap. "Bad news about Allyn, I'm afraid. Looks like she's gone back to that sleazebag who cheated on her."

It came out exactly the way she'd practiced in the car, candid and unemotional. If Wendy knew how dejected she was, she'd feel bad too because there wasn't anything she could do to help.

"I knew something was wrong," Wendy said glumly. "You haven't talked about her."

"Nothing to say. I was hoping she'd come around, but it's been about ten days since the last time we talked. Melody got her job back at the UW, so she'll be moving back to Seattle any day now."

"That's just wrong. Allyn loved you."

"Evidently not enough."

"So that's it? It's over."

"Appears that way." At least she hadn't told anyone else she'd been in love with Allyn, so she wouldn't look like an utter fool when she got thrown over for the ex-wife. "But I can't complain, you know. I got an awesome camera out of the deal."

"You're so full of shit."

"I know. I'm just trying not to let it get to me."

"It should get to you," Wendy said sharply.

A steady rain precluded her escape into the backyard with Dexter, but even that was preferable to another drubbing from Wendy on why her romantic life was such a disaster. "It's not my choice, obviously. She wants what she used to have. I understand that, probably better than most."

"If you'd still pick me over her...you're crazy as hell."

Her tone was bitter, and if Bea didn't know her so well, it might have sounded self-pitying. Instead, it was anger and frustration that she'd steadfastly refused to move on.

"What do you expect me to do, Wendy? Knock her over the head and drag her back to my cave? She wants Melody. End of story."

"Because you won't fight for her. You're afraid to lose."

There was more truth to that than she wanted to admit. "Losing would suck. At least this way I can keep my pride."

"Is your pride worth that much?" She was clearly still angry, and she waited two beats for the respirator before she continued, because yelling took more air. "You're being a chickenshit...just like when I decided...to have the surgery."

"In the first place, calm down." She stood and took Wendy's hand again. It was true she'd been terrified when Wendy insisted on having the surgery in hope of regaining use of her hands, but her fears were ignored. "And about your surgery...not to be too obvious, but look how that turned out. You lost control of your lungs and you nearly died again, so forgive me if I don't take your advice."

"It's all about the reward, Bea. If you lose Allyn...you won't die...and you won't be paralyzed. The only risk is your pride."

"But it's her decision, not mine."

"Very noble. Does Melody feel the same way?"

Bea huffed. "She's probably doubling down. Flowers, candy, the whole nine yards."

"While you're sitting on your ass."

No answer to that except to agree.

"Melody is showing her that she wants her. What are you showing her?"

"That I...respect her. That I trust her to make the right decision. That I...shit. That I can't be bothered to show her how I feel about her."

"Yes, that one." Wendy finally smiled, albeit smugly. "Go see her. She needs to know that you love her."

Bea sighed and nodded her agreement, grudgingly conceding that it was her pride talking when she told Allyn she wouldn't "play the game." She might as well have pushed her out the door. "I'll go sometime this week."

"Go now."

"Right now? We drove all the way up here to visit you."

"Chickenshit."

"What am I supposed to say?"

"You're stalling. Go."

"You can be such a terrorist," she groused, even as she pulled on her jacket and grabbed for Dexter's leash. After a parting kiss, she started toward the door, calling out over her shoulder, "I love you...and I'll love you even more if you're right."

* * *

Allyn walked again through her apartment to see if she'd left anything undone, any little chore to keep her busy. Weekends were almost unbearable. A steady rain kept her indoors, and with no work to fill her day, she had too much time to mope.

A week and a half had passed since Bea broke things off, and the hurt hadn't eased at all. No calls, no updates on Dexter. A friendly night out for a movie would have been nice. She'd been tempted to show up at the volleyball game and at least offer her hand in friendship. Then she'd played back Bea's hurtful words in her head. *Fuck that*.

In contrast, Melody seemed to be everywhere all at once, calling several times a day, texting, sending photos and links, and writing long, drawn-out emails detailing every facet of her day.

Allyn had taken to dodging many of the calls, most of the emails and all of the texts. It annoyed her that Melody increasingly behaved as if their reconciliation was a foregone conclusion. She hadn't agreed to anything.

At least Melody wasn't pressuring her to remarry, though she repeatedly said she would prove her love as long as it took for Allyn to take her back. If only Bea had shown her that kind of patience.

She felt trapped by Melody's attentions. Bea told her she would, and that she'd end up choosing Melody and justify it because Bea had refused to play.

No one ever took responsibility for their choices. Why should she be any different?

She'd fallen into her old habit of not eating, but the moment she realized she was losing weight again, she bought a jar of protein powder to mix with yogurt and orange juice. A scoop of this, a cup of that, a splash of the other. As her blender whirred, another sound caught her attention and she turned it off to listen. A knock at the door.

Sunday afternoon. It couldn't be anyone else but Bea, and she excitedly raced across the room and flung the door open wide—to Melody.

Clad in a calf-length raincoat with the hood up, she produced a bottle of champagne from one of her oversized pockets. "Guess who officially lives in Seattle again?"

"What are you doing here? I thought you had another week in Tucson."

"I had a few vacation days and I blew off the rest. Naomi was making it impossible to stay, so I rented a truck and moved everything up here myself. I thought maybe we could drive out to Snoqualmie Falls for dinner."

She invited herself in and hung her raincoat on the hook by the door, revealing a disturbing coincidence—she was wearing the same brown pinstriped pantsuit and ankle boots she'd worn the day she came home and announced she was leaving. She looked sharp, especially compared to Allyn, who was wearing yoga pants, a Seahawks jersey and bright blue bedroom slippers.

Making herself at home, she began opening cabinets in search of wineglasses.

"Top shelf over the dishwasher."

As she popped the cork and poured, she told of her twenty-three-hour drive from Tucson and how Jillian and Tiff had picked up her apartment key and met her last night to help her unload. "I would have been over here sooner but I was up half the night unpacking."

Allyn walked behind her and emptied the contents of the blender into a glass. "I just finished making a protein shake. You want one?"

"Ditch it. Wouldn't you rather have a nice big steak at the Salish Lodge?"

"I can't. I have…other things to do." Another lie easily told.

Melody's face fell for an instant but she recovered with a smile and handed Allyn a glass of champagne. "At least do me the honor of celebrating with me. No matter how everything turns out, I finally feel like I'm back where I belong."

Allyn went through the motions, clinking her glass and taking a sip as Melody took a seat on one of the barstools. The strength of the bubbles took her by surprise, and she vividly recalled the last time she'd had champagne. Dom Perignon. They'd shared a bottle with several other couples after their wedding.

"I have to admit it's kind of nice having my own place," Melody went on. "Nobody yelling at me…or worse, giving me the silent treatment. Living alone is way better than that. It isn't something I want to get used to though."

The last bit was a none-too-subtle hint about moving back in together, and Allyn found it irritating, especially given the teasing grin that came with it. "Don't you think you're being a little presumptuous?"

"I didn't mean to be. Just…hopeful. I honestly don't want you to feel rushed about anything. I know this isn't easy for you and I don't blame you. We'll take everything nice and slow just like we said."

"Just like *you* said. I never told you I was coming back."

Melody's smile faded again but there was still a twinkle in her eye that said she wasn't taking Allyn seriously. "No, but if I keep showing up with flowers and champagne, I'll wear you down eventually. I could see it last weekend when you were playing with Hunter. Plus Mom said if we didn't get back together, she was going to kick both of our asses. You don't want to get on Sheryl Rankin's bad side. Nobody does."

Allyn was tired of seeing her tune out everything she didn't want to hear. "That's exactly what I mean. You're just so sure of yourself. I'm not the same person you walked out on. It was hard on me when you left, but I learned I can take care of myself, and being alone is a perfectly fine way to live. I also learned even the people you trust most can lie to you, so don't think you're going to win me back with flowers and champagne, or with cute stories about Hunter and your mom."

"Whoa, I hear you. I'm not asking you to do anything you aren't ready for. All I'm trying to do is find a way to get back to where we were. Whatever it takes."

"We're never going to be where we were. I don't want to be your housekeeper anymore. When I've worked all day, I want to go out with friends—*my* friends, people who care about *me*. If I'm going to be with someone, I want her to care more about me than she does about herself."

Obviously taken aback by her assertiveness, Melody leaned backward slightly on the stool as though pulling away from a possible slap in the face. "I've changed too, Allyn. I'm not that asshole who cheated on you. I learned my lesson. All I ask is a chance to prove it."

Practically speaking, Allyn wasn't even sure what that meant. Dating? Sleeping together? Melding their lives again? Her gaze moved down the pinstriped pantsuit to the polished ankle boots. She couldn't envision herself doing anything with Melody. Not now, not ever.

With startling clarity, she put her finger on exactly the reason Melody didn't have a chance. It wasn't because of her affair or the cruel way she'd cast her aside, and it had nothing to do with Bea.

It was because she no longer loved her.

No attraction, no chemistry. And no desire at all to know her again.

CHAPTER TWENTY-FIVE

"It's over, Melody." Allyn marveled at the steadiness of her voice, a sign of her certainty. "We had some good years but now it's time for us to go our separate ways."

Melody's eyes went wide with panic and she began to shake her head. "No. I don't accept that. It can't be over, Allyn. I watched you at my mom's, and you were so happy. That's exactly how you used to be. I know we can get it back. I swear I'll never hurt you again."

"I love your family very much, and I hope I'll be able to keep them in my life. I hope you'll be in my life too, but it won't be as my partner. There isn't anything you can do to change that. I just don't feel that way about you anymore."

"That's it. We need to talk this out, get all our feelings out in the open. Maybe we can go to counseling or something."

"I don't want to. And I don't want to listen anymore, because it isn't going to change how I feel. You should just go."

"That's all I get? No explanation? Just...it's over?" Increasingly agitated, Melody pointed a finger across the counter. "I fucked up—I don't deny that—but after all we've been through together, I deserve better than that."

Allyn sneered at the wagging finger, Melody's go-to gesture for asserting authority and putting her in her place. "Do you really want to have a conversation about what you deserve? We could start with all the lies. With the calls and emails of mine that you ignored."

"That wasn't the same thing. You already knew all the hows, whats and whys. You just wanted to keep talking because you couldn't accept it."

"And how is that different from this?"

"Because I don't have a clue why you're saying this." Melody squeezed her eyes shut and rubbed her head with both hands. "Look, I know it's going to be hard for us, but I'm willing to put in the work. I believe we're worth it. I also believe we'll be even stronger for going through all this together. If that means we have to start over at the beginning, then I'm willing to do that." She thrust her hand across the counter. "Hi, I'm Melody Rankin. Pleased to meet you."

Allyn ignored her hand, recognizing her attempt to trivialize her words and retake control of the conversation. She didn't want any more of Melody's apologies, nor to hear another string of senseless pleas. Only cold, harsh words would shut her down once and for all. "I forgive you for Naomi. I forgive you for how you treated me. But it doesn't change anything. Even if I got past all the ways you hurt me, it wouldn't make any difference. I don't have feelings for you anymore. I'm not attracted to you and I don't see that ever changing. In fact, I…I'm not sure what I ever saw in you in the first place. I didn't want to have to tell you all that, but you keep acting like it's just a matter of time before I come around. You need to understand that it isn't going to happen. Not ever. That's all there is to it."

Melody stiffened on the stool but made no move to leave. With her chin jutting out and her eyes closing to a squint, she looked ready to spit nails. "That's not all there is and we both know it."

Allyn bristled at her tone.

"You're trying to make it sound like it's all about me, but not once did you mention Bea Lawson."

"What about her?"

"It's obvious you're using her to get back at me. Jillian told me how you two put on a big show in front of her so she'd run back and tell me about it. I guess it worked, because I couldn't stand to think of you settling for someone like that."

Allyn could feel the hairs stand on the back of her neck, and she gripped the edge of the kitchen sink. "Settling for Bea Lawson? Someone who loves and respects me, who always thinks of me before she thinks of herself? Someone who doesn't have a deceptive bone in her body? I'd hardly call that settling."

"Bea Lawson isn't who you think she is." The veins on Melody's forehead were bulging with anger and her voice rose with every word. "Do you have any idea what she did to Wendy Huang? That poor woman broke her neck and now she's paralyzed. Did Bea think of her? Hell, no. She thought of herself. Divorced her, dumped her back on her parents and left her to rot in a wheelchair for the rest of her life. That doesn't sound like love and respect to me. She's a loser, a low-life scumbag, and you'll be left high and dry the second you need her most."

"Everything you think you know about Bea Lawson is a lie. Wendy Huang too. I know them both. I've seen them together and it so happens they're more devoted to each other than any two women I've ever met."

"Great, so you're settling for a woman who's in love with somebody else."

Never before had Allyn felt such an urge to slap someone, but she couldn't lower herself to do something so deplorable. "Isn't that the same suit you were wearing the night you came home and told me you'd fallen in love with another woman?"

Melody looked down to check herself and then gaped at Allyn with bewilderment. "What the fuck?"

Allyn flung her sticky protein shake across the counter, landing most of it on Melody's face and chest. "Let's call that your Asshole Suit. Dry clean only, isn't it?"

"Jesus Christ, Allyn! You've totally lost it."

"No, I've found it. I finally have closure with you once and for all. Now get out of my house. And get out of my life."

Melody opened her mouth for the last word but thought better of it when she saw that Allyn had grabbed the blender jar and was threatening to throw its contents as well. Muttering under her breath, she stalked out and slammed the door behind her.

Allyn's hands shook wildly but not from fear or fury. She was proud. She was thrilled. She was whole again.

Holding onto the counter and then the barstool for support, she carefully navigated the slippery floor, laughing aloud at the awful mess she'd made. Besides soaking the floor, the spray had also drenched the couch and coffee table. Papers, magazines, pillows. It was well worth it to see the shock on Melody's face.

She plucked the stepladder from the closet by the door and carried it into her bedroom. Still trembling with exhilaration, she climbed up and retrieved the box she'd stashed only a few months earlier on the closet shelf. Photos, cards and mementos of her life with Melody. Still in her bedroom slippers, she marched unflinching in the rain to the trash bin where she'd dumped the cake. With a giant heave, she tossed the whole box inside, along with all the stress and doubt she'd wrestled with since Melody's return.

If it wasn't too late, she could turn her focus to Bea. Only now she was in Melody's shoes—trying to win back a woman she'd mistreated. Ironic indeed. It would serve her right to lose everything.

She'd learned from Melody that being sorry wasn't enough. She had to start back at the beginning…be a friend first and hope Bea would fall in love with her again.

Melody had shaken off the biggest globs of goo as she walked toward the door, making a mess all across the room. It took an hour to rub it out of the carpet, and all the while she laughed to recall the sticky liquid dripping from Melody's face. If only her phone had been within reach, she'd have taken a photo to preserve the moment forever.

Another knock on the door tightened her gut. Surely Melody hadn't come back for more.

This time it was Bea, and she was struggling with Dexter's leash to keep him from jumping. Both were dripping wet as though they'd timed their dash from the car during the worst part of the downpour.

She brushed her damp hair from her eyes and looked at Allyn solemnly. "I was wrong about what I said. If this is a contest between Melody and me, I'm in. More than anything in this world, I want you to pick me."

Tears of joy welled up instantly and she threw her arms around Bea's shoulders and squeezed hard enough to nearly send both of them tumbling. Then she tugged her by the elbow toward the door. "Get in here!"

"What about Dexter?"

"Bring him. I don't care if I get thrown out."

* * *

It was supposed to have been Bea's moment for a bold declaration, and on its heels, a sweeping off the feet Rhett Butler would have envied.

Allyn clearly had other ideas.

Bea had barely closed the front door when Allyn yanked her into the bedroom and pushed her across the bed. What followed was a tender, determined assault in which their clothes were strewn in every direction and the bed linens thrown to the floor.

She found herself flat on her back with her arms pinned above her head while Allyn covered her face, neck and shoulders with wet kisses that left a cool trail in their wake. By the time her arms were released, it was all she could do not to take herself.

Allyn lowered her mouth to the tender skin just below her hipbone, where she sucked until it left a purple mark.

For a moment Bea was sure she intended to mark the other side as well, but instead she looped both arms around her thighs and captured Bea's most sensitive spot between her lips. No teasing, just an unrelenting onslaught of lips, tongue and teeth that brought every neuron in her body to focus on that one tiny space.

Bea was torn between clenching the muscles in her hips and giving Allyn what she wanted now, or going limp in an effort to make it last. But then Allyn began to moan, and the intermittent vibrations made her options moot.

"Oh, God." She began to writhe, driving her heels against the mattress to push herself deeper into Allyn's mouth as her climax erupted.

Allyn never moved her lips, not even when Bea's bones turned to liquid and she soaked languidly into the bed.

The love bite on her hip throbbed like a brand—Allyn's brand. Bea was owned.

* * *

Allyn lolled beneath the covers and checked the clock. Almost midnight. After nearly five hours of making love, dozing and making love again, her body was sated but her heart wanted more.

Bea returned from a clandestine walk with Dexter and stripped off her clothes again. Before getting back into bed, she settled him on a blanket in the corner.

Allyn savored the picture from behind as Bea bent over to nuzzle him with sweet talk.

"I can feel you looking at me," Bea said without turning around.

"I was memorizing that sight so I'd have something to think about tomorrow when I doze off at my desk. I have this mental slide show…it starts with those big green eyes looking up at me through all that rain dripping off your hair."

"I had no idea you'd be so glad to see me." She turned off the lamp and climbed into bed, where she molded into Allyn's side. "Something must have happened to change your mind."

"What makes you think I changed my mind? I never decided on Melody. I tried, though. I admit that. I thought it would be easier for everybody, and I probably could have forgiven her for cheating if I still loved her. I kept waiting for my old feelings to come back. I imagined us being together again and all I could think was how empty it was. That's because I love you now, and

I don't have room for anyone else in here." She placed Bea's hand over her heart. It was remarkable to hear her own words tumble out so easily. She knew exactly what she wanted.

"I felt the same way. It killed me to think about you with anyone else, and even more to think about being with anyone else after being with you. You're it for me, lady."

Allyn kissed the top of her head and smoothed her hair, noting that it was softer than usual after a rinse in rainwater. "I know how hard it must have been for you to let me see Melody again, to have dinner with her and go down to Olympia to see her family. That made me love you even more because it showed you cared more about me than you did yourself."

"There was a little self-interest too. I didn't want either one of us to ever have to look back and wonder." Her arms tightened around Allyn's waist. "I was hoping you'd realize right away you didn't want Melody back. When you didn't, I got scared you'd leave me so I left you first. That was stupid because I love you."

"For what it's worth, I was already planning to show up at your house tomorrow with my suitcase. If you hadn't let me stay, I was prepared to camp out in my car in your driveway."

"You need to be careful with this pillow talk or I'm going to keep you up another hour past your bedtime."

"About that...we need to work on our schedules because I have a feeling this sleeping together and staying up half the night making love is going to be a regular thing."

As Allyn closed her eyes, she took a mental inventory in search of doubts, fears or regrets. None, though one important question remained: Would there ever be a place in her life for Melody, or the history they'd shared?

She didn't have to answer that tonight.

EPILOGUE

Kit grunted and steadied her legs beneath the heaviest corner of Allyn's desk. Even with her bad shoulder, she was still stronger than anyone else in the house. "Back it out. It won't fit this way. We have to turn it."

Bea obliged, walking it back into the widest part of her newly-configured hallway. "We should have put the desk in there first and built the office around it."

The addition, a twelve-by-fourteen room with large windows and a sliding glass door leading onto the back porch, had taken ten weeks to complete. It was hard to know which excited Allyn more, a new office or the peace and quiet from having the construction workers leave, taking their noisy hammers, drills and saws with them.

Their second attempt to maneuver the desk was successful, and after a couple of false starts Allyn chose its final resting place where she could view the backyard. Then she walked from one corner to the next admiring the layout.

Remembering how pleased she'd been when first presented with the idea of an addition, Bea reveled in her look of pride and satisfaction. Allyn had moved in gradually over a period of several months, leaving her apartment for good at the end of February when her lease expired. However, she soon realized Bea's second bedroom was too cramped and cave-like, not at all pleasant as a home office. This was a giant step for them—a permanent one, since Allyn had laid out over twenty thousand dollars for improvements on a house that was still in Bea's name only.

That would change in about two months on the last weekend in August, which happened to be their one-year anniversary of running into one another at the Pak & Ship in Broadview. It was the day their lives changed forever, and they planned to commemorate it with a simple backyard wedding among friends, including Wendy, with Krystal nearby. As far as Bea was concerned, August couldn't get here soon enough.

Allyn dropped a box of files on the corner of the desk. "This is going to sound weird, but I can't wait to start work tomorrow morning."

"You like it?"

"It's awesome." She kissed Bea on the tip of her nose. "Just like you."

Kit groaned and yelled loudly so Marta would hear her in the kitchen, "They're doing it again."

"You should try it sometime," Bea said, wrapping her arms around Allyn's waist.

Marta appeared in the doorway with her purse slung over her shoulder. "You could have told them to get a room, but they already did that. We need to hit the road if we're going to make it home in time for the Storm game."

"You guys can watch it here if you want," Allyn offered. "I owe you dinner. We can order a pizza and some wings."

Kit snorted. "You're not getting off that easy. Bea comes in every day bragging to Grady and me about whatever you cooked the night before. We want the works."

"You're on."

Allyn insisted on cooking at least four nights a week because she enjoyed it, while Bea insisted on going out or ordering in for the other nights. They had a chance to fix the mistakes they'd made the first time around, and she didn't want Allyn to fall back into the domestic role she'd had with Melody. Theirs was a partnership.

After Kit and Marta left, Bea spent another half hour setting up the computer, printer and phone while Allyn arranged her office supplies and files in a credenza that fit neatly beneath the window. The only other furnishing in the room was a stationary bicycle. Over the winter they both had added a few pounds, but the longer days of summer meant more playtime after work, and softball started up again in two weeks.

"You were right. It's awesome," Bea proclaimed. "I vote we call it a day."

Allyn checked her watch. "It's four o'clock. That gives us a couple of hours to check one more thing off our list."

"Oh, no. Not today."

"Today." Ignoring her objections, Allyn went into the bedroom and changed her T-shirt, which had gotten dirty in the move. "Today!"

Bea sighed as she walked down the hall, her feet slapping the floor as though she were being pushed from behind against her will. "I can't believe I let you and Wendy talk me into this already. You two make a diabolical team."

"It's for your own good." She tapped Bea's chest with a finger. "There's a hole in there and we need to fill it."

Dexter had indeed left a gaping hole, succumbing to lymphoma after only seven months, well short of the year Kyle had optimistically predicted. Their time together had been worth all the effort and expense, joyous until early April when his tumors returned and he began showing signs of distress. Her decision to let him go was resolute, but her sense of loss was still raw and unrelenting. She wasn't ready for another dog. But Allyn and Wendy insisted another dog was ready for her.

Or ready for them. Allyn had stepped seamlessly into the role of caregiver for Dexter, and losing him was as hard on her as it had been for Bea.

"I don't want another dog that looks like Dexter. I'm not replacing him."

"Agreed. There's no replacing Dexxie anyway. Maybe we should get a girl."

"That's a thought."

More apprehensive than excited as they drove toward the shelter, Bea considered asking if they could postpone it for another month or two. Or six. Or more. But Wendy especially was insistent they adopt another right away.

"What is it with you and Wendy? Why can't I have some time to grieve? It feels disloyal to Dexter to run out and get another dog. Like he was just a little gadget or something that broke, so I have to go buy another. He was more than that."

"I know." Allyn reached across the console and wiggled her fingers for Bea to take her hand. "Wendy was worried about you dragging your feet. I told her you might need some time, but she said you were capable of a lot of love. She didn't want you to waste it."

"I know exactly what she's doing. She's comparing it to all the time it took me to start dating again after her accident, how stubborn I was because I wouldn't take any of those women seriously." She curled her wrist to bring Allyn's hand to her chest. "Turns out I was right to wait. Otherwise I could have been tangled up with the wrong lady when you came along."

"Hmm."

"See, I got you." Bea pulled into the parking lot at the Seattle Animal Shelter, but didn't turn off the engine. If Allyn conceded her point, she was prepared to drive back home without going inside.

"No, you didn't. In fact, you made my point. So thanks for playing."

"How do you figure?"

"What if I'd played it your way? Let's say I decided not to go out with you last year because I wanted to brood a little longer over Melody. What do you suppose would have happened if she'd come back around after things fell apart with Naomi?"

That was, frankly, a terrifying prospect. Their window for being together had been quite narrow. If either of them had chosen to wait, they wouldn't be sitting here together. Allyn would be back with Melody, and Bea would be mourning Dexter by herself.

"Our next dog is waiting for us in there right now, Bea. What if she goes home with someone else instead?"

Bea couldn't begin to push back against an argument like that. With one hand, she brought Allyn's fingers to her lips, and with the other, opened her car door. "Let's go get her. Maybe she can be our ring bearer."

Bella Books, Inc.

Women. Books. Even Better Together.

P.O. Box 10543
Tallahassee, FL 32302

Phone: 800-729-4992
www.bellabooks.com